We'll Never Be Sixteen Again

Part Deux

By

Mick Whitehead

For Sue and Craig and all my family

Very special thank you to my editor
Paul Osman

Part Two of the Mark Byrne Trilogy

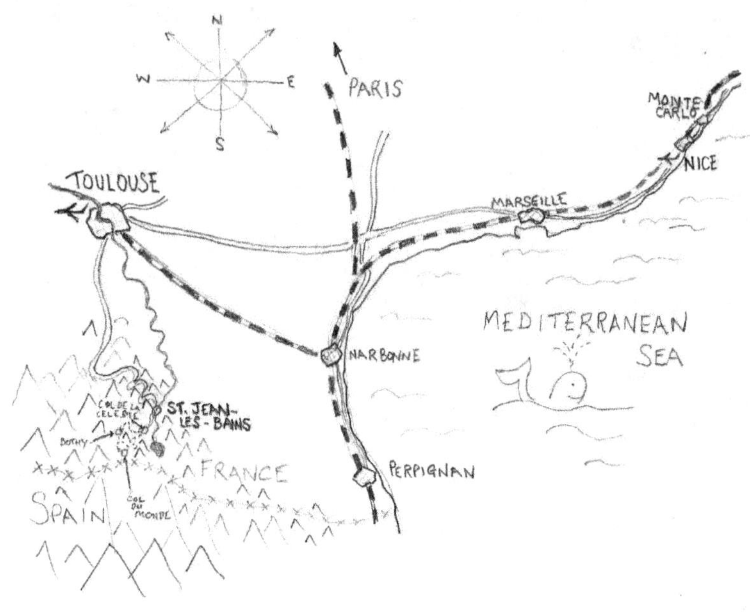

RUINS
ON THE
COL DU MONDE

Chapter One

The Tail

There were eight pubs in the centre of town. The Prince of Wales, was probably number eight, on everyone's list. It was an old, brick built, coaching inn, that had been in a steady decline, since the end of the eighteenth century and it's popularity had been decimated further, around ten years ago, when the old cattle market, had relocated to a purpose built industrial estate, on the outskirts of town. Only a few, sad, old, rusty, wrought iron, livestock stalls were still visible, above the nettles, just beyond the empty car park, at the rear of the pub. The direction taken by the Town Council back in the sixties, the so-called 'modern initiative' plans, had quite literally, as it turned out, given us all a bum-steer. Back Lane, which ran parallel to the high street was redeveloped and widened, to allow traffic to flow through unhindered. And so, ever since, cars, lorries and buses have filed past, along the new, traffic managed, inner ring road and have been treated to the arse end view, of our town's oldest and grandest shops, pubs and hotels, which line the now unseen, quaint and narrow high street. To all intents and purposes, in the eyes of passing motorists, our lovely town has, unwittingly, gained, a split personality - so much for progress.

Despite the enclosing march of modernisation, the interior of The Prince had stubbornly remained, largely unaltered. It was still divided into three separate rooms. The Tap Room was inhabited by a small, select, mustering of cloth-capped pipe smokers, all puffing and sucking away with their weary boots resting on a dull brass rail, which ran the length of the bar, about six inches, above the stone flagged floor. Anyone had a right to drink at this little exclusive bar, provided they'd been a regular at The Prince for the last twenty years and only then, if the rest of the old sweats thought you 'was alreight'. They stood lifelessly, with their arched backs bent away from a single square table, to the drone of a time worn clatter of ivory and glass hanging around in the thick, smoke filled room. The Tap Room door strangely jammed in it's frame whenever a stranger tried to enter, but three or more of these snuggly patrons and there would no longer be enough room to swing a cat round. In any case, to do anything other than pour drink down one's neck, or play a game of 'Doms', would have meant changing the habits of a lifetime. The ghostly presence of these old dinosaurs to drinking always lingered in the stale smoke, long after the bar was empty.

At the back of the pub was The Games Room. This white-washed room narrowed down to form the rear passageway, which led to the toilets and the back door. There was precious little furniture wasted here. If it hadn't been for the pool table, you'd be forgiven for thinking this room was actually part of the toilets as it permanently stunk of urinal de-odourising balls.

The décor of The Lounge Bar, by comparison, was positively glowing - mainly from the grey, filtered light, which streaked in through the half-opaque, glass windows. These thin, luminous shafts again spotlighted the perpetual cigarette smoke, rising from the overflowing table top ashtrays and swirling back and forth between conversations. The Sunday lunch time session at The Prince was like an unmarked, country crossroad, on a damp day. Odd people from all walks of life, lounged about without purpose, their favoured interests betrayed only by their clothes. Like the poacher for example, enjoying a rewarding pint after a long and profitable morning, leaning casually against the bar in a dark overcoat and muddy rubber boots. Next to him a brigade of Argyll patterned, Pringle jumpered golfers, gaggling over their wines and the dog-collared Vicar, joyously knocking back a crafty dram after Morning Service.

No one paid any notice to the lonely figure, sat buried behind a folded broadsheet, held high and covering the hardened features of his face. The only evidence of a human presence was a thick, ginger thatch of hair and the several, sausage-like fingers which gripped the edges of the paper. They belonged to Bryn Davies, a.k.a Lofty: ex-boxer, ex-rugby player, ex-policeman. The ex's were not by choice. He'd been thrown out of most organisations, due to his hidden temper. He sat motionless, his laced-up boots firmly planted on the hard, wooden, parquet floor, which was littered with un-swept, stubbed out fag ends. If ever there was a position like 'stand to attention' for a seated posture then Bryn had perfected it: arms parallel, in line with the body, elbows bent at ninety degrees exactly, heals together, toes pointing at ten to two. All he needed were two peepholes cut into the paper and he was in C.O.M, Classic Observation Mode. But that wasn't required just now. He'd been contacted previously and had been instructed to wait here today, at twelve-thirty precisely. He liked to arrive early and reckie his surroundings first. Every five minutes or so he flicked and straightened his newspaper, folded it neatly over to the next page and momentarily glanced at the front door. He was lapping up the titillating tales he was reading, in The Weekly News. Why bother to buy a *daily* paper, when you can catch up on all the sleaze, in one go? His almost empty glass of beer hadn't moved for a while. It had reached that lifeless, flat stage, waiting for someone to top it up. That someone had just walked in and was leant over the bar, jumping the queue, and placing his order with the landlord.

Inspector Derek Atkinson, CID turned around, reached inside his breast pocket and pulled out a leather cigar case. He was still wearing the same, dark, crumpled suit he'd had on all week. He looked over at Lofty, bent his head down and lit up a fresh smoke with his silver Ronson lighter. He savoured the first few puffs of Cuban tobacco, twiddled with the lighter inside his pocket and studied the man opposite, who was still submerged in the printed word. He walked swiftly across to the corner of the room and introduced himself. Lofty rested his newspaper on the table and shook hands. Both men were evenly matched and they both recognised that in each other too.

"The drinks'll be along in a minute," said Atkinson as he flicked a chunk of spent cigar ash onto the floor. Lofty folded his newspaper several times, until it was precisely the correct size to slide, snuggly, into his blazer jacket pocket.

"So what's it all about? You made it sound very S.A.M. yesterday, over the phone."

"Sam?" said Atkinson, looking puzzled.

"S.A.M - smoke and mirrors," corrected Lofty.

Atkinson was staring straight into Lofty's eyes, ignoring his last comment. He had a knack of reading people quickly. He'd also done some homework on Lofty too, prior to this meeting. He'd read Lofty's police file, which was surprisingly thin, for someone who'd been booted out of the force for gross negligence and for being responsible for almost killing a suspect, he was questioning. The poor, middle-aged man he'd suspected of wife beating had been hand cuffed to a chair in the interview room, at the time of his so called interrogation. Luckily, there'd been an ambulance crew at the station enjoying a tea break, otherwise Lofty would now be doing time for man slaughter. Up until that point, Lofty's police career had been moving speedily forward, in an acceptable direction. Reading between the lines, Atkinson had come to the conclusion that Lofty possessed the right kind of blind subservience, to keep his mouth shut when asked.

"There's someone I'd like you to keep a discreet eye on for me. He's not been proved guilty of anything just yet, but I'd like someone to let me know what he's up to."

The Landlord arrived with two fresh pints of ale and placed them down on the table. Atkinson waited for him to turn away before continuing. He took out a photograph from his pocket, slid it across the table and picked up his pint. "That's Mark Byrne, works at a café called The Friary in Crowston. Do you know it?" Lofty wiped the froth from his top lip and shook his head. "Doesn't matter," Atkinson continued. Lofty picked up the photo and stared at the young face as he listened to Atkinsons' brief. "Just see what he gets up to for a week and report back to me."

Lofty was still none the wiser. "What's Byrne done, that requires this kind of covert surveillance?"

"I can't say at this stage, only that it could be a nice little earner for both of us, if I'm right."

"I'll need some expense money up front," complained Lofty. "Things haven't been great lately," he muttered, raising his glass to his lips again. Atkinson was one step ahead of him and reached inside his wallet for five Ten Pound Notes which he handed to Lofty, but he didn't let go of them until Lofty understood that this money was to be used for travel expenses and not frittered away at the bookies.

"And one more thing, under no circumstances are you to approach Byrne, or intervene. Is that clear?"

"Yes Boss," replied Lofty, smiling as he buried the banknotes in his trouser pocket.

"I mean it! I don't want Byrne getting suspicious. He's only a kid and the sort to scare easily. Just keep your distance and call me at this number, every evening at six-thirty sharp." Atkinson passed over a scrap of paper. "There's no need to follow him in the evening or at night time. His address is written down on the back too. He normally starts work at nine in the morning."

"The Friary at Crowston," repeated Lofty confidently.

"That's right. Good man!" Atkinson looked around the room, downed the rest of his pint, placed the empty glass firmly on the table and stood up and cocked a finger like he was drawing his gun from a shoulder holster, "Keep me posted."

Lofty jumped to his feet and shook hands again, firmly. "You can rely on me," he said sternly. Atkinson nodded and marched straight out of the pub as Lofty sat back down. He pulled out one of the Ten Pound Notes, raised it above his head to catch the landlord's attention and ordered another pint. He was feeling pretty chuffed with himself. He wasn't as dumb as he was making out. He was adept at playing the part of licking the boots of people in power. Atkinson's call had come completely out of the blue but was very welcome all the same. He scanned over his memory to a year ago and he could just about remember the unathletic looking Sergeant Swindlehurst who'd taken over from him at the station, but he couldn't recall Atkinson at all; he was a complete unknown.

He was thinking about what Atkinson had said just now and two things stood out from their conversation. The biggest of these was 'a nice little earner for the two of us', which sounded very promising and the other thing was 'Byrne scared easily'. This is going to be a pushover, he thought. The bell rang inside the room awakening Lofty to his current surroundings.

"Last orders at the Bar, please!"

Early the next morning, Lofty was already in position, outside Bowland Mobile Home Park. He was sat in his car, trying to prevent the windows from steaming up inside by wiping them with his clean, white handkerchief, whilst the rain tap danced on the tin roof above his head. He'd showed up at seven a.m. and positioned his car: away from the road, but facing the entrance to the caravan park.

Earlier, when he'd arrived, it'd been dry and clear and he'd taken the opportunity to explore around the derelict ruins of the old hotel, in whose brick littered car park, he was now waiting. The old, abandoned hotel was in a dangerous state of dilapidation. All the windows had long since been vandalised. The rooms were open to the elements and the neglected shards of broken glass and pools of water lay in permanent despair, on all the floors. He'd climbed the metal fire escape at the rear of the building and casually examined the piles of litter, scattered inside, by turning them over with the toe of his right boot. When the chill, damp air took it's natural course on him, he relieved himself in the corner.

He'd nothing else to do, but wait and watch. On the passenger seat of his car was: a square Tupperware box of sandwiches, a Thermos of black coffee, his field glasses and a pencil and notepad. The discarded Weekly News and an umbrella were on the back seat. He felt good about being involved in proper detective work again. Since he'd *moved on* from the Force, a year ago, worthwhile jobs had been pretty thin on the ground. His private detective business was practically, non-existent. The most exciting assignment he'd been hired to do was finding a lost puppy, which turned out to be hidden in a neighbours shed. Most of his recent income had come from security work. He enjoyed being one of the doormen at The Clouds Nightclub in Preston. He'd a knack for turning most situations to his own advantage. He especially liked talking to the ladies, as they waited outside and he had his favourites amongst them, whom he helped jump the queue. When things, inevitably, became heated and rowdy, his training as a boxer came in handy too.

From his pocket, he removed the photo of Byrne which Atkinson had given him and began talking to himself, as he often did. "Now what have you been up to, my bonny lad?" (It's surprising how quickly this comforting habit establishes itself, when you're forced to live alone.) Lofty looked up as he heard a car pull out of the caravan park. He watched its single female occupant turn the wheel and move off in a northerly direction, up the main road. Then a chubby youth appeared, riding into the site on a bicycle, with an empty, newspaper delivery bag, slung across his handlebars. At least things were starting to happen at last, he thought. The residents of Cayburn had begun to wake and stir on this wet start to another, new, working morning.

A slim looking lad, a little under six feet tall, in a black leather bomber jacket, came walking through the entrance towards the main road, carrying a sports bag. Lofty noted the time. "Eye, eye, bonny lad, gotcha!" he said, as he watched Byrne cut across the brick littered car park, a little too close for comfort, as he headed up the footpath to the Bus stop. The steamed up windows inside the car had at least concealed his presence. Five minutes later, a red double decker bus pulled up and Byrne climbed aboard. "Here we go." Lofty started his Austin 1100 and let the bus almost disappear from view before he pulled out into the main road, heading north towards Lancaster. The window wipers were groaning and slapping away the rain on the outside, as he wiped the inside of the screen again and again. He took care to maintain a good distance. After ten minutes, with the heater blower turned up fully and a jet of fresh air rushing in through the narrow opening at the top of the driver's window, the front screen began to clear enough for Lofty to relax at last.

Byrne eventually jumped off at Lancaster Central Bus Station. The dark blue Austin 1100 rolled up into a parking space opposite and Lofty adjusted his rear view mirror, to note the direction Byrne was taking. So far, so good, he picked up his field glasses, newspaper and brolly, locked the car door and ran after him, in the rain. When he had Byrne firmly fixed in his sights, Lofty opened up his brolly and followed at a steady fifty yards behind. Byrne hadn't looked around once. This was going to be a P.O.P he thought, a piece of piss; but later when his belly began to rumble, he regretted leaving his flask and sandwiches behind, inside his car.

By the time Lofty had made his fourth, routine call to Atkinson on Thursday evening, a clearer picture of Byrne's movements and intentions had already formed. On Monday; Lofty had followed Byrne to: the Post Office, two Banks, W H Smiths, Thomas Cook's and the photo booth in Woollies. Tuesday, Byrne had visited a private residence in Wyresdale Drive, Firton and emerged with a rucksack. On Wednesday, Lofty had been forced to gain access to an adjacent field, at the side of Byrnes mobile home because, worryingly, he hadn't set foot outside, all day. Lofty had observed Byrne through his field glasses, sat inside his lounge, although he couldn't see, in any detail, what was keeping him occupied. Thursday morning, Byrne had ridden over, on his moped, to The Friary again and later into the centre of town, to visit two more Banks.

"Well, clearly he's planning to make a move. Although I haven't worked out why he's been to so many branches of the Midland bank," Lofty concluded.

"Don't dwell on that that," said Atkinson curtly, "I think we need to concentrate on where he's moving away to. I've got a gut feeling it'll happen this weekend. Byrne's obviously not working anymore. That short visit to The Friary, this morning, was probably just to say his farewells." There was a lull in the conversation. Then, Atkinson continued, "So, apart from

Tuesday, have you seen Byrne out and about carrying his rucksack again?"

"No, not since he came away from Wyresdale Drive at two-thirty, Tuesday afternoon."

"So, apart from visiting The Friary, has he met with anyone else?"

"No Boss"

"Then he's acting alone," Atkinson said to himself.

"Do you want me to go back to the house in Wyresdale Drive and squeeze whoever it is that lives there for more info?"

"No need Lofty, I know exactly who he is. He's not connected with this at all. He's just one of Byrne's colleagues from The Friary."

Lofty was getting wise to Atkinson's dismissiveness. If Atkinson didn't want someone interfered with, it probably suggested he was saving that one for himself, he wrongly assumed. However, there was a lot more to Byrnes activities than he first realised. For Atkinson to be taking this much trouble meant whatever it was had to be big and all Byrnes visit to banks meant, somehow, it had to involve money.

"Let's see what tomorrow brings, Lofty. Get yourself settled into position, at the usual time."

"Ok Boss."

When Lofty pulled onto the brick littered car park, the following morning at seven-thirty, Byrne was already stood at the bus stop, on the opposite side of the road, wearing his rucksack. Lofty parked up and stopped the engine. Looking through his rear view mirror, he could see Byrne watching him from across the road. When Byrne turned to look up the main road, Lofty quickly got out of his car, raised the bonnet and stood in front of it so that he was shielded from view. He noticed there was no one else around. If Byrne comes across to speak to me, he thought, now's my chance to grab hold of him, drag him into the derelict Hotel and force him to spill the beans, by whatever means it takes. Disappointingly for Lofty, within a couple of minutes a bus drew up next to Byrne and pulled off again down the main road in a southerly direction. This was not

Byrne's normal routine, thought Lofty - time to make a move. He was counting his blessings, too, that had he arrived three minutes later this morning, Byrne would have been clean away by now and no one would have been any the wiser. He slammed the lid of his bonnet down and scrambled round to the driver's door.

The bus had been caught by a set of red traffic lights, at the junction to Cockerham Road. Once the lights changed to green, Lofty pulled out onto the main road and recommenced following his quarry. "So, it's Preston is it, my bonny lad and what's inside that rucksack of yours, eh? I'll bet you'd like to hand it over to your Uncle Bryn?" Talking to himself, helped him to concentrate; he didn't want to lose the bus, not at this critical stage of the hunt. After a forty minute stop-go journey, the bus reached its terminus at Preston Coach Station. There were no parking spaces available nearby so Lofty ran up the kerb and pulled up, half on and half off the pavement, to observe Byrne getting off the bus.

The time was still only eight-fifteen and the town centre shops hadn't yet opened up. He could see there were several lorries parked on the high street, unloading their goods. Byrne was taking a very leisurely walk in front of the shop windows, occasionally pausing and looking inside them. "What's he up to I wonder? Time to take a walk." Lofty found an empty parking meter and dropped fifty pence inside, giving him two hours grace. He followed Byrne reasonably closely, as there was lots of cover on the busy street. In addition to the criss-crossing of delivery drivers, shop entrances were being unlocked and staff were toing and froing, setting out their stands on the pavement. Further down the high street, Byrne had stopped for several minutes, outside the Armed Force Careers Information Office, staring at the contents through the window. When he eventually moved off towards the Railway Station, Lofty followed and paused only momentarily, where Byrne had stood, transfixed; he could see nothing of interest to him.

Inside the Railway Station, he finally spotted Byrne, sat down outside the passenger waiting room on Platform Two.

"F.M.O.B" said Lofty out loud. "Fuck my old boots! This is it!" He looked around anxiously for a public telephone box. He had to get hold of Atkinson quickly as it seemed likely Byrne was now heading for London. He grabbed a Railway Porter and asked him if he knew the nearest place to make a call. At this time of the morning, if he was in luck, Atkinson would be just arriving at his office.

"What is it Lofty?" said Atkinson looking at his watch and sounding more niggly than normal.

"I'm at Preston Railway Station, following Byrne," answered Lofty, still sounding slightly out of breath. "It looks like he's heading down to The Big Smoke, London."

It was not a complete surprise to Atkinson, but at the same time he felt genuinely frustrated. "I thought this might be on the cards, but he's a day earlier than I expected." Atkinson rested his telephone receiver between his right shoulder and his right ear and slid around his desk reaching for his telephone index directory. "Right, are you listening? Here's the plan. I'll call the British Transport Police at Preston Railway Station and tell them you're assisting me with a case. They'll probably want to send one of their own with you, so keep *schtum* about our little enterprise. I'll invent a cover story, as to why we're following Byrne. Make your way to the Transport Police Office now and wait for my call. Have you got that?"

When Lofty and PC Burke of the non-uniformed British Transport Police eventually boarded Byrne's train, seconds before departure, they were relieved to have embarked without arousing any suspicion. Atkinson had told the Transport Police, that Byrne had recently left Borstal and that he was a known drugs courier, and was planning to pick up a consignment today, in London. They should follow him, but they should hold back until he met up with his contact. Lofty, of course, had been given different instructions. Atkinson was taking a big risk, but he had no choice, other than to place even more trust in Lofty. He had instructed him to discreetly search inside Byrne's rucksack, for clues. He'd stopped short of mentioning there could be a bag full of cash inside. Atkinson had previously planned to pay Lofty off this evening and take up the surveillance personally, thinking Byrne would be making his move the following day, Saturday. Unfortunately, it was not to be. "Whatever you do Lofty, make sure Byrne doesn't catch you near his rucksack. It's a long journey to London and Byrne won't be expecting anything, so you're bound to get an opportunity to take a quick look. If all else fails, get the Transport Police bod to create a diversion, whilst you ferret about. Remember, whatever happens, give me a call on this number, as soon as your train arrives in London."

Lofty and Burke were sat at the rear of the carriage with their eyes tirelessly peeled on Byrne.

****

"So Fi, how's your French doing, Par Lez Voo Fron Sez?"

Fionn began to giggle and reached into her coat pocket. "I've bought one of these," she said, holding up a new copy of Collins French Phrase Book. She pointed to the cover. "Look, it says 'clear and concise'."

"You mean, just like wot I said - Par Lez Voo?" It was too early in the morning to be drinking beer, but I was feeling better about myself than I had for a long time, certainly since Max had taken her own life and perhaps even before I'd been roped into robbing the Post Office in Crowston. "Have you been to France before, Fi?" I said, looking at her innocent face. For the first time today, I could see she was looking slightly apprehensive. Maybe the enormity and uncertainty of our hasty adventure was beginning to daunt her. Her face soon lit up again, as she recalled a funny story from her past.

"The only time I've been abroad before was when I was nine years old," she began and took a sip of her beer to wet her lips. "It was a school trip to Bruges - "

I interrupted her, "Which junior school did you go to?"

"Firton Primary"

"Right, sorry Fi, carry on."

"It was an overseas football tournament and I'd been asked to go along by one of the boys, Simon Wilshaw. My mum was good friends with his parents, so that was why. We were only away for about four days altogether, watching the football and visiting some castle and other stuff. I think the boys almost reached the final. Anyway, when we were coming back on the boat, most of the teachers were buying boxes of cigarettes and they put them all in my little red suitcase." Fionn began to laugh.

"You're joking," I said, half seriously.

"No, it's true. I was very sweet and innocent in my pony tails," Fionn grabbed her own hair, at the sides, to demonstrate, fluttering her eyelashes at the same time. "They obviously thought that the customs police people wouldn't check inside *my* case." She took another swig of beer. "The funny thing is, when we were lined up to go through customs, after we got off the ferry in Dover, we all had to hand our cases over, as we passed through. When it was my turn, I gave the customs chappie my case and I blurted out something like, 'there are no cigarettes in there'. I was trying to put him off. He looked at me, frowned and said 'I should hope not little girl' and he handed me back my case, without bothering to check it." I started to laugh as Fionn continued. "When we got back to our coach the teachers emptied my case and gave me my clothes back. I think they were quite relieved really. Up to now, that's the sum total of my experience of being in Europe."

The green and pleasant countryside was flashing past our windows as the train raced along, rocking from side to side. I'd not been paying much attention as to how far we'd travelled, until we slowed up into the damp, dark subterranean world that blindly heralded our arrival at Birmingham New Street Station. The iron wheels screeched and hissed and we were jolted to a halt. We looked out onto the platform; it was noticeably busier than it had been up at Preston. Lines of waiting passengers gathered at the doors to board our train. We tucked in our feet and elbows, as the cumbersome passengers began to stream and fill our carriage, dumping their baggage in overhead, netted racks. Fionn's red tartan rucksack was still clearly in view, protecting my army rucksack, which lay beneath. The clamour of people shifting about soon died down, once everyone had settled into their seats. Not long after, we were zooming along again. The ticket inspector passed through our carriage, merrily clipping away, maintaining his natural balance by resting against the back of seats with his feet placed a stride apart. He was closely followed by a tired looking buffet trolley and matching attendant. Fionn insisted on buying us both another beer, as it was her round. There wasn't much of a choice: McKewans Tartan Bitter, or Tennents Lager. Fionn chose the Tennents because she liked the picture on the front can, but the back of our cans portrayed different pictures of scantily clad models, wearing bikinis. Mine was called Pat and Fionn had Heather, but they both tasted the same. I bought a sausage roll but regretted it, as soon as I took my first bite. I showed Fionn the inside of the roll.

"Look at that, it's like staring down a tunnel." There was a cavernous gap between the thin layer of meat and the top of the pastry. "I could park my moped in there!"

Fionn was still laughing at my misfortune, when the train suddenly began to slow down and eventually came to a halt, in the middle of nowhere, between Birmingham and Milton Keynes.

After a while, our fellow passengers grew weary of staring out of the windows and became even more restless. Some were beginning to move back and forth, when an argument erupted, at the rear of the carriage. We heard some angry shouting and several businessmen, next to us, got up to investigate. Between the backs of standing onlookers, I could see two men grappling with one another and to prevent them from tearing strips out of each other, they had to be forcibly wrestled apart by some plucky passengers. Moments later, the ticket inspector appeared. The fracas dissolved, as people descended back into their seats. Fionn asked one of the men next to us, who was settling down again, what all the fuss had been about. Someone had tried to pickpocket one of the passengers and he had mistakenly accused an innocent bystander. When I heard this, I quickly glanced down the aisle to check our rucksacks. A wave of panic swept over me, when I saw that Fionn's rucksack was missing. I jumped up and told her I was going to check our luggage. When I reached the storage compartment, I could see Fionn's rucksack had slipped down into the empty space where mine should have been. Shit! I looked around and fumbled through all the bags and cases, but to no avail. Then, the connecting door suddenly opened. I turned around and just about jumped out of my skin. Facing me was the mean looking, big, ginger-haired guy, the same one who'd got on the train at Preston.

"Is this what you're looking for?" he asked, forcing a smile and held the rucksack up, for me to take. "I found it on the floor in the passageway, outside the toilets,"

I noticed one of the buckles was undone and the other was loose. Gingernut hurried off back to his seat, at the rear of the carriage without waiting for my reply. I opened my rucksack and checked inside. Nothing appeared to be missing, but my stuff was all jumbled up. My electric razor, which was at the bottom, was now on top. More importantly, I could see, immediately, that the frames had not been tampered with - things could've been worse. I carried both rucksacks back with me, banging into a few extruding elbows and shoulders along the way.

"Hey, what's wrong?" asked Fionn, looking shocked.

"Someone's been rifling through my rucksack."

"Really, has anything been stolen?"

"Not as far as I can tell."

I had my hand inside, having a feel around and pulled out a pair of nylon, orange underpants, with contrasting purple trim. "Maybe the thief was put off by these?" I joked, holding them aloft. Fionn blushed and one or two other passengers began to laugh.

I turned to Fionn and said, "Luckily, that bloke at the back of the carriage, the one with the wedge of ginger hair, found my rucksack in the corridor."

"Yes I noticed him go past, just before the fighting started."

I turned round to check the back of the carriage and noticed Gingernut was sat next to the guy, who'd had his pocket picked. There was something not quite right, about those two. "I'm going to keep my rucksack between my feet. I don't fancy losing it again," I said, pulling down the flap and fastening up the buckles. "You'd better do the same."

The train pulled forward and accelerated away, as the ticket inspector swept through the carriage once again, this time apologising for the unscheduled stop. It had been caused by a signalling fault.

When our train finally coasted into Euston Station, it was over an hour late. I grabbed Fionn's arm and suggested we let everyone file out of our carriage first, as we'd plenty of time to kill, before we had to make our next connection. As we stood next to one another, amongst the hustle and bustle on the platform, I couldn't help having a look around for Gingernut and his mate. Happily, they were nowhere to be seen.

"Right then," I said. "I guess we need to find, an underground map."

"Is that it, there?" said Fionn, pointing at a large board on the wall, between the toilet doors.

"Yer, looks like it. Follow me." I looked at Fionn who was smiling like a little girl in a sweet shop. "Nice one, Fi," I added. We found Victoria Station on the map and I traced the route with my finger.

"The Victoria Line's what we need," I said laughing at my own gormlessness. "Do you fancy something to eat first?"

"Yes, I could murder a burger," she said, dumping the remains of her mum's sandwiches into the nearest bin. Our plan was to go to Victoria Station and buy two tickets, for the Night Ferry to Paris. Fionn was really excited about this leg of our journey, for two reasons. One, she was so looking forward to seeing the Eiffel tower and two, The Night Ferry sounded so romantic. That's so girly, I thought.

"Imagine," she said with delight, "We'll be in our bunks on the train, on the ferry from Dover to Dunkirk, being rocked asleep." I didn't want to shatter her illusions. I didn't think, for one minute, she'd considered the possibility there might be a gale blowing across The English Channel.

At Victoria Station we were feeling nicely fed, tired, excited and perhaps a little anxious about whom we'd be sharing our bunks with. We'd discovered from the ticket office, that the compartments on the sleeper carriages all had four berths in them. We sat, leaning together shoulder to shoulder, waiting for The Night Ferry Train to arrive and playing a game, to see who could spot the most outrageous looking Punk Rocker amongst the evening commuters moving about the station.

"Wow, look at him," whispered Fionn, nodding her head in the direction of a guy with half a scrapyard stuck to his face. It looked bloody painful too. It was the first time I'd seen someone with so many safety pins through their lips. I was scanning around when, suddenly, my heart froze. Stood with his back to me, in front of the large timetable screen, was the unmistakable figure of Gingernut. He was by himself, studying the latest timetable information and when he'd apparently found what he needed, he left climbing the stairs. I followed him with my gaze as he walked across the overhead walkway and disappeared into a throng of passengers, heading for the exit. I thought this was *too* much of a coincidence. Who was this guy? But at that moment, I was feeling too tired to think of a reason that connected him to me, or why he appeared to be following me.

Just before nine p.m., the diesel engine pulling the shiny, blue carriages of The Night Ferry pulled up on Platform Five. I pointed to the white destination sign, on the side of the carriage.

"Look at that Fi, London to Paris." There was no time to stand and stare. As soon as the carriage doors were flung open, there was a mad rush to get on the train and find an empty compartment. Inside the corridor, in front of us, were a very smartly dressed, middle-aged couple, carrying matching suitcases.

"Quick, follow them," I said, pushing Fionn to the front. We watched them opening each compartment, until they found an empty one.

"Fi, ask them if we can share with them."

Fionn turned around, giving me a quizzical look, "are you sure?"

"Yes, they look like nice people. Better the devil you know," I said.

"Excuse me," said Fionn, in a soft voice, directly to the couple in front of us. "Would you mind if we came in with you?"

The middle-aged man turned round to face Fionn and smiled, "of course you can, it'll be our pleasure." His wife smiled at us both too, as we naïvely put our rucksacks down on top of our bunks.

"Those are your wardrobes there," said the lady, pointing at the lockers. "Is this your first time aboard The Night Ferry?"

"Yes!" we both said together.

"Oh lovely," said the lady, smiling again. "Enjoy."

After a few minutes to store our things away and place our pyjamas and toothbrushes on our pillows, we locked our wardrobes and went to find the buffet car.

"I fancy a nightcap, Fi. What about a cocktail?"

I'd not tried another cocktail since that night at Eve's house, with Max, when we'd both got completely legless on Singapore Gin Slings. Disappointingly, for Fionn, the buffet bar was not the romantic experience she was hoping for. There was no silver service and no uniformed waiters, wearing white gloves. In fact, the whole carriage looked worn out and scruffy. We ordered two Manhattans from the barman, just because we liked the picture on the menu card. The drink had a warm, red colour and was topped with a cherry on a stick. We clinked our glasses together and our eyes squinted at the first taste.

I was still keeping one eye peeled for Gingernut, but judging by his hasty departure from Victoria Station, I was guessing, he was now long gone. At ten o'clock, with the train bumping along gently, we decided to call it a day and headed back to our compartment. The nice, middle-aged couple were both sat up reading, in the half-light from their bunk lanterns. They smiled at us as we took it in turns to slip out with our toothbrushes and visit the loo. I drew back my curtain on the top berth and wished everyone goodnight.

"Goodnight Byrney," said Fionn from her berth below. "Thanks for a lovely day."

I lay awake for an age, listening to the heartbeat of the train, of the endless beating of wheels along the rails and the gentle snoring from one of our hosts, on the opposite side of our compartment. I felt curiously protective towards Fionn. She seemed unaware of her own vulnerability and I made up my mind to look out for her, until I could tell she no longer needed me. I was feeling guilty too, about running out on my family. I couldn't help noticing dad hiding his disappointment about my change of heart on joining the RAF. Neither of my parents understood my reasons. Perhaps I should have told them the truth about my intentions: to locate where Eve's husband had met his death, at the hands of the Gestapo, so that I could reunite Eve and Paul's ashes. Mum would have thought I'd gone mental. More than anything, I had to put some distance between me and the Police too. I was beginning to realise the huge sum of money Max and I had stolen was becoming an unwanted millstone around my neck, now that it was no longer possible to use it to fulfil our dreams. My eyelids were beginning to feel heavier. "Goodnight Max," I whispered under my breath, achingly. "Wherever you are."

****

At around ten to nine earlier that evening, it had become obvious to Lofty that the two young kids from Cayburn were skipping the country, on The Night Ferry. There was no way he was going to follow them, any further. He'd already been fretting half the day about how many parking tickets were stuck to his car windscreen, or whether it'd been towed away to the

Vehicle Pound. He should have rung Atkinson at Euston, but he had to follow Byrne, through to his final destination. At Euston Station however, PC Burke had split with him, to catch the return train to Preston. This was after Lofty had owned up to having, supposedly, followed the wrong suspect and apologised for wasting his time. There was much to tell Atkinson and the fifty pounds, he'd received at the beginning of the week, had all but disappeared.

"PARIS!!" shouted Atkinson down the phone.

"Sorry Boss, but that's definitely where they're heading for."

"What's this girl like, the one that Byrne's travelling with, did you get her name?"

"Yes, I heard Byrne calling her Fi. Well, she's a brunette, average size tits, average height, pretty, do you need to know more?"

"No, I think I know who she is now." Atkinson was checking a list of names he'd copied into his notebook from the condolences book at the Crematorium, the day after Eve's Funeral. "Here she is," he said to himself, underlining her name. Lofty was still complaining about how, or when, he was going to get back to Lancashire this evening.

"Did you get a look inside Byrnes rucksack?" Atkinson enquired casually.

"Yes, just clothes and personal stuff: paperback, shaver, pair of trainers."

"Was that all?"

"Nothing you wouldn't expect to find. I tipped everything out and put it all back again." Lofty thought it was wise not to mention he'd accidentally bumped into Byrne, almost getting caught in the act.

"Listen, you'd better get yourself back here. There's a Goods Train leaving Euston at midnight. I'll speak to the Station Master and let him know you're on your way."

"A Goods Train Boss? Where am I supposed to sleep?" grumbled Lofty.

"Use your initiative, man. You should be able to make up a bed, out of some old sacks or something. Give me a call tomorrow, when you get back and we'll arrange to meet up. I suppose you'll need a bit more cash."

"Too bloody right I do." Lofty suddenly remembered his parked car, on the meter in Preston. He asked Atkinson if he'd been able to have it picked up.

"Sorry Lofty, by the time I managed to get hold of someone it'd already been recovered and taken away."

"Bloody charming!" complained Lofty. "J.M.F.L - just my fucking luck!"

"Slight problem," said Atkinson trying to keep a straight face. "There was no room in the yard at Preston Nick so they had to take your motor down to Chorley. You'll have to catch a bus from Preston. Call me tomorrow."

Lofty could hear Atkinson laughing in the background just before the phone cut off. Bastard, he thought, I'll get my own back on you one day. Christ, it's going to be a long night.

Atkinson was still chuckling away to himself, as he sat down behind his desk and took out his bottle of Scotch and a glass, from the bottom drawer. He poured himself a good measure and held the glass in front of him, at eye level, staring at the clear, amber spirit and began to mull over what Lofty had reported. If Byrne's rucksack had only contained what Lofty said, then that must mean, the loot from the Post Office raid was still somewhere in West Lancashire, more than likely at Byrne's home. But why go to all those lengths and preparations before departing and quitting his job too? Doesn't feel like Byrne and his new partner are just away on a little holiday. Well, that's perfect, he thought. It'll give me time to find the money for myself before he returns. He threw back the whiskey and placed the glass down onto his desk, next to his notebook. His eyes were drawn to the line he'd scored under Fionn Terry's name. As his eyes slid further down the list, right at the bottom, one name suddenly flashed up - Henri Larouchamps.

Chapter Two

A Train Full of Vikings

I woke with a start the next morning to the sound of our compartment door being slammed to. Where was I? It took me a few moments to work out, exactly where I was - on the train to Paris. It was already broad daylight outside. I stared at my watch, eight-thirty. I drew back my berth curtain and immediately noticed our hosts opposite had left. Their berths having been tidily made-up.

"Fi," I called, "time to get a move on. I think we've missed breakfast."

By the time we'd dressed and visited the loo, the train had slowed to urban speeds and was cantering silently along, threading through the grey, backstreet suburbs of Paris that appeared to have woken hours ago. The everyday rush hour of stationary cars, cyclists and pedestrians queued behind closed crossing gates, waiting for us to pass. An uninterrupted rolling film show of back gardens, plastered walls, telegraph poles, concrete pillars and hoards of old, abandoned goods carriages flickered by our window, from right to left.

Neither of us had had a pleasant nights sleep. We'd been woken up several times during the early hours, as the Night Ferry train was shunted and coupled up, again and again between the land and the sea and from ship to shore. It was no surprise we'd slept in until now.

"Have you got your Passport handy?" I said, looking at Fionn as she buckled up her unmistakable, brightly coloured, rucksack.

"Yes, it's here in my coat pocket," she confirmed.

On the lengthy platform at the Gare Du Nord station, we joined the back of the queue for the French Douane checkpoint. I showed Fionn my awful passport photo.

"Do you think they'll let me through?" I said laughing.

"I shouldn't worry," replied Fionn, "mine's just as bad."

There was no sign of the middle-aged couple who'd kept me awake with their chorus of snoring. No doubt they'd be at the front of the queue.

After a nervous few moments, whilst the armed Gendarmes and Border Police looked over ominously at everyone, we were soon outside in the cool, morning sunshine of a noisy, Parisian Boulevard. On the crowded pavement across the street, we noticed some people sat at tables drinking coffee. Behind them arose a tall building, with red canopies above the shuttered windows. This ornate, three-storied building, with its decorative iron balconies occupied a prominent position at the convergence of two boulevards and was called Café Le Bistrot.

"Let's try there," I said, pointing at the inviting tables in front of us.

There were simple, one-sided menu cards on each table, together with a Martini ashtray and a plastic cruets. 'Le Formula' Continental breakfast consisted of jus d'orange, croissant and a café and was only Fifteen Francs. We enjoyed our terrace breakfast 'a la Parisienne'. All around us was a mesmerising bedlam of furious activity, interspersed with the rapid service provided by our two waiters as they weaved amongst the tables. There was also an open market in full swing, lining one side of the boulevard that built a temporary wall of wooden crates behind it. Spilt and rotten vegetables languished in the gutter beside vans and lorries, all casually double parked, forcing the passing traffic to funnel and share a single carriage way. Between the tall impressive buildings that lined the boulevard, echoed shouts of merchants, the bleeping of car horns, a traffic policeman's impatient whistle and in the background the constant rumbling clatter of car tyres, relentlessly thumping over the cobbles - which all blended together, to form a Parisian street symphony - accompanied by the intoxicating smell of the fresh merchandise, mixed with car fumes. Popping in and out of the café, a steady flow of merchants frequented the bar to buy cigarettes and tiny glasses of a thin, milky fluid, which they drank quickly, marked only by the exchange of a few coins.

"How would you like to work here?" I said to Fionn. She was still staring in wonderment at the scenes of everyday life that were being played out in front of us.

"It's better than watching television," she remarked. After a richly satisfying breakfast, our dirty plates were cleared, encouraging us to either order again, or give up our seats. Fionn was looking around to get a sense of her bearings.

"Aren't we supposed to catch our next train from the Gare de l'Est?"

I had my Paris map open on the table. "Yer, it's only about five minutes away," I said, pointing down an adjacent side street.

"I think we should get our tickets first, before we start looking around the city."

"Good idea," I said, smiling at her.

After buying our train tickets for Nice, we stumbled upon some luggage storage lockers at the station. We dumped our rucksacks and locked them inside. Next, we made our way to the nearest entrance to the Metro. The plan of the underground was remarkably easy to follow. All the underground trains had a route map in each carriage, along the internal edge of the roof line, above the doors and windows. We settled down, relaxed and watched the Parisian commuters, in their remoteness, as they went about their normal everyday business. Most of the ladies I saw were dressed to perfection, like shop mannequins with their quaffed hair-do's and their artistically made-up faces. They stood silently and majestically with their beads and jewellery hung all about them. I noticed some ladies were even carrying small dogs inside their handbags. My mum was missing out on a lot of potential sales in her fashion shop, if only there had been a pet shop next door. We were heading for a station called Invalids, which I thought was a nice, charitable thing for the Parisians to provide.

Once we were outside at ground level again, we were slapped across the face by our first sighting of the Eiffel Tower which stood, larger than life and directly in front of us. It was such an amazing sight. I was shocked at the actual size of the base too. Between the four, giant feet which sat at each corner, there was enough space for a football pitch. Hundreds of tourists were milling around, taking photographs and buying little replica souvenirs. Almost everyone was gawping upwards at the maze of metalwork.

"Come on Byrney," said Fionn, impatiently, "put your teeth away. Let's go up it."

The view from the second stage literally took our breath away. Luckily, neither of us suffered from vertigo and we were able to ascend the stairs reasonably quickly, overtaking some of the slower climbers. We held back the temptation to look out, until we reached the platform. According to Fionn, the gleaming, white church of Sacre Coeur, on the opposite hillside, looked like a giant cake of blancmange. Down below, we could see the traffic, snaking along the quaysides by the River Seine and tiny, ant-like pedestrians, walking through the parks and gardens. Fionn reached inside her coat pocket for her Kodak Instamatic camera and began clicking away. I asked an American tourist to take our photo, with Notre Dame in the distance behind us.

The day continued in much the same way for the remainder of the daylight hours. From the base of the tower we walked up the length of Boulevard St. Germain, pausing for lunch at the famous Café Flore, before heading down to the Place St. Michel and onto Notre Dame itself. Inside the ancient ornate arena, the light was very dark and the damp and the hushed atmosphere felt oppressive and unwelcoming. It's like being back at Junior School, I thought. Outside, we queued up at the front corner, away from the crowded, gigantic arched entrance doors and paid our five Francs to ascend the curved, stone staircase to the giant bells, made famous by Quasimodo. We stood high up on the gusty ramparts, guarded by the cheeky gargoyles, which, like us, were sticking out their tongues to the world. By the time we were sat once more on the underground

Metro, our feet were aching with all the walking we'd done, despite only having seen a fraction of the Paris sights. In the cobbled streets leading up to the Gare de l'Est, we called in at a small Supermarché, to buy some food for our overnight journey to the south coast.

"Look at this Fi, a bottle of red wine for just three Francs! I've got to buy one," I laughed.

On the platform at the Gare de l'Est, we could see we weren't the only young people hanging around with rucksacks. This was obviously still a popular route to the French Riviera, even at this late stage of the holiday season. We walked further down the platform, consciously trying to find a less rowdy group of passengers to wait amongst, until our train arrived.

At eight-thirty exactly, our TGV express train drew up and we noted the position of the sleeper car along the long column of SNCF carriages. Once inside, we found an empty compartment and settled in.

"Oh bollocks," I said, "I've forgotten to buy a bottle opener."

"Don't worry, I've packed one in my rucksack," said Fionn, digging into one of the large front pockets, where she had stored some cutlery and her enamel mug.

Our little picnic was abruptly interrupted by two boisterous, blond-haired lads with daft grins on their faces.

"Are those beds free?" said the tall one, pointing at the two spare berths.

I looked at Fionn who just shrugged her shoulders, so I stood up and said, "er yes, help yerself."

The two lads were very muscular and looked incredibly strong and healthy.

"My name is Lars," said the tall one, "and this is my friend Arne. We are from Sweden." We all shook hands and once the introductions were over, they joined us in our picnic. They supplied baguettes and slices of ham, which perfectly complemented our cheese and tomatoes. Lars and Arne were part of a large group of students from Scandinavia, on an organised trip to France. After a couple of days in Paris, they were now travelling down to the Riviera for the rest of the week, before heading back up to the snow around Chamonix, for a week's skiing. This explained why there'd been so many of them on our train. After a couple of hours, our compartment was becoming loud and raucous as we joked about how they looked like Vikings. We were visited by the Chef de Train who, after clipping our tickets, demanded that we make less noise, otherwise he would eject us from the train at the next station. After he'd moved to the next compartment, the two Vikings gave him a two-fingered salute, followed by more hearty laughter. I could tell Lars and Arne both had their eyes on Fionn, so I deliberately sat right up against her and told them she was my sister. When the two Swedes went off to buy some more beer, I checked that Fionn was okay. We decided that she should have the top bunk tonight and got herself tucked into bed behind her curtain, before our hot-blooded Vikings returned.

It was an education listening to Lars and Arne speak about their homes in Sweden. My life was not so very different to theirs, I thought. I was also surprised to hear that they had both seen lots of Rock Bands too in their home town of 'Vesta Ross', sounded like a frozen curry. By the time we all climbed into our separate bunks, I'd really warmed to them and their funny stories about swimming in the lakes and about how, as students, they are permitted to drive cars on the roads, but only at speeds of thirty kilometres an hour. "My moped can do the equivalent of eighty." I drunkenly boasted.

Predictably, Fionn was the first to rise the next morning. By the time we three lads had awakened, she was dressed in her shorts and sweatshirt, ready for her first day on the Cote D'Azur. We eased our thumping Viking heads from off our pillows as the bright sunlight burst through the carriage windows, stinging our eyes. Lying flat on top of my bunk, I dressed as best as I could whilst Fionn sorted through the pile of mixed clothes on the carriage floor.

Our two Swede's were staying on the train as far as Menton. They swapped addresses with Fionn and we hugged each of them goodbye, shouting 'Skål tamma fan' at them through their carriage window, as we walked down the platform. They'd been a lot of fun.

Chapter Three

Nice La Belle

"Are you nervous about going to work for a stranger?" I asked Fionn, as we headed towards the railway station exit.

"Yes, a little bit, but he's not really a stranger. He said some nice things about Eve, at her funeral. I'm more worried about whether he'll like me or not."

"You're a natural Fi, he's lucky to get you." I could see Fionn smile to herself, then she turned to me and said,

"Does Henri know *you're* coming?"

"No, not yet. Besides I'll only be in Nice a couple of days at the most. Just long enough for him to point me in the right direction."

"You're still going ahead with your plan then?"

"Of course." I said confidently.

After leaving the station, the obvious thing to do was to head south, knowing we would soon stumble upon the Mediterranean itself. In front of us, the twin spires of Nice Cathedral dominated the skyline. In France, they certainly know how to build glorious churches Although it didn't look quite as spectacular as Notre Dame had yesterday, it was still extraordinarily ornate and put to shame anything I'd seen back in Lancashire. Since we'd entered France, I was pleased with how well our journey was progressing. Already, there was a lot of mileage behind us and the nervousness that took hold of me during that unsettling journey, from Preston down to London, had subsided completely. I'd almost convinced myself too, that Gingernut's actions had been just a coincidence after all. It felt like we were now walking in a different world altogether, the bright and beautiful world of a millionaire's playground. I was enjoying my first days of being an adventurer and it was impossible not to feel totally free. It was a great time to be alive and it was difficult to imagine how very different it must have felt for Eve, thirty odd years ago, living under the tyranny of 'The Occupation', when imprisonment and death had stalked her every move. I was more determined than ever, to visit the place where her husband, Paul Larouchamps, had met his death. I was certain his brother Henri would be only too glad to help me with this simple quest. He had obviously been connected to the French resistance in the past, in some way, as he'd organised the reception for Eve, when she'd visited France again, some twenty years ago. Perhaps he'd be able to show me exactly where his brother's grave lies. I reckoned on a couple of days in Nice, a couple of days in the Pyrenees and back again in Nice for the weekend, to enjoy a bit of a holiday, before flying back home to Lancashire, from where I would plan my return trip, with Eve's ashes, providing of course no-one else had claimed them.

After twenty minutes walking in the bright morning sunshine, we suddenly came upon a wonderful, old, open air market. My eyes had never seen such colour. Most of the market stalls were effectively covered and decorated with enormous bunches of cut flowers.

"Look at all the Chrysanthemums and Lavender," gasped Fionn, "It's unbelievable." It looked to me like everyone in Nice too, had turned out to buy flowers this Sunday morning. And why not, the vast array of flowers did have a remarkable, uplifting effect. Like an operatic finale, it made you almost want to stand and applaud.

The beautiful buildings around the square were much older than the offices and commercial premises we'd walked past earlier. I was beginning to recognise a particular style that seemed to sum up the French. All the windows had wooden louvred, shutter doors, which were painted a pleasant pale blue colour and were often flaked and faded by the strong sunlight. The stonework too, was very pale but had an amazing, weathered patina, which reflected many subtle shades, from pink to ochre. The gable ends, which were most prominent, presented worn, painted publicity brands: such as the blue and white of RICARD and the red and white of DUBONNET. My stomach was beginning to feel envious at the sight of all the food stalls, so I looked around for somewhere close by to eat. We were spoilt for choice: the market appeared to be surrounded on all sides by a continuous terrace of wicker chairs and tables all laid out invitingly.

"Come on Fi, over here. I'm starving."

We found a free place amongst the local shoppers and settled outside the Café des Fleurs. As we rested our rucksacks under our table, I was surprised to hear the waiter address us in English. Perhaps we did look odd and out of place. He pointed to the breakfast menu board and recommended an Omelette Niçoise and a glass of the local Rosé wine.

"What the hell, let's go for it," said Fionn, with a smile.

We soaked up the scented, vibrant atmosphere. It felt like we could just sit there all day.

"Thanks for sticking up for me last night, on the train," she said. "I quite liked pretending to be your sister."

"That's ok," I replied. "I always wanted a sister."

"That's funny, I always wanted a brother," said Fionn, laughing and she bent forward and kissed me on the cheek.

"Hey, that's arson," I joked.

"Don't you mean incest?"

"Well as long as we keep it in the family," I laughed. "Your secret's safe with me."

The waiter was passing along the tables, topping up everyone's glass with the chilled Rosé wine. "If we have another one, I don't think I'll want to leave," I said.

"That's probably the idea, anyway don't you think it's time to go and look for the Hotel Les Moulins?"

"I suppose so, can't put it off any longer."

Having received a few vague directions from our waiter, we shuffled off towards the beach. We'd decided to follow the promenade around to the old port. "Can't be that difficult to find," I said, with an air of confidence.

It can be quite alarming how reality differs from your imagination. For some reason I'd imagined the Hotel Les Moulins to be a grand palatial residence on the sea front, overlooking the old marina. The only sea view to be had here, I thought, was probably from the roof. The tired looking Hotel *was* situated in the old port, but at ninety degrees to the harbour and several doors up a side street, called Rue Lazarette. The ground floor entrance had two, tall, solid glass doors which opened into a small vestibule. It was paved with an old, mosaic floor tiles, portraying three windmills, in reference to the name of the hotel. Resting in the left hand corner was a giant ceramic pot containing a dangerous looking cactus plant. Facing the entrance was a dark, studded, oak door, which lead through to the reception desk and restaurant. To the right of the vestibule, the mosaic tiled floor continued through an open entrance into a sparsely furnished coffee bar, or Bar Tabac as it was called above the opening. It had a long, tall bar counter with a large decorative mirrored glass panel below, which reflected the sunlight back into the room. Behind the bar was a complicated looking coffee machine, with chrome tubes and pressure gauges and levers that resembled something you might see in a fifties science fiction film. On the rear wall of the bar, was a large picture mirror with the hotel name and again, more windmills. The outer wall to the front of the building consisted mainly of glass panelled frames looking out onto the street and a café opposite, called Le Sardine. I was beginning to think learning to speak French would be a doddle. Just think of an English word and put 'Le' in front of it, Le beer, Le sandwich, Le fish and chips.

From behind the bar came the familiar sound of someone washing crockery and glasses. In front of it, two customers were seated on bar stools. One was a dark-skinned middle-aged man with dark curly hair. He was reading a copy of the Nice-Matin. The other customer was just in the process of leaving. "Salut Jean-Paul," he said, as he walked away. The young man behind the bar I recognised immediately, from three weeks ago at Eve's funeral. It was Henri's son. I nodded to the departing customer, allowing him to pass in front of us before we stepped inside and introduced ourselves.

"Good to see you, entrée, entrée." said Jean-Paul, he appeared to be genuinely pleased to see us. "Sit down, what can I get you to drink? You must be very thirsty, non?"

"I'll have a Cola, please," I said.

"And for mademoiselle?" enquired Jean-Paul.

"I'll have a Cola too, please."

The dark-skinned stranger next to us was taking an interest in us too. He folded away his newspaper and spoke, "Are you going to introduce me to your friends, Jean-Paul?"

"Pardon Patrice, this is Fionn and Mark from England. Fionn is going to be working with us here at Les Moulins."

"Enchante, I'm very pleased to make your acquaintance."

Fionn blushed as Patrice bent forwards taking her hand and placing a kiss upon it.

"Asseyez-vous, please sit down." said Jean-Paul, gesturing for us to take a bar stool as he placed two slim bottles of Coke-Cola and two glasses half full of ice, on the bar top in front of us. "We are about to close the doors for the day. I'm sorry my parents are not here right now, but would you like to join us on the beach? You can leave your bags here."

We looked at each other and nodded.

"Yer, why not. We'd love to." I said. "I'll keep hold of my rucksack, just for now."

"Do as you please," replied Jean-Paul.

From the opposite side of the street, a concrete path led down to the quayside. We followed Jean-Paul and Patrice, by the side of the marina and past lots of immaculate gleaming yachts, all firmly tied to their moorings. At the end of the quayside, there was an archway cut into the harbour wall where the concrete path continued and eventually sunk into the sandy beach, just a ten minute walk from our Hotel.

"I could get used to this," laughed Fionn.

For a Sunday in October, there were still lots of bathers lying on the sand. Parked cars lined the low wall that marked the edge of the promenade. There were few free spaces available. People were still entering from the promenade, through a gap in the wall. A group of beach goers were playing a game of volley ball, patting and passing the ball to each other and throwing themselves energetically on the sand. It looked like a lot of fun. Jean-Paul stopped about ten feet from the edge of the sea, pulled his t-shirt over his head and sat down, staring out over the bay. We sat down, four abreast, all facing the same direction. We sat on our rucksacks and Patrice on his newspaper. In the distance, several fishing boats were being gently raised and let down again by the swell of the sea.

This tranquil scene was rudely interrupted by the urgent sound of Police sirens. We all turned around and together with everyone else on the beach, we watched as four Police cars went racing up the promenade, in the direction of the airport.

"Just like a Saturday afternoon in Preston," I joked, not expecting anyone to understand, but trying not to let my paranoia with the Police re-emerge.

"Probably some important Politician flying in for a holiday or something," said Jean-Paul cynically. "They are always wasting our taxes." I was beginning to understand the mind of a French student. Politics appeared to be very important to them. I couldn't say that it interested me very much.

Fionn kicked off her trainers and said, "Lets go for a paddle Byrney."

We stood, like a pair of Scotsmen at Blackpool, me with my jeans rolled up to my knees and Fionn in her cut-off jean shorts letting the cool waves gently break over our bare ankles. All that was missing was a knotted handkerchief perched on each of our heads. I asked Fionn what she thought of Jean-Paul?

"Seems okay. I'm just really glad he speaks such good English. My biggest worry before we arrived was not understanding anyone." She turned around to look behind her before continuing, "I'm not sure about his friend Patrice, he's very handsome, but he's a bit old to be hanging around with a teenager, don't you think?"

"Yer, I suppose." I hadn't thought of it like that, but I guess we'll get to know him better, soon enough.

Bathing over, we went and sat next to our new French friends and Fionn retrieved her *Collins French Phrase Book*, from out of her rucksack, to brush up on her vocabulary. Before long, we were passing the book between us, Fionn and myself reading aloud the French version and Jean-Paul and Patrice speaking the English translation. Some of the phrases in the book were so corny, like: 'la femme de chambre ne vient jamais quand je sonne - the Chambermaid never comes when I ring' - that had us all howling with laughter. We discovered that Patrice was an old family friend to the Larouchampses. Patrice's father had been a printer, here in Nice before the war and his studio was on the same street as Les Moulins. Patrice had carried on the family business when his father retired and before we parted for the day he said, "you must come round and have a look at my place, tomorrow. We print many posters and sketches for the cinema and rock bands also. You'll probably find some of them very interesting."

"Thank you Patrice, we will."

When we returned to the hotel, Jean-Paul took us upstairs to show us to our rooms. I had already explained to him that I would only be staying a couple of nights, but decided not to reveal anything about my plans to him, because I wanted to discuss them first with his father, Henri. I was given a small, but pretty guest bedroom, on the second floor. It was small by hotel standards, but felt like a palace, compared to our mobile home back in Lancashire. To my surprise, my room was given to me free of charge. "Gratuit, gratuit," said Jean-Paul. I looked up the translation later in Fionn's phrase book. She was given a spare room to herself, on the third floor, which was part of the Larouchampses' private accommodation. We were both wacked out by nine p.m and we made our excuses to retire early to our rooms. At this hour of the evening, Henri and his wife Juliette had still not returned from their weekend trip to Milan.

Around two a.m., there was a faint knock at my bedroom door. I opened it to find Fionn, standing there in her pyjamas, illuminated by the light in the corridor and looking slightly sorry for herself. "Henri and his wife got back around midnight," she said. "The sound of them moving about must have woke me up and I've not been able to fall back to sleep since. So I thought I'd come down and see if you were awake too." It was a warm night and I'd left my window open. The sound of metallic tapping drifted in from the harbour as the yachts nodded from side to side, gently pulling on their moorings. I switched on my bedside lamp and ushered Fionn into my room. I drew back my curtains so that we could look out of the window as we sat together, at the end of my bed. Earlier in the evening, we'd both used the telephone in the coffee bar to phone home. My mum and dad were both very pleased to hear that we'd reached Nice, safe and sound. They were even happier when I'd let them know that Fionn had travelled out with me too. At least it would give my mum something different to talk about when she next bumped into Fionn's mum, over at the Newsagents back in Cayburn.

"What did your mum have to say Fi, when you called?"

"Just the usual stuff about staying away from strange men," she laughed, "but I got the feeling she was definitely missing me and I suppose I'm missing her too, a little."

"What do you think of it here then, do you like it?"

"Oh yes, I'm really looking forward to starting work tomorrow and learning what goes on here. There doesn't appear to be any guests staying here at the moment, so I've no idea what I'll be doing to begin with."

"Yer, it's not like the Friary, is it? Couldn't imagine Madge and Joanie putting up with it being so quiet. They'd be dragging people in off the street by the scruff of the neck and standing over them, until they ordered something. I think I'm going to miss them both really, Edward too. When you look back, you have to admit, they looked after us all like we were their own children."

"Well at least there's the Friary Christmas Do to look forward to," remembered Fionn. "I wouldn't miss that for anything."

"Are you going to be alright by yourself here, when I go away for a few days?"

Fionn looked at me inquisitively, " sure, don't worry about me. I'll be fine once I get used to everything." And with that she squeezed my leg, got up and walked to the door.

"Goodnight Byrney. Nice underpants by the way," she laughed.

"Goodnight Siss." I turned out the light and sat staring at the boats in the harbour a little longer. It was kind of comforting to watch them calmly moving in the breeze. It was also reassuring to see millions of pounds worth of property floating around unguarded. I collected all my Francs and Pesetas from inside my coat and placed them into ten equal piles and stored them inside my ten pairs of socks, storing them in the bottom drawer of my dressing table. Yes, I was feeling very confident, everything would work out just fine for the both of us.

The next morning, I wandered down to the restaurant to find everyone sat at the large dining table. Everyone that is, except Henri's wife Juliette who was already serving customers, inside the coffee bar. Fionn was first to say good morning then Henri came forward out of the kitchen and shook hands with me.

"Hello Mark, it's good to see you again. Welcome to Les Moulins, I hope you will have a pleasant time here."

"Please call me Byrney," I replied "and thank you both for allowing me to stay here." Jean-Paul looked up from his newspaper and drew back the empty chair next to him.

"Asseyez-vous, please sit down Byrney."

There was a large, blue enamel coffee pot on the table, which I helped myself to.

"The coffee and croissants are delicious, Byrney," said Fionn, taking a bite and spilling crumbs everywhere.

"So how do you like Nice, you two?" said Henri, but before we could answer, Jean-Paul was stabbing a finger and pointing at an article he was reading in The Nice Matin.

"Ecoutez, listen to this," he said, looking directly at Fionn. "Remember those police sirens from yesterday? They have arrested the leader of 'The Sewer Gang' at Nice airport."

"What's the 'Sewer Gang'?" asked Fionn, with her hand over her mouth to prevent more crumbs falling onto the white table cloth.

"They were a group of ingenious thieves, who used the sewers to tunnel into the vaults at the Societe Generale Bank, here in Nice. They got away with millions of Francs in jewels and cash. It was the largest bank raid ever in France. The leader arrived back from America yesterday, incroyable, it's all here in the journal..."

Once again I was reminded about my own exploits. It appeared to me that the whole world had been *at it* this summer, nicking stuff. Henri was stood next to me and offered me a wooden bowl full of croissants to choose from and as he went to sit down next to Fionn, asked, "so Byrney, what are your plans? Jean-Paul has told me you're only staying with us for two or three days."

I wasn't sure if this was the right moment to mention my mission here to Henri, but I guessed I had to start my enquiries sooner, rather than later, so:

"Well, Henri, there is something I'd like to ask you." Henri was all ears. I continued. "It's a bit sensitive, but I'd like to visit the place where your brother Paul died, so that I can scatter Eve's ashes over his grave." Henri suddenly looked very pale and the others were looking at me like I'd just mentioned a big, taboo subject, like I was asking for the whereabouts of Lord Luchan. Jean-Paul was the first to break the spell.

"That's a very nice idea, Byrney."

Henri immediately interrupted his son. The creases beneath his receding hair line grew deeper as he spoke. "Actually, I don't think you should do that. To be blunt with you, it could be very dangerous to start disturbing the dead, even after all this time." I was taken aback by Henri's reply. I hadn't expected to be brushed aside and what had he meant by 'disturbing the dead'?

"Is it forbidden?" I asked.

"No Byrney. It's just that there are people around today who have never been punished for their crimes during the Second

World War. If you start turning over stones from the past, you never know what will come out from under them."

"But don't you know where your brother's grave is?" I asked.

Jean-Paul had been getting restless and looked directly across the table at his father. His young, sharp, blue eyes were clearly angry. He took a deep breath and said impatiently, "what mon Papa is avoiding saying to you Byrney, is that he is a coward. He doesn't know where his own brother is buried because he spent the whole of the war hiding away."

I didn't like the way the atmosphere at the table was changing. I now wished instead that I'd spoken to Henri in private. Fionn, I could tell too, was feeling very awkward.

Henri slammed his palms down on the table, making us all jump. "That is enough, Jean-Paul. Please, go back to reading your newspaper."

"Even the Sewer Gang had more nerve and bravery than you, Papa. What risks did you ever take?"

"You weren't there Jean-Paul. You don't understand the dangers we all faced."

Just then, Juliette appeared in the dining room looking alarmed. "Garcons arrêtez, boys, what is all this shouting? The customers can hear you in the bar." Jean-Paul stood up and moved away from the table. "What is wrong?" she asked.

"Rien," he shook his head. "It's nothing. I will see to the customers," he said as he left.

Henri spoke softly, "I apologise to you, Fionn and Byrney. Jean-Paul can be a little head strong sometimes." Juliette raised her eyebrows and forced an innocent smile. She was dressed in a pale blue cardigan, open at the neck, to reveal a small gold cross and chain. She turned to Fionn and myself, explaining that we shouldn't pay too much attention to Jean-Paul. Then she retrieved something from the top of the pine dresser.

"I have a letter for you Mark," she said, waving a brown envelope in the air. "It arrived this morning." I recognised my own handwriting on the address. It was my travellers Cheque Book, which I'd posted from Lancaster the previous week.

"Thank you Juliette, and please, call me Byrney."

"More café Fionn?" said Henri, having regained his composure.

I now realised my task wasn't going to be as easy as I'd thought. I'd not reckoned on dangerous either, just how dangerous could it be? For the moment I brushed those thoughts aside. There was certainly no love lost between Henri and Jean-Paul. Perhaps I would find the son more helpful than the father. After breakfast, I left Henri and Juliette to fuss over Fionn. They had obviously taken a shine to her. Although the hotel was quiet at the moment, it was an ideal time for Fionn to learn her duties and improve her spoken French.

I'd decided to take up Patrice's offer of having a tour around his studio, but before that, I thought I would just have a chat about it first with Jean-Paul. When I walked into the coffee bar, I was surprised to see Patrice was already sat at his stool, leaning over the bar in conversation with Jean-Paul. He saw me approaching and held out his hand. "Salut Byrney, cafe?"

"Salut Patrice, oui s'il vous plait."

"That's not bad," he joked. "Already he's talking like a real Frenchman. Jean-Paul has been telling me why you have come to Nice." I was about to explain that it might after all, just turn into a holiday, when Patrice continued to say that he might be able to help me. "Don't worry about Henri, I think he feels a responsibility to you and doesn't want to see you come to any harm." Harm? I thought. I only want to sprinkle a few ashes over a grave, not climb into one.

Half an hour later, we were outside on the busy pavement, amongst the parked cars and dodging the happy shoppers. Patrice had an arm over my shoulder as we walked up the street, towards his studio. He was giving me a brief history of his family printing business and was waving his free hand aloft, to exaggerate the finer points. Patrice's father and Paul Larouchamps had been at the same school and had remained life long friends, right up until Paul had to flee the country. In fact, Patrice's father, Andre, had been best man at Paul and Eve's wedding in Paris. He was also involved with the FFI, the French Resistance.

Patrice unlocked his studio door. There was a wooden name plate fixed to the pillar at the side. Patrice tapped it with his keys, "C'est moi, that's me." The sign read, 'Hard Hat Graphiques.'

"Why 'Hard Hat'?" I asked

"It's a phonetic play on my family name, Arnatte," joked Patrice. Nothing phoney about that, I thought.

As soon as we walked inside I was hit by the smell of paints and turpentine. It was much larger inside than had been suggested by the shabby entrance on the front street. The one, rectangular shaped room was around fifty feet long with an iron, spiral staircase. This led up to a balcony on the first floor, which hovered and extended over half the room, where we stood. Dominating the studio floor, were two, large, metal, work tables, which both had a pair of chrome rollers across them, like old clothes mangles. There were two, long, wooden racks, each splashed with a thousand drips of differently coloured paints which had presumably been deposited by an array of used paint tins haphazardly placed on top of the shelves together with various bottles of chemicals.

Spaced evenly around the room, were several pieces of old, plain, wooden furniture. Some I recognised as map drawers. They reminded me of my old Art Classroom at school. Art had been my favourite subject all through school. In the final year, which seems like a lifetime ago already, our weekly art class had been a triple lesson every Wednesday afternoon. Whilst we perfected our landscapes, we'd spend hours staring out of the first floor windows and having deep, meaningful, unforgettable discussions like: what we'd do if we woke up one morning to find you were the only person left alive.

Patrice was stood against his desk, lighting up a cigarette. I noticed the same distinctive, blue cigarette packet as the one that Eve had smoked too - Gypsies. He was watching me as I moved around the room. Inside one of the half opened long chest of drawers, I could see rows of wooden printing blocks with letters of the alphabet, in different sizes and styles. The colourful posters on the wall in front of me caught my attention.

As I was browsing the framed artworks of film posters and rock concerts, my admiration was growing for Patrice. He was a curious character. He'd a handsome face and an open honesty about him and although I'd only known him a couple of days, I felt relaxed in his company. At the end of the gallery I reached the last poster. It was dated thirteenth of June this year - *The Rolling Stones in Nice*. I turned to face Patrice, who was anticipating my question. "Wow, I'm impressed."

"Yes, that is my favourite too. I was lucky enough to see them play at the sports arena. It was a great concert. When they came out onto the stage and played "Honky Tonk Women", fifty thousand people went wild. It was an unforgettable day, the day that music came to life."

"I'll bet," was all I managed to say. I'd been a Stones fan myself for a few years now too, although I'd not had chance to see them play live yet. One of my first LP records I'd bought was a compilation of theirs called *'High Tides and Green Grass'*. It came with a poster inside the record sleeve, which is still hanging on my bedroom wall at home. I was enjoying the tour of Patrice's studio, but one question was still burning on my mind.

"You mentioned earlier that you might be able to help me find Paul Larouchamps's grave?"

Patrice smiled. "Did you know there are certain organisations in France today, who are still concerned with bringing fugitives to justice, for the crimes they committed during World War Two? One of the guys who still does this is quite famous in the south of France. I remember him, on two occasions, standing in exactly the same place as you are now. The first time was in the winter of 1943, when I was ten years old. That was the day your friend Eve was leaving for England." Patrice handed me a stool from under the workbench.

"So you met Eve too?" I said, almost disbelieving it might be true.

"Yes, many times." Patrice pulled up another stool and began to talk again. "Like I already told you, my father and Eve's husband were very close friends." Patrice was lost in thought for a moment. "Now, where was I? Ah yes, 1943. My father as I said worked for the Resistance, not in a combative way. He was a forger. He supplied documents for people who were escaping from the Nazi's. My father used his printing equipment to produce ID cards, travel permits, underground journals, all kinds of things. This studio was very different in those days, before I made all the alterations that you see before you. The upper floor was used for storing the reels of paper. They were lifted up through a hatch, using a winch. I was looking down through the open hatch when my father handed Eve her false ID card. It was a very tearful farewell between her and Paul. When she left, she was in the company of one of the many guides who helped to take people to the safety of Spain. The guide on this occasion, although I didn't know it at the time, was a man called, Gastin De Bourges. He was also escorting some English airmen, with whom he had travelled down from Geneva. Eve was only going as far as Marseilles but, because she was English, she ran the same risks of being captured as the airmen."

"So who is this person who can help me find what I'm looking for?" I said, impatiently.

"I was just coming to that, attendez. You must understand a little of our history first. Immediately after the Liberation, there were many reprisals. Ordinary people, who had been too afraid to resist, came out of their shells and took revenge on those they believed had assisted the Nazis. Some underground criminals even used this time of upheaval to rid themselves of their rivals. It was a lawless few weeks, hundreds of people died and when order was restored again, many weapons were never handed into the authorities. Despite the joys of the Liberation, it was a shameful time too. In the confusion, many of the worst perpetrators managed to escape justice. Some of them even bribed their way back to their pre-war positions of power. A few years after the war ended, Gastin De Bourges became a kind of a bounty hunter. He knew my father kept records of the identity cards he had produced and he turned up here one day to speak to my father. He hoped to find evidence, or clues, to the whereabouts of some of the perpetrators who were still at large. That was the last time I saw him, almost thirty years ago. He must be about sixty years old now, but I know he is still alive. His name appears in the Nice Matin occasionally, usually in connection with the trial of a former member of the dreaded Milici." Patrice walked over to his desk and took down a framed photograph that was hanging on the wall above and handed it to me.

"What am I looking at?" Patrice remained silent and then smiled when he saw that I recognised Eve, holding the handlebars of a bicycle, at the centre of a group of six men.

"Those are some of the Resistance Fighters, here in Nice at the beginning of the occupation." I was still staring at the old, faded, black and white photograph. Eve looked so young. "There is a famous story," continued Patrice. "Eve was part of a group of men who rescued a Resistance Fighter from the hands of the Italian Army, who were in charge of Nice when it was still part of the Free Zone in France. She pushed her bicycle into the road in front of a car that was carrying an important prisoner, forcing it to stop. She could easily have been run over. When the car was stationary, her armed comrades sprang the prisoner, who eventually made it all the way back to England. The prisoner was Georges Coulombier, one of the organisers of the escape route, known as the Renard Line."

That was some story, I thought. If I wasn't able to find Paul's grave, then at least I was getting to know more about Eve's past. Patrice offered to locate Gastin De Bourges, as he was perhaps my only hope of finding out what I wanted to know. "Do you think, he'll want to help me?"

"Yes, of course," said Patrice, looking slightly shifty and evasive.

Chapter Four

Toulouse

It was another three days before I finally had some good news from Patrice. It was Thursday afternoon and I was in the middle of a strange conversation with Jean-Paul, at the time. We were both sat on the beach, admiring the view and Jean-Paul had been inventing stories about the young girls lying on the beach, about how they came down here in the hope of being spotted by a movie director, or a bonbon daddy.

"You know, since they let the girls go topless on the beach it has been terrible for me," admitted Jean-Paul. I had no idea what he was he was referring to; it seemed like a good thing to me. This is France after all, I said to myself.

"Yes," he continued. "I have been having trouble with my weanus."

I was trying not to laugh, "you mean, your penis?"

"Yes, my weanus, ever since the girls have been coming down to the beach and taking their tops off, every morning I have had to beat my weanus with a stick, just to get my jeans on." I didn't know if he was being serious or just joking, but looking around the beach, at all the pretty girls, I could see he had a point.

"Bonjour, Byrney" said Patrice as he approached, looking very pleased with himself. "Good news! De Bourges has agreed to see you on Saturday afternoon. Just one small problem, you have to meet him in Toulouse." Patrice shrugged his shoulders as he referred to a scrappy piece of paper in his hand, "Hotel de Lion"

"Wow, that's great. Does he know where to find Paul's grave?"

"Yes, he confirmed he is familiar with Paul's story. There is one other thing to tell you and that is, he has insisted you must make a donation to De Bourges's organisation, one thousand Francs." I was doing a few sums in my head, converting the figure back into English money. It was only about one hundred pounds.

"Sounds great, thanks you very much Patrice."

The following evening I was packing my rucksack in readiness for my imminent departure to Toulouse. I'd also decided that this would be an ideal time to call my parents and let them know what my plans were, but played it down a little by saying I was going across to Toulouse, to meet a friend. However, as soon as I began talking to mum, her conversation had me reaching for the panic button. Yesterday afternoon, our mobile home had been burgled. She was almost certain that nothing had been taken, apart from, my moped. I couldn't believe it. She said that a fat Police Sergeant (yes, I know the one) had called round that morning to investigate and had informed her that there had been a recent spate of thefts in our area, involving motorcycles. 'Probably a gang from out of town', had been his exact words. When mum told the policeman that I was currently on holiday in Nice, he said not to worry, but I must call in at the Police Station to make a statement, as soon as I returned home again, to West Lancashire. I put the phone down. My thoughts were jumping about, all over the place. The police now knew exactly where I was. But why would anyone want to steal my moped and how had it happened, without anyone seeing anything? Then I began to panic about the cash buried beneath the garden shed. There was absolutely nothing I could do about it. So, for now, I would just have to put it to the back of my mind. At least I'd enough cash on me to keep me going for a while and hopefully see me through until I was back home again.

Henri very kindly gave me a lift to the Railway Station in his Renault 12 estate car. It was an early start for us both. My train was leaving Nice at twenty minutes past six and was due to arrive in Toulouse approximately seven hours later. He was doing his best to be cheerful. I felt a touch of deja vu, having been taxied about so often by Edward at the Friary, in similar circumstances, during the last eight or nine months.

"You have our telephone number? Please call us if you need any help and please, be careful Byrney."

I was feeling upbeat about being on the move again, not that I didn't enjoy being in Nice. It was a beautiful city and exploring the old quarter with Patrice, listening to his stories, had been a fascinating way of learning about some interesting pieces of French history. I had also discovered that there were a lot of other English people living in the south of France. There was even an English-speaking radio station, called Sovereign Radio.

The express train from Genoa was already waiting at the platform as I emerged from the ticket hall. I climbed aboard and found an empty seat in the first carriage. I sat by the window, facing forwards, with my rucksack on the empty seat opposite. Juliette had made up a packed lunch for me: fish paste sandwiches, some fresh peaches and a bottle of water, so I'd everything I needed. I'd taken the precaution of leaving some of my clothes behind with Fionn: meaning the socks, where my spare cash was hidden. Better safe than sorry, I thought, just in case I ran into trouble, or had my rucksack stolen. Hopefully, Fionn wouldn't decide to wear my socks, otherwise I'd have a lot of explaining to do.

There were three stops on my journey and just after the second stop in Marseilles, an argument broke out amongst some of the passengers, but it subsided as quickly as it had begun. I was still sat with two seats to myself, with my legs stretched out opposite, resting on my rucksack. I wasn't taking any chances. The SNCF train was rocketing through the arid and scrubby countryside, which was strewn with hidden, ramshackle sheds and the occasional herd of nomadic goats. I was still bemoaning the loss of my wonderful moped. I knew I would have to replace it, when I turned seventeen, but for the time being, I would be stuck without any means of getting around with my mates, when I eventually returned home.

****

Just the sight of seeing Atkinson walking out of the Police Station had got Lofty's back up. He'd still not forgiven him for the debacle around retrieving his car from Chorley Nick. He had the memory of an elephant and could hold a grudge as long as the next man. Lofty also had a nose for sniffing out a back hander and he knew full well that Atkinson was holding out on him, especially as he was no longer a part of Atkinson's covert operation against Mark Byrne. Lofty was turning the tables on his former partner and had started his own covert surveillance, to see if his suspicions held any water. Shortly before lunchtime, on the fifth day, things were beginning to pay dividends. There was definitely something odd about seeing Atkinson climbing into the driving seat of a Police 'Black Mariah'. Perhaps he was just doing something as innocent as a spot of moonlighting? "S.T.Y," said Lofty out loud, "Smarter than you." Through his field glasses and from the opposite side of the park, he observed Atkinson, pulling out of the yard car park. He glanced down at his watch, eleven-thirty - a bit early for lunch, he thought.

Lofty followed the dark, blue, Ford Transit van: through town, around the inner ring road and out the other side up Cockerham Road. At the traffic lights, he turned right and headed up towards Cayburn. Then the van turned left onto Bowland Mobile Home Park. Lofty drove past the entrance and just caught sight of the police van, slowly turning off the brick littered car park and disappearing around the back of the derelict hotel. "What's he up to then?" Lofty pulled on to the old Transport Café lay by opposite and switched off his engine, concealing his car behind some overgrown Buddleia bushes. He picked up his field glasses and went to investigate.

The Black Mariah was parked facing back towards the exit. There was no sign of Atkinson. Moving quietly to the back of the van, he saw the rear doors had been left open and a steel ramp was resting on the ground. There was only one course of action to take. He clambered up the fire escape and entered the

48

first floor of the derelict hotel, pausing to listen for signs of movement from within. The last room, at the end of the corridor, faced directly over the mobile home park and he stood staring at the flat, rectangular, roof tops of the caravans. Lofty peered through his field glasses, but despite their twenty times magnification, the narrow space between each caravan and the angle of his line of sight meant that it was impossible to see what was occurring at ground level. It was obvious to Lofty that Atkinson was paying a visit to Byrne's caravan. Lofty knew from previous experience, when watching Byrne two weeks ago, the best vantage point to get a clear view, was to take up a position opposite, from across the adjacent field. At the top of the fire escape, he saw the Black Mariah was still unoccupied. He ran down the steps and through the gap in the fence and into the meadow. The ground was saturated and he cursed as the cold, dirty, rainwater splashed above his ankles and ran down inside his shoes, soaking his socks. "J.M.F.L" he moaned. The meadow dog-legged away from the fence and he rested up behind the hedge, about fifty yards from Byrne's caravan. He could see Atkinson inside, moving from room to room. "You sneaky sod," he said to himself. Atkinson appeared at the door and moved around to the back of the caravan, behind the shed. He removed the rain cover from Byrne's moped and wheeled it along the path and out of the garden. "He's nicking Byrne's moped," said Lofty, lowering his field glasses in shocked surprise. 'He's got some brass neck. No doubt he'll have an excuse already worked out, if he's caught,' he thought.

Lofty ran back to the top of the dog leg in the meadow and waited for Atkinson to appear by the police van. He reached into his raincoat pocket and whipped out his Rollei XF35 compact camera. He captured that decisive moment of Atkinson pushing Byrne's moped into the back of the van, making sure he got the number plate in focus too. His feet were sodden, his shoes and trouser bottoms were caked in mud, but he never felt more pleased with himself. "Gotcha!"

****

Luckily, my train was terminating at Toulouse Station, as I'd fallen asleep for the final hour of my journey. It was only through sensing the other mumbling passengers, shuffling about my carriage, that I had woken up to discover the train had actually already pulled up, at the platform.

Once again, I was in awe of the size of French cities. Apart from the absence of an Eiffel Tower, Toulouse looked every bit as magnificent as Paris, with a large river, old Roman bridges and cobbled streets. The only other obvious difference between the two great cities was the setting: the dark, looming stumps of the Pyrenees that lay, waiting for me, on the southern horizon. I could almost stand in their shadow. I took out the scrap of paper on which Patrice had written down the address of the Hotel de Lion and quickly figured out that the best way of finding it was to simply get in a taxi. The train had arrived at the station exactly on time, which meant I'd half an hour to kill before my rendez-vous with Gastin De Bourges. I passed the scrap of paper to a scruffy looking taxi driver and he grunted, "Montez-vous, climb in." He eyed me, suspiciously, through his rear view mirror. He had very bad body odour and I'd taken the least offensive position on the back seat and had wound down my window fully. After tussling with the traffic in the stale heat, the smelly taxi pulled up right outside the door. I was glad to get out.

The Hotel de Lion was a five-storied, pale coloured, sandstone building, with ornately framed, circular windows, which protruded from the attic space of the steep, slanted, slated roof. I particularly liked the coloured glass in the front door and in the fan shaped window above. It reminded me of the hotel which my great-aunty Ethel had run with her husband Leslie, at the seaside resort of Hoylake. When me and my brother Anthony were very small children, our parents used to take us to stay with them for a week's holiday. It was sited just behind the promenade and sand from the beach used to drift up by the front garden wall, which always seemed very exotic to us. Every visit, we would ritually rush off to the nearest souvenir shop on the promenade and buy a plastic golf set. We had hours of harmless fun, whacking the plastic golf balls as hard as we could, only for them to travel just a few feet at a time, until the club heads were bent out of all recognition. Sadly for great-aunty Ethel, she became crippled with arthritis and they had to close the hotel. She's still there, confined to a downstairs apartment, being nursed by Leslie.

The mosaic coloured lettering, directly above me, spelt out the name and the date underneath read 1885. The front door looked out onto a park opposite, which had a gravel path running through it's length with an avenue of trees, interspersed by wrought iron benches. It was a very popular spot amongst people of all ages, who were either taking a stroll along its path, or playing a game of Boules, or lazing around listening to a portable radio, or even just sitting on one of the benches, with spoilt, pet pooches in their laps. The inside of the hotel had a very similar layout to 'Les Moulins', only in reverse. To the left was a café/bar and to the right, a busy restaurant, which had a great atmosphere: orchestrated by the diners and the uniformed waiters, dashing about, carrying trays of drinks and uncorking various bottles. Their movements were very fluid and the service was fast as they glided between the tables, with two plates of food balanced on each arm; how did they do that without dropping them?

I waited for an hour, playing a game with myself to imagine which one of the customers might be Gastin De Bourges. The only clue I had to his identity was that he was around sixty years old. For some reason I pictured him to look like the grandfather figure, César, from the TV program Belle and Sebastien. I couldn't have been further from the truth. The busy restaurant was beginning to empty quite dramatically when in walked a tall guy, wearing knee high, suede boots, a brown leather jacket and leather cowboy hat. All his costume needed was a bullet belt slung across his chest and he'd look like a real bandit. "Bonjour," he said in a gruff voice without the slightest hint of an apology for his lateness. "Vous ettes Byrney?"

I stood up to greet him. "Oui, parlez-vous Anglais?"

"Yes, Gastin De Bourges, a plaisir." We shook hands and before he sat down, he turned and clicked his fingers, which resulted in a glass of red wine being hurriedly delivered to our table and placed down in front of him. He was looking me up and down and I could tell he had his doubts about me. "Arnatte has told me, you are looking for the grave of Paul Larouchamps?" But before I could answer he asked, "Do you have the money?" I hastily took out my wallet and presented a thousand Francs for him to count, expecting he would hand it back to me, but instead he folded it in half and stuck the thin wad of cash inside his breast pocket. "Bon." He took a large slurp of wine and continued. "So, you are a friend of Eve Larouchamps and you want to find her husband's grave - well, you are not going to find it dressed like that." His large, bushy eyebrows, which looked like African caterpillars stuck to his grainy forehead, were pointed at the rucksack sat next to me. "Do you have any strong boots, or warm clothes?" When I replied to the contrary, he brushed this inconvenience aside and announced, "we will get you the correct attire from my office."

It was only a short walk along the busy gravel path to the modern office complex at the other end of the park. As we were rounding the hotel and just before we crossed the road, Gastin grabbed my arm and pointed to a long, grey, three-storied building behind a walled garden. "You see that house there? That was the Gestapo Headquarters during the occupation. You did not want to be in there, thirty five years ago." He rolled up his left sleeve to show me a faded, tattooed number on his arm, "otherwise you were in a lot of trouble." It was the first piece of evidence I had seen so far in connection to the war. Even now, the house looked unwelcoming and sinister. I had a feeling I might see a lot worse in the coming days and I was starting to feel slightly unnerved. I was putting a lot of trust in Gastin De Bourges, which was probably exactly how escaping airmen had felt towards their guides, on their long journey to safety, during World War Two.

Gastin's office was on the top floor of a five storey, concrete building. "I'll make a deal with you," he said to me as he stepped into the lift, "If you can get to my office before me, I'll take you to where you want to go." The lift doors began to close in front of him and I ran up the ten flights of stairs like my life depended on it. I heard the elevator doorbell ping as I rounded the bottom of the last flight of stairs. When I reached the top of them, Gastin was holding open his office door. I was bent over double, trying to catch my breath. "Not bad," he said, smiling. "Okay, come in." Once I had my breath back, I was able to take in the interior of Gastin's environment.

There was a world map on the wall with several marker pins stuck to it. There were filing cabinets, propaganda posters from the 1940's, black and white framed photographs and a French flag, draped on top of a blackboard. He had attached a series of portraits down the left hand side, with comments written in chalk along side them. The comments referred to the date, place and witness of the last sighting. On the wall behind his desk, was a glass fronted cabinet, protected by steel bars. Behind the glass, I could see several hand guns and a rifle. Gastin detected my interest and said, "souvenirs from the war. Don't worry we won't be needing any of them where we are going." I looked away from the blackboard for a moment as Gastin opened up a big locker and handed me a pair of hiking boots, a parka jacket and a small, canvas rucksack. "You are going to need these. Do you have any spare socks? You will need to change your socks twice a day. We will be walking for two days. Leave the rest of your things here." He looked at me, eye to eye. "Don't worry no-one will steal them." He sat down behind his desk, cleared the paperwork in front of him and locked it away inside a drawer. He placed a duplicate canvas rucksack on top of his desk and added a washbag and a bottle of spirits. "Essential supplies. When we took airmen over the Pyrenees, during the war, we assembled just around the corner from here at a safe house, right under the noses of the Gestapo. The airmen were always referred to as 'Parcels'. When it was time to move up to the mountains, we always travelled under cover of night. So you see you are very lucky because nowadays we can travel in daylight. It's less dangerous and no one will be trying to stop you or will even be shooting at you."

"I'm very pleased to hear that," I replied smiling. I thought he was trying to put the wind up me. I didn't doubt for one minute the dangers they'd faced all those years ago. Although I'm not so sure how I would have coped, living with those constant horrors and fears.

"This afternoon we will be travelling by bus to St. Jean-Les-Bains. Take with you only the items I have mentioned. Are you ready?" My own large, military rucksack was placed inside the locker and Gastin checked it was safe and secure. Then he took his fur coat from the back of the door and locked up his office. Gastin didn't strike me as someone to be messed with. He'd given me the impression I would have to prove myself in his eyes. Just because I was an ex-colleague of Eve's cut little ice with him. I felt I could trust him one hundred percent, but at the same time he made me nervous. I wanted to get to know him better and my hope was that after a few days together he would look upon me as a friend.

On the bumpy, three hour bus journey, Gastin was happy to talk about his exploits and successes since 1945. His knowledge of the Pyrenees and the escapes routes used by the Allies had paid dividends when he was chasing down ex-Nazis - who were on the run by then, in large numbers. "We called them the 'Rat Runs'. They were using almost the exact same Escape Lines that we had used, for several years previously. How ever did they think they would get away with it? But, despite our best attempts to stop them, some of the worst offenders slipped through our net and are still at large. You saw some of the photos in my office: Paul Touvier, Klaus Barbie, Jean Leguay and some prominent members of La Milice." Although he admitted he'd spent almost eighteen months in a Labour Camp at the end of the war, he didn't confide any details. His passion was the mountains. "When you climb the mountains, it's an extraordinary feeling. You will find out what you're made of when you are tested physically, at the same time alone with your thoughts. There is real freedom, but it can also be a place of real danger too, especially if you are caught in a 'White Out'. You have to watch the sky, read the clouds, watch for sudden changes in air pressure and wind speeds. It's a beautiful, but very unforgiving world. When we start walking tomorrow, you must do everything as I say; is that clear?" I nodded in agreement. "I don't want your death on my conscience, accidental or otherwise." Cheers, I don't want my death on my conscience either, I thought.

Outside the bus window, the shaded portion of the hillsides we were passing was creeping ever higher towards the summit, as the sun sunk lower in the evening sky. The hills grew higher, above the sight of the window frame and I craned my neck up against the cool glass, to see their snow capped ridges. I was interested in learning more about Gastin's organisation and to begin with I asked him what its name was.

"A.T.C. Agence Trouver les Collaborateurs. We play a small part in helping to bring traitors, collaborators and torturers to justice. There are bigger and more important agencies than mine, but we share information to help keep the costs down. It's very expensive tracking fugitives in places like South America and Australia. I suppose you want to know why I do it?"

The noisy bus was beginning to labour at the steep inclines we were now ascending. The twisty, narrow road was now snaking through the foot of the mountains. I looked over the edge of the curb. There was only a wheel nibbled six inch step protecting us from plummeting down, hundreds of feet to the base of the ravine. My palms began to feel uncomfortable and clammy and I was hoping that Mum's pink kittens weren't about to spring out of my bum, so I looked the opposite way and tried to concentrate on what Gastin was saying to me.

"I bet in your home town there is a cross with the names of the soldiers who died in the war? They are all heroes too, correct?"

"Yes, they sacrificed their lives," I replied proudly.

"When the Germans bombed your cities are the names of the civilians also on the cross?" He didn't wait for an answer. "Non. They are forgotten. In France there were many victims like this too. If people died in their homes because English or American bombs fell on them, no one ever complained or condemned these regrettable actions, as long as the bombs were killing Nazi's too. This we accepted." Hearing these words, my pride had quickly changed to guilt. "But much worse things happened to us," continued Gastin. " Innocent people were dragged from their homes in the middle of the night, their possessions stolen and looted. Whole families disappeared that way, or they were sent away to die: either quickly or slowly, through hard labour. Their names are forgotten forever. The only way to remember them is to bring the perpetrators to face justice, so that we can record the names of the victims. And hear about their anonymous suffering and allow these tormented witnesses to lay their fears to rest. This is why I hunt them down. When I was in Mauthausen Concentration Camp, I promised myself that, if I survived, I would dedicate my life to ensure that the victims of the last war, would not be allowed to be forgotten and that the truth of how they were treated would be known to the world. How else can we make the world a better place today? Do you understand?"

Gastin's words gave me a lump at the back of my throat. "Do you know what happened to Paul Larouchamps?" I wanted to hear the truth from Gastin and was hoping he could tell me that whoever had betrayed him had also been brought to face justice.

"I wasn't with his group. That particular day, I was over two hundred kilometres away, collecting some 'Parcels' in Montauban. I have searched for the truth for over thirty years and yet I still believe that, one day, the person responsible will be uncovered. At the time, we didn't know that Paul's group had been betrayed, by someone who had infiltrated the Renard Escape Line. The German Patrols had been able to follow their tracks in the snow. They never stood a chance. Perhaps if there had been some Allied airmen amongst their group, it would not have ended the way it did."

"You mean they would have lived?"

"Yes, they would all have been taken in as prisoners. It was normal for the Gestapo to interrogate captured airmen for information about the Allies and they would not have wanted them to witness a massacre. It was I who eventually found the burnt remains of those two Jewish families whom Paul had been travelling with. It was on my very next run a week later when I came upon the chard remains of the last staging post. The bodies were so badly burnt it was impossible to count them. It's thought that the Spanish guides were amongst the ashes too. There was very little time to search for clues. The day afterwards, I was arrested in Toulouse. Our escape network had been completely compromised."

As the dark sky descended, the giant shapes of the mountains became heavier, almost overbearing. What mysteries did they still hold onto, in the dark recesses of days gone by? Gastin removed his hat and parked it on his knee. Turning directly to face me, he said, "I'm going to tell you a secret, Byrney." The dim, interior lighting of the bus shaded this grey haired man who sat next to me. For the first time, he looked much older than he had six hours earlier. His eyes flickered and he spoke sorrowfully.

"One of the Spanish Guides, that day Paul Larouchamps died, was my father."

Chapter Five

Anna

When the coach finally chugged it's way into the deserted bus station, surprisingly, it was still only early evening, although it felt and looked to me like the middle of the night. As the rest of the passengers who'd endured the journey up from Toulouse trundled off into the darkness, I turned around in a full three hundred and sixty degree circle, to get a feel for my new home. So this was St. Jean-Les-Bains; there wasn't much to see; it felt like the very edge of a wild frontier. At the entrance to the bus station, by the low, stone wall, I noticed an old, stone water trough which immediately made me think of Crowston:

"Byrney, this way," said Gastin, who was already several paces ahead of me. I caught up with him on the narrow main street, which rose steeply from the cobbled square in the centre of town. In daylight, on a sunny day, it must have resembled a stairway to heaven. My ears popped. They'd already popped several times on the latter stages of our journey up here, due to the changing air pressure; it was either that, or fear. On both sides of the street, old-fashioned street lanterns glowed with the dim light, of worn out torch batteries. Apart from our shoes crunching the gravel beneath our feet, the only other sound we could hear was a distant murmur of water cascading over rocks, somewhere down behind the houses and shops. They all appeared to be closed and were already dressed for the night too, with shuttered up windows, or drawn down blinds. The chill air was scented with the organic aroma of wood fires, the merging of their floating smoke failing to forestall a falling mist. The short, uphill walk momentarily revived my legs after the confinement of the bus journey. It had been a long day and I was starting to feel tired, but mostly I was just relieved the bus had actually made it here too, without breaking down or plunging into a ravine.

"Here we are," announced Gastin as we paused beside an orange glow on the pavement, bestowed by the ground floor windows of an old hotel. It was the only building along the empty street to show any signs of life. Hand painted on the brickwork above the solid oak door, the name, Hotel Coraline. "It belongs to an old acquaintance of mine. He was also a mountain guide during the war," said Gastin, as he led the way and stepped inside. We were greeted by the warmth from a large, open fire radiating into the reception hall, from one of the adjoining rooms. The reception desk was set back in a dismally lit alcove. Gastin rang the counter top bell and I looked around at our intriguing surroundings. At the foot of the dark wooden staircase, to my great surprise, stood a real, stuffed, grizzly bear, displaying his fangs and claws, like he was about to pounce on anyone who'd dared to leave without paying. Mounted on the walls too, were various trophy heads of other wild animals: several species of deer, boars and foxes. As the light danced from the flames of the open fire, their black eyes shimmered, almost tricking me into thinking they were still alive. I found myself wishing that they still were, and that they could be somewhere other than part of the dishonourable display, lining the oak panelled stairway.

The opaque glass door behind the reception desk gave a creak as it opened and a paunchy figure, wearing a blue denim apron and a kindly, middle-aged face, appeared. He immediately recognised Gastin and placed his outstretched arms over his shoulders and greeted him warmly, in the traditional French way, with a kiss on each side of the face. It seemed odd to me at first to see grown men kissing each other like this. Back home in Lancashire a greeting like this would have been fiercely batted off had a bloke tried that on with my dad.

"Gastin, good to see you again. How long has it been since you were last in the mountains?"

"Probably not as long as you think, Jacques. You can take the man out of the mountains, but not the mountains from the man, n'est ce pas?"

"Bon, we have two rooms ready for you. Who is your friend?" enquired Jacques cordially as he stepped forward to greet me and held out his hand.

"Pardon, let me introduce Byrney. He's from England." said Gastin, urging me to shake hands with our 'Patron'.

"Jacques Casson, welcome to Hotel Coraline. Any friend of Gastin's is always very welcome here, bien. Please sign the register, Byrney. " As he turned around to remove our room keys from their hooks, Gastin said, "Byrney has come to the mountains to find Paul Larouchamps's grave." The keys Jacques was reaching for fell on the floor. When he resurfaced from behind the counter, he was staring straight at me and smiled,

"In that case, I hope you enjoy your time with us, here." Gastin took the keys and asked if it was possible to get something to eat. "Yes, it's all prepared. Please take your things up to your rooms and come back down to the restaurant. I have a table ready, waiting for you." I paid for my room, for two nights. Gastin must have had his own private arrangement with Jacques as no money was exchanged between them, which made me curiously wary of them.

Gastin ordered a meal for us both, which sounded to me like 'handy wheel it' - it actually turned out to be the grizzliest sausage I'd ever tasted and I found it almost impossible to swallow the slimy, fatty meat by itself. I hid half of them under my scrunched up napkin and concentrated on absorbing the rustic surroundings of the room, which had a random display of several pairs of long, wooden ski's, some old, tennis racket style snow shoes and a gruesome collection of gin traps - Pyrenean style. As we ate, Jacques pulled out a chair at the next table and talked to us about the history of the hotel. He told us a sad tale about how he'd changed the name of the hotel in honour of his deceased wife, who had died giving birth to their daughter. Then his reminiscences stepped further back in time.

The two Frenchmen had obviously known about one another during the Second World War, but they had never worked together. The red wine was having a detrimental affect on my eyelids and when the bottle was empty, Jacques insisted on pouring us all a glass of cognac, 'compliments of the house'.

"It was the worst of times when Paul Larouchamps and those two Jewish families were killed on the mountains," said Jacques. "It was the death of our Escape Line too. The unimportant ones amongst us who managed to avoid arrest had to go into hiding, for many months. No one knew who to trust. Merde, if I could get my hands on the rat who betrayed us."

Gastin was staring at the tumbler of cognac in front of him. He seemed to be making a mental note of everything Jacques was telling us. I looked at Jacques as he spoke. Beneath the chubby face were signs of an intelligent guy who could quickly draw a ready smile, which gave me the impression it might be used as a lever to wriggle out of an awkward situation and he appeared to be someone who was now enjoying a very comfortable life. After the war he'd made a success of his business, becoming a well-respected member of the community too. I noticed he certainly liked to spend his money on jewellery, judging by the number of gold rings on his fingers and the chains around his neck. He must have been about the same age as Gastin, but he looked so much younger. I thought I'd try to break up the monotony of Jacques voice by raising a question of my own, one that had been preying on my mind.

"What happened to the guides who were helping Paul Larouchamps's group to escape?" Gastin looked up from the table and waited to hear Jacques reply.

"The Spanish guides, or the French ones?" asked Jacques, looking slightly perturbed at my interruption.

I shrugged my shoulders. "I'm not sure."

Gastin answered first. "The Spanish guides are believed to have been locked inside the refuge with the escapers. That's right isn't it Jacques?"

"It wasn't me who was delivering those parcels, that day. I never did the run from Nice. I was waiting in Toulouse for the next consignment of parcels to arrive, so I can't say for sure what happened. As far as anyone knows, they all died: Paul, the two families and the guides who had taken charge of them for the final walk into Spain."

"You mean they almost made it to freedom," I said. "How unlucky." Jacques poured another liberal measure of Cognac into the glasses, but I'd had enough already so I covered mine with my hand and he nodded and continued to speak.

"The Gestapo came down on us hard. They had acquired all our names and addresses. They waited in the dark at one of the safe houses and arrested anyone who knocked on the door. I had been warned not to go. My only chance was to make my own way to Spain."

"So no one knows who betrayed you all?" I asked in all innocence.

Jacques waited for Gastin to speak this time and then, offered his own theory. "After November '42, the Germans had taken over running the whole of France. We were no longer in the Free French Zone. Everything became much more dangerous. We had begun to suspect that the Gestapo were starting to train their own agents to pose as escaping Allied airmen. Normally, we would uncover anyone who didn't look right; you just knew, instinctively, but the more people that helped us, the more unsafe our security became. Someone in our organisation was working for the Germans."

Gastin shifted uneasily in his chair and raised his glass and said, "Well, here's to finding out who that bastard was." I looked at him. He was deadly serious.

The next morning, after dressing in my warmest clothes, I knocked on Gastin's door, but there was no reply. So, assuming he was already at breakfast, I descended to the dining room. I was feeling dead excited about getting out onto the mountains at last, but the buzz inside me immediately subsided, when I saw that there was no one inside the restaurant. There was only the faint clatter of pots coming from the kitchen. I sat down, facing the kitchen, just as it's door burst open and in walked a girl, carrying a metal tray with two silver jugs on top. She had shoulder length, dark brown hair and looked about my own age.

She placed the tall, silver jug down on the table. turned over one of the white coffee cups then poured me a cup of dark coffee.

"Du lait?" she said, smiling, holding the smaller jug before me.

"Milk, yes please."

Her smile formed a slim dimple in her left cheek as she introduced herself as 'Anna'. She spoke to me in English, with a hint of an American accent. She was Jacques' only daughter.

"Pleased to meet you," I said and for some inexplicable reason, I bowed my head, which made Anna giggle. She had the kind of distinctive beauty, which always had the effect of making me feel nervous. "Do you know where Gastin is?" I asked as I took a sip of the hot, strong coffee.

"Yes, he has already departed. My father is taking him back to Toulouse." I was a bit shocked and annoyed that he'd run out on me *and* I'd already paid him too. My expression must have given my thoughts away.

"Don't worry," replied Anna. "He said he would return in two or three days, when the fog has lifted." She pointed to the windows with her eyes. "See?" I looked out of the window behind me and all I could see was a pale, grey mass, obscuring all before it. Looks like Gastin has taken the rest of the village with him too, I thought.

"Would you like some eggs and bacon?" enquired Anna, holding the empty tray with both arms behind her back and patiently swaying from side to side.

"Yer that'd be great," I said forgetting my manners and added, "S'il vous plait."

Anna sat opposite me, watching me devour my plate of deliciousness. She poured herself a cup of coffee au lait and allowed me to finished eating before asking me where I was from and how I came to know Gastin. As we'd been unceremoniously left to our own devices, Anna offered to show me the sights. I thought she was joking, what sights?

It was still eerily thick with fog, out on the streets. The houses, which we walked past, were like ancient tombs, deathly quiet. It felt like we were stranded inside a Victorian graveyard, surrounded by unfamiliar shapes, unable to find our way out.

"I can't see a thing, where is everyone?" I said, having lost all sense of place and time. I was glad to have Anna for a guide.

"What do good Catholics normally do on a Sunday morning?" she teased.

"Go to church?"

"Exactement."

"How come you're not in church then?"

"Church is for old people," she replied, smiling and grabbing my arm before I accidentally stepped off the pavement. As we levelled off at the bottom of the street, one or two signs of life began to slowly creep into view. I could hear the familiar rumble of vehicles, approaching along the cobbles in both directions, their yellow headlamps emerging from the strange mists at the last moment. "Do you like the cinema?" Anna said, excitedly. "There's a matinee performance starting soon. I go there all the time, it's just around the corner from here."

"What's on, anything good?" I imagined it would take films a lifetime to reach such a far away, outback place such as this and was expecting her to say, 'just the usual silent movies.'

"Jaws. I've seen it twice already, but if you want to watch it, I don't mind seeing it again," she laughed.

"Why not?" I'd seen it too, but at least it would help to pass the time away and anywhere I could see further than the end of my nose would be an improvement.

****

Sandra Atkinson sat staring at her reflection in the bedroom mirror. These days, it was taking her longer to look as good as she used to and she wasn't happy with the results. She picked up the small, silver framed photograph from the right shoulder drawer of her dressing table. The black and white photo showed a happy couple, drinking champagne on the terraces at Aintree

Race Course, a mere nine years ago. They'd hit the jackpot that day, in the big race, on the eighth of April 1967, Grand National day.   Sandra remembered closing her eyes and pressing her finger down on the race program, on a rank outsider, called Foinavon. She had placed her usual one pound bet. Little did she realise the excitement that lay in store that day. With only seven fences from home, Foinavon came from nowhere to take the lead, when he was able to waltz past the twenty or so leading horses, who'd all been caught up in one of the biggest pile ups ever seen on a horse track, let alone in the biggest race of the year. By the time all the unseated jockeys had remounted, Foinavon was uncatchable and he romped over the finishing line, at a starting price of one hundred to one. Although they'd attended the same race every year since, they had never been able to repeat their luck. Sandra was beginning to believe that luck was running out on her marriage too.

She gave up on fixing her wayward, bleached, blonde hair. It looked presentable enough to get her into town and besides she was going to cover it up with her favourite Hermes silk scarf. She stood up and straightened the seam of her mini skirt and heavy-footed it downstairs. She grabbed her packet of Consulate Cigarettes from the top of the glass topped coffee table and placed them inside her coat pocket which rested in readiness over the chair arm. She squeezed into her stilettos and walked through into the kitchen, to leave a saucer of milk down on the floor for her adorable cat. The house, like her marriage, had long since lost its excitement. She was looking after numero uno and that meant spending whatever it took to keep her looks. Monday was manicure day. She paused by the hall mirror, to check her lippy and pulled down the front of her lamb's wool cardigan, until she showed just the right amount of cleavage to ensure she'd attract a little attention. Since she so very rarely received any from her absent husband, she felt she still deserved some reward for her efforts. Her mother had tried to warn her off, about marrying a copper and she'd been proved right - 'married to the force' and only one holiday a year to show for it. She slammed the door behind her, walked up the drive and out onto the close, crossing the pavement behind the blue, 'parked up' Austin 1100 and headed down the ginnel, towards the bus stop.

"I'll bet she's high maintenance," said Lofty to himself. He followed the long, swaying pair of legs, walking away from his rear view mirror, watching her until she disappeared. He then turned to face the semi-detached, 1930's style house - the Atkinson residence.

Three days earlier, after losing Atkinson outside Bowland Mobile Park, he'd returned to the recreation park opposite the Police Station and waited for him to knock off. It being a Friday afternoon, he didn't have long to wait and after a brief pit-stop at The Prince, he'd followed Atkinson back through town to his home in Churchtown Close, which ran down towards the old canal. Lofty quickly realised there hadn't been sufficient time, or opportunity, for Atkinson to dispose of Byrne's Moped and you didn't need to be Mastermind to work out where it was.

In front of him, the driveway was covered in freshly fallen leaves, but was pleasingly empty of vehicles. The front and side of the house were guarded by a rickety, wooden panelled, fence. At the bottom of the drive was an old, painted, wooden garage. Lofty gave a smug sigh at the imagined ease with which he would be able to gain access - not what he'd come to expect from a Police Inspector. Whatever Atkinson spent his 'ill gotten' gains on, it certainly wasn't home security. He pulled on his leather gloves and quickly crossed over to the opposite side of the quiet Close. Like Atkinson, the majority of the neighbouring residents were all professional types and at nine-thirty in the morning, they had already left for the office.

The double garage doors were locked from the other side, but round the back he was able to ease open a wooden, planked, single door, without causing the slightest damage. There was enough light passing through the single side window for Lofty to explore the interior. Like most garages these days, it was only used for storage: a workbench, a noisy chest freezer, some old garden furniture and a rusty lawnmower. However, in front of the workbench, Lofty immediately clocked an old, grey blanket, draped over a motorcycle. He removed it with an exuberant movement of his arm, like a matador, evading the charge of a bull with his cloak. It was Byrne's Moped alright, although he hardly recognised it: the fuel tank was on the floor, there was an empty space where the seat should be, part of the hollow frame had been sawn in two and the white fibre glass top box had had it's lid broken off. 'He's had a right go at this,' thought Lofty, casting an eye over the tools still scattered about the floor. He noticed the double seat, lying on top of the workbench, with its leather cover ripped open and fistfuls of padding removed. Then, at the back of the bench, a group of newspaper cuttings, pinned to the wall and set out like a police incident room, also irked his curiosity. They had all been taken from the front pages of The *Courier*. He read each headline in turn: "Post Office Raided", "Crowston Girl in Suicide Tragedy", it was all starting to fit. Lofty read further along, until a hundred watt light bulb suddenly lit up inside his head. 'Twenty-two thousand pound," he said out loud, "so that's his game, F.M.O.B.'

He replaced the grey blanket over Byrne's Moped, slipped the catch back on the side door of the garage and casually walked back up the drive. It didn't take Lofty long to reach the same conclusion as Atkinson; the answer to the puzzle lay with Byrne himself. He'd just have to bide his time until he returned from France.

****

"What else do you normally do for fun around here?" I asked, as we stepped out from inside the plush surroundings of the Cinema St. Jean into the cold, early evening air. The white blanket of dense mist had not improved one iota whilst we'd both been tucked away watching the movie. In fact, the air was so thick it seemed to me like I could slice it in two with a Kung Fu karate chop. "I'm glad you're here," I said, not realising I was talking to myself, " I don't think I could find my way back to the hotel otherwise." Anna was busy talking to a friend behind me and fortunately, she'd missed my daft attempts to disperse the fog.

67

"Pardon Byrney, did you enjoy the movie? It was quite scary, uh?"

"That bit made me jump, when that blokes head rolls out of the hole in the boat," I laughed.

I was feeling more upbeat about being stranded with a stranger in the middle of a cloud, in a forgotten corner of France. Anna's open friendliness was slowly conquering the disappointment I'd felt first thing this morning, on learning that Gastin had run out on me.

"Are you hungry, Byrney? Let's go back to the hotel, I will cook something for you."

"Sounds great," I said.

As we walked back up the narrow street, I asked Anna how come she spoke such good English. Apparently after leaving school two years ago, she had gone to America for six months to study wildlife conservation. She was very aware of the changes taking place on the mountains. During the hot summer, earlier this year, the mountain glaciers had melted, shrinking back to their shortest length, this century. The Hydro-Electric plant that powered the area had also been forced closed due to the low volume of water in the river. It was incredible to believe that whilst I was chasing after Max, during those sun kissed days in Crowston, so much more was being affected in other parts of the world at the same time.

When we stepped back inside Hotel Coraline, Anna took me through to their living accommodation, which was at the back of the kitchen. There was a small lounge room, with a T.V. It was very basically furnished, with an old fashioned green fabric sofa and a wrought iron candelabra, hanging from the centre of the ceiling, with part worn candles. It resembled something you might find in Dracula's castle. I followed Anna back into the kitchen and she lifted a large, cast iron frying pan onto the range cooker. "How do you prefer your steak, bloody?" She worked very quickly and efficiently; she was well used to preparing food. I looked around for some drinking glasses.

"Shall I get us something to drink?"

"Yes, there's a 'Cave' through that door there," she said, pointing to the opposite side of the kitchen. "It's where we store the wine. Chose any bottle you like, watch out for the bats."

"Okay," I said. Anna followed me to the door and switched on the lights, illuminating the stone steps leading down into the cool vaulted room below the house. The bottles of wine were stored horizontally, in large metal cages. Half expecting to see an old coffin somewhere I walked all the way to the end and back again. There must have been several hundred bottles to choose from. I chose the one which was covered with the most dust.

"Formidable, a Margaux 1960, I'm impressed," said Anna, when she saw the bottle I was proudly showing off.

"That was a great year," I said, wiping the dust from the label. "It's the year I was born."

We ate inside the restaurant, simply because that's where Anna and her father always ate, even if they had clients dining there too. In October the hotel was normally closed. There was a steady trickle of customers throughout the summer, mainly hikers and climbing adventurers. The winter ski season was when they made their money, from mid November right through until the end of February. Anna had such a busy life, balancing her time between her studies and helping her father to run the Hotel. She loved to ski in winter and even found time to volunteer for the regional Mountain Rescue and Search Team. Last year there had been a large slab avalanche and several climbers had been caught up in it. "We only found the last two bodies this summer after the snow had melted away," said Anna gloomily.

"Wow, does that happen often?" I said.

"No, not really, but this springtime was the worst anyone could remember. Afterwards in the summer, we even found two skeletons from the war. They were taken to Toulouse University Hospital for identification."

Anna asked me about my interests and ambitions. I began by telling her about Eve and how I planned to bring her ashes back to the Pyrenees, so that she and her husband Paul could be reunited at last. "That's so romantique." Anna was really taken with my idea. "If you need any help with finding the place, just ask. I know these mountains really well. I grew up exploring them."

After a few glasses of wine, the conversation inevitably got around to boyfriends and girlfriends. I told Anna about my summer with Max, at The Friary in Crowston. It was the first time I'd spoken in detail to anyone about my friendship with Max. Although Anna was a relative stranger, I found it easy talking with her. I think she could sense my loss for Max. She spoke about how she'd never known her maman. The only stories she knew about her were the ones her father had told her. Anna's mother, Coraline, had been orphaned at the start of the war and spent most of it with around thirty other children, who were cared for in an old chateau tucked away in the Haut-Garonne countryside. Her journey had begun as an evacuee, on the road in Northern France, after she had been bombed out of the home, in which the lives of her parents had been claimed. Eventually, she was taken under the protection of the Croix-Rouge Française. As the number of children travelling with her through France increased, they were compelled to move on, from shelter to shelter, continually moving south until they reached the safety of the Free French Zone. Life at the old chateau, despite all it's hardships, had felt idyllic compared to the dangers and uncertainties of a life in transit. But even then they all lived in constant fear of being discovered by the authorities, who were under orders to send all Jewish children to the camps in Germany.

In 1946, when she was sixteen years old, she had been working in a hotel in Toulouse, when she met Jacques Casson - and shortly after, she came to St. Jean to work for him. They fell in love and were married in 1952. Coraline suffered from numerous miscarriages and her doctor warned her against having a child. Five years later Anna was born, but joy quickly turned to tragedy when Coraline died from a haemorrhage, only a few hours afterwards.

We both heard the front door of the hotel open, followed by a gust of cold air blowing around our table. It was Anna's father, Jacques. He struggled out of his thick overcoat and placed his keys on the reception counter, then noticed we were watching him and quickly said "Hello. Oh, I think Gastin will be returning tomorrow evening." There was a look on Jacques face suggesting either he'd forgotten I was staying here, or maybe I wasn't welcome, or maybe he was just tired.

"Ah, great," I said, feeling slightly relieved. Gastin hadn't abandoned me after all.

"Yes, he said he had some business to attend to at the Gendarmerie. He didn't say what, probably some fugitive he's hunting down."

I stood up and immediately felt the effects of the wine on my balance. I noticed Anna had hidden the empty bottle under her chair. "Would you like me to help you clear away?" I said, winking at Anna.

"No, it's okay, we can manage, merci."

"Well, thank you for a lovely meal." My words sounded a bit naff. What I really wanted to say was how much I'd enjoyed being with her all day, but I could see her father was staring at me impatiently, as I turned towards the staircase.

"Bonne nuit, Byrney," she said, as she picked up our dirty plates.

The next morning sounded much busier outside my bedroom window, overlooking the front street, than it had the previous day. I lay listening to the rush hour, which had begun around seven a.m. I drew back my curtains and looked out onto the cobbles. Buses were gathering up school kids and vehicles of all forms of commerce were doing their rounds. The snow capped mountains in the background were almost clear, dressed only in a few, wispy, white streaks of cloud and early morning mist. They looked so close I could almost reach out of my window with a broom and brush the snow from them. I took my time getting ready, as I'd nothing in particular to rush for. So, after a hot shower and a shave (the half dozen hairs on my top lip and chin), I skipped down the panelled staircase to find Anna and Jacques, already seated and eating their breakfast.

Seeing them both together made me realise how much Jacques doted on Anna and how very proud she was of him.

After a plate of oeufs brouilles I asked Jacques if I could make a phone call.

"Yes, there is a public phone on the reception counter, please help yourself. I'll add it to your bill."

I rang Fionn at Les Moulins and spoke to Juliette first who was very pleased to hear my voice. Fionn asked me how I was getting on and was surprised that I still hadn't been up the mountains. She sounded very confident about her work and mentioned Jean-Paul by name at least three times and how he was being very helpful. I was going to warn her about his weanus, but thought I'd better let her find out for herself. And besides he struck me as someone who was almost as inexperienced as I was. I ended the call by saying I should be back in Nice in two or three days time.

Later that morning I discovered another surprise about Anna when she showed me her Mobylette Scooter which she kept in a garage in the rear yard of the hotel.

"Come on Byrney, don't be shy. I promise not to go too fast," she said, obviously teasing me. Anna's father had to spend most of the day attending a meeting at the local community office, about the upcoming tourist season, so Anna insisted on taking me for a ride. "It's such a lovely day, let's not waste it."

It felt wonderful to be zooming along again with the chill air on my face, even if I was sat behind a girl aboard a pip-squeak of a step-through scooter. Anna handled the flimsy machine very confidently, besides she'd promised her father she'd be careful, as always. Once out of town, the ground soon levelled off. The wild river we were following criss-crossed beside the ancient road until we reached a ninety-degree corner and it was our turn to cross the river over a single-track bridge. Anna paused at the entrance to inform me that this was just a temporary bridge, built around two years ago when the old one had been swept away, in the storms of December '73. So far, we'd not met another vehicle, or another person, for that matter.

After another sharp turn, we passed a few, lonely, impoverished farmhouses. The land behind them had been terraced and cultivated with olive groves. It looked to me like a hard way to scratch a living from the land. The road continued to rise steeply again as it zig-zagged between two sides of the mountain, one side in the full light of the sun, the other tucked into the shaded part of a deep ravine. I was impressed with how the little machine we were sat astride was coping with the load and the gradient. The river in the plateau below us became more like a white ribbon as we climbed ever higher. After a further twenty minutes we'd traversed the valley to the point where the faded, scrubby grass had become lost under a covering of hard, frozen, shiny snow. It was almost blinding when it caught the full reflection of the sun.

The tarmac surface suddenly came to an abrupt end, into a large car park. In front of us, I could see a complex of single storey cabins. One was obviously a restaurant and the remainder must have been for accommodation. We stepped away from Anna's scooter, removed our helmets and walked over to the edge of the car park to admire the view. As far as my eye could see, there was only peak after peak, disappearing into infinity. It was impossible to imagine how any human being could get beyond them. There was a huge wall of snow that slid down between the two nearest peaks, like a huge white tongue, a monumental sculpture, created by nature, which a thousand architects couldn't match. It was then that it suddenly hit me, about the enormity of the task I was undertaking.

"This is where you'll start from tomorrow morning," said Anna, taking in a lung full of the clear air, savouring it's life affirming quality, then blowing out her white, vaporous breath, like some indigenous mountain creature.

"I don't see how it's possible to get any further."

"You're not changing your mind, are you Byrney?"

"No, but…" I was lost for an answer.

"Don't worry. You don't have to climb over the top of each one; there are passes between them. Okay some of the paths are a little dangerous, but many people have walked along them, including pregnant women and children. You'll be fine, as long as you're not afraid of heights," she joked. "It's a bit late for that now."

I looked back down the valley to retrace the route we'd just taken. "Well I guess it's just a case of follow the leader. I think I can manage that," I said, trying to convince myself too.

"Come on, I'll show you around," said Anna cheerfully.

The whole complex of cabins and barns was completely deserted. Anna took me to a small wooden cabin with a white cross, painted on the door. Attached to the side of this wooden building was a tall, steel mast, about twenty-five feet tall. She removed a key from a zipped pocket in her glove and unlocked the door. Inside the room were two sets of bunk beds and a desk with a large metal box sat on top of it, which had lots of dials and thick black wires protruding out the back. She went into a smaller room behind and I could hear her unclipping a metal cover, then the thud of a large switch and all the lights flickered on inside and the dials of the radio receiver came to life with a humming buzz. At the same time, a crackling sound came out of the speaker, which was fixed higher up the wall and that I'd not noticed, until now. Anna emerged from the back room and announced, "This is our mountain rescue base. When the station is closed, someone has to check the batteries and the function of the radio once a week." Anna pulled out a worn chair from underneath the desk and picked up the hand held receiver. She checked the setting on the dial and pulled down the trigger on the back of the microphone stand.

"Attention, Celeste Station. Casson appeller - tu me reçois?"

Surprisingly, a French voice crackled out of the speaker. Anna smiled at me and said "Impressed?"

After a short, routine conversation with the operator at the Gendarmarie in St. Jean, Anna switched off the radio and asked if I'd like a coffee. Then she disappeared into the back room again, to sort out the gas bottles before lighting the stove. She filled an aluminium saucepan with snow and set it down to boil. I was looking around at the lack of privacy over the sleeping arrangements. "Do you sleep here too, when there is an emergency?"

Anna looked at me with a sarcastic smile, "are you prudish Byrney? Yes, of course. Sometimes we are out here for seven or eight nights at a time." She passed me a steaming metal cup of coffee and we walked outside to check if the mountains still looked as awesome and scary as they had ten minutes ago.

The journey back to St. Jean seemed much quicker. Once we reached the single-track bridge we were back into the cold shadow of the mountains, as the sun swung over into Spain.

When we returned to Hotel Coraline, Anna took me up to her bedroom to show me the black and white framed portrait photograph of her mother. It had been taken around the time when she first moved here with Jacques. I studied the photo in detail. It was remarkable to see so much of Anna in her, her slender waif like figure, the same thick brunette coloured hair and the same shape eyes and full lips, with a narrow dimple in her cheek. I noticed too, she was wearing a distinctive necklace, which had a fruit shaped object at the end. I made a comment to Anna about how beautiful she was and what a lovely necklace.

"Yes, my father gave her that as a gift of their engagement." Anna opened the small drawer of a music box and took out the very same necklace, so that I could feel its beauty. The pendant was in the shape of a long aubergine. "It's for luck," said Anna softly. "It's said that if you dream of an aubergine on New Years Eve it will bring you luck for the following year." I looked at Anna's smile and in that moment, I felt a strong compulsion to kiss her, but she lowered her head and placed the necklace back inside the music box.

At eight-thirty that evening, I was sat enjoying another meal in the restaurant at Hotel Coraline. Gastin had returned with more equipment, but for some unknown reason he seemed more edgy and uncomfortable. The equipment he'd brought consisted of two pairs of snow shoes and two large wooden staffs. I couldn't work out what was troubling him. The large wooden staffs, he explained, would be needed when we were descending on the loose shale. He also explained they protected the back and helped with your balance as there would be plenty of shale to negotiate. During the meal there was a lot of discussion in French regarding the route and the timing. Anna had disappeared and returned with a large, detailed map, which she spread out on top of the next table. Jacques seemed to be protesting to Gastin about something I didn't understand. When the conversation settled down and we each had a glass of cognac in out hands, Gastin announced that Anna would be travelling with us also. He appeared to accept this. It had been almost a decade since Gastin had last been so far up into the mountain and although he knew the paths better than the lines on his own face, he admitted that some of the landmarks would have changed over the years, especially since the glaciers had retreated further up the mountain, exposing beds of broken boulders which would, inevitably, be impossible to cross quickly and safely.

"I think it would be wise to take to our beds earlier than normal this evening. It is at least eight hours from the Col de la Celeste to the Col du Monde, where the ruined refuge lies. Anna informs me there is a rescue cabin halfway that is stocked with blankets and food, which we can use on our return." I looked at Anna and we both smiled at one another. "Jacques is going to take us as far as Celeste in the morning," continued Gastin. "So we need to take breakfast around six a.m."

We all looked at one another satisfied with our plans. Then I raised my glass and said, "to the mountains."

"Aux montagnes," they all replied.

Chapter Six

Le Col Du Monde

I'd no idea what to expect, or what we'd find, on top of the Col du Monde. Perhaps there'd be nothing left of the burnt out ruins of the refuge shelter, where Eve's husband had died at the hands of the Gestapo. Perhaps time and the effects of the extreme weather had taken its toll and what remained there had since slowly dissolved and been swallowed up by the mountain. I only had two pieces of evidence to reflect on, both from 1943 and both relating to the immediate aftermath of the massacre.

According to Eve's reminiscences, Paul's mother, who was still living in Nice at this time, had written to her to say that Paul had perished in a barn, along with two Jewish families and that the guides had been arrested and taken away for questioning, to the nearest Gestapo headquarters. The letter, which Eve referred to, had sadly arrived only two weeks before VE day, in May 1945. It was a double edged sword, graciously putting an end to her despair at never knowing what had become of her husband, but at the same time crushing her adventurous spirit, with the knowledge she had lost the only man she had ever loved.

According to Gastin, who had found the smouldering remains a week after the massacre, it had been impossible to say precisely how many had died there. Gastin has since spent the last thirty years tracking down collaborators, torturers and members of the Milici, the Vichy paramilitary group who had fought against the French Resistance fighters. He had also chased fleeing Nazi's across the Pyrenees who were, ironically, using the same paths to freedom which had been used by the Allied Escape Lines, during World War Two. These escape lines were known as 'Rat Lines'. Very few of these wanted men got the better of Gastin in the mountains. He had been highly successful in tracking them down, relieving them of their weapons and arresting anyone who had dared to evade French justice or their just desserts.

The last time Gastin spoke to me on the bus journey up to St.Jean-Les-Bains, he had realised, at sixty years of age, that he saw my adventure as his last chance to find out anything new about how his own father had died, or who had betrayed him. We shared a common goal: the person responsible for Paul Larouchamp's death and the death of Gastin's father had almost certainly been the same man.

***

Jacques Casson's Peugeot 504 Estate car was doing a fine job at hitting every pot-hole in the road up to Col de la Celeste. Anna and I were bouncing about on the back seat, doing our best to avoid hitting our heads on the roof. Jacques was also giving us his tour guide raconteur, trying to impress Gastin in particular. As we approached the single track bridge over the river, Jacques pointed out where the German Army sentry huts had once stood, either side of the bridge.

" Gastin, do you remember?" said Jacques. "We had to ford across the river during the war, when we were taking parcels up to the mountain. It was a very difficult and dangerous task in winter, especially if the parcels we were escorting refused to cross. Sometimes, we had to drag them along. We didn't dare risk leaving anyone behind, for fear they would be caught by the German patrols and give away all those who had helped them to escape. Lucky we were paid for our troubles, n'est ce pas?"

"It wasn't about the money for me," answered Gastin. "It was about fighting back in the only effective way we knew. Every allied airman that made it back home to England was able to re-join the war and start fighting the Germans again."

"And killing more innocent French civilians with their bombs too," bemoaned Jacques.

Anna and I looked at each other, thank goodness the killing was all over now, I thought.

At the car park, at the top of Col de la Celeste, we unloaded our equipment and shared the load equally between the three of us. The snow capped mountains in the foreground looked wonderfully inviting. The weather conditions were perfect. It was the clearest I'd seen the sky look since I'd arrived. Anna checked the straps were tightly secured on our rucksacks and we each carried one of the tall, wooden staffs. Allowing for additional time for any mishaps along our route and back, Jacques agreed to meet us back here at noon tomorrow. We walked through the complex of cabins and barns, which Anna had shown me yesterday and picked up the path, which was traversing the valley towards the start of the Glacier di Aureola. Gastin was out in front and Anna was beside me, but she dropped in behind when the path narrowed to a single track.

It was one of those days that made you feel glad to be alive, walking along in the crispy, cool air, with the morning sunshine warming our faces. Below, the blue sky was reflected in a large lake, which had been partially frozen. In front of me, Gastin was striding out at a steady pace, which neither slowed nor speeded up with changes to the gradient. Immediately to my right, the shear cliff face rose fiercely, scarred and encircling. Anna commented that this was where many climbers liked to test their skills, which often lead to her rescue organisation being called out to deal with a fall, or someone trapped high up on a ledge.

We zig-zagged upwards in single file for a couple of hours, as our horizon stretched away, further and further. I found the wooden staff, which Gastin had provided for me, a great help with my balance and it gave me confidence with my footing along the narrow, shingle covered path. I could hear Anna, behind me, humming a tune to herself and whenever I looked around she smiled back at me. As we rounded the cliff face, I heard the squalling wind blowing in the distance. On the nearest peaks, small showers of snow were being driven across the length of the sharp ridge. Our path now fell away, sharply. It was so steep in places, it made me feel dizzy and I was in danger of falling arse over tit. Gastin was descending quite fast. He was using his staff like an anchor, to pitch himself forward from side to side, causing the shingle to splash away. After a few go's, I soon got the knack of transferring my weight and throwing my staff forward digging it into the loose shingle to break my descent.

The base of the path levelled off into a field of pale, grey boulders, some the size of a detached house. When all three of us reached the bottom of the path, Gastin removed his rucksack and took out his flask of black coffee and filled each of our tin mugs.

"What do you think of the Pyrenees, Byrney?" asked Gastin.

"Amazing!" I replied, " It makes me feel so miniscule." I turned to Anna, "look at the size of those boulders, how did they get here?"

"The glacier pushes them down the mountain," she smiled and pointed to an odd shaped boulder next to us. "I think this one is from Spain - wouldn't you agree Gastin?"

Gastin played along with Anna's joke, "yes, definitely looks Spanish to me. Isn't that a Gaucho hat on top of it?" he joked. "The good news is," continued Gastin, "we're about half way. The bad news is it's all uphill from here and it's going to get colder. How are you feeling Byrney, you don't have a headache or anything?"

"No, I'm fine - easy peasy." I was hoping I wouldn't later regret saying that.

After a small snack of raw ham and goat's cheese, (if only my mum could see me now - a year ago I'd turn my nose up at such insignificant foods, like garden peas and tins of spam.) it was time to start moving again. The landscape on this side of the mountain looked like a scene from another planet. There was no vegetation whatsoever. We could have been on the surface of the moon, that's if the moon had been covered in snow. The snow was still frozen beneath its soft surface, so we were able to crunch our way through it quite easily, but I could feel my shins beginning to ache. Even Gastin's pace had slowed slightly. Then we came across some lines of evenly spaced exposed rock, which looked to me like the top of a toast rack, half buried, in the white powdery snow. At this point, Gastin stopped and turned towards the glacier, then passed around the crampons for our boots - these weird looking contraptions made perfect sense to me now, as I stood stamping my feet to test their grip.

We had somehow to get onto the top of the Glacier. There was only one short but ridiculously steep access point and I watched Gastin as he began to climb the treacherous looking wall of ice, by kicking away at it, to make steps as he ascended. It was slow and arduous. I suggested to Anna that we could just walk straight ahead, "it would be much quicker." As I took a few steps forward, Anna shouted at me to stop.

"Those are snow capped ravines in front of you, Byrney."

"But they look so tempting," I argued.

"Some of the ravines are twenty-five metres deep or more. If you fall through the snow, you will seriously injure yourself."

I stepped back and began to climb the steps, which Gastin had made. "I think I'll go this way," I said, feeling myself blush.

Once we had climbed onto the smooth surface of the glacier, Anna informed us that this was roughly where her colleagues in the mountain rescue team had found the two bodies, earlier that summer. Despite having been covered by the glacier since the war, they still had items of clothing attached to their skeletons, suspended in deep freeze for over thirty years.

"They would have started their journey in the ice much further up the mountain," said Anna. "The glacier is constantly on the move, but you can't see it with the naked eye."

I could see Gastin, calculating the distance to the nearest ledge, which was still at least a mile ahead of us.

"Everything okay, Gastin?" I asked.

After a while, he turned around and looked at us both, "Yes, we need to keep moving," he said reassuringly.

After another hour of plodding up the frozen glacier, we reached the foot of the final climb to the Col du Monde. We scrambled our way up a slippery, shale slope, sometimes on all fours. It was an exhausting, back bending walk, carrying our packs and digging in with our wooden staffs to prevent ourselves from sliding backwards. When we reached the long, gritstone ledge at the top, there was a large semi circular opening, cut into the rock face as if it had been quarried out, but on moving closer, I could see the rock face had several, natural, jagged ribs. It was as if we were stood inside the stomach of the mountain. The clearing was in the full face of the sun, which was now almost horizontal to our line of sight and all the snow had melted away to reveal a little, green oasis of alpine flowers. As we entered the opening, the first signs of a structure came into view, behind the rocks to our right. A lone brick chimney, about ten foot tall stood at the centre of four, lumpy stumps of stone boulders, which formed a rectangular base. We all walked a line abreast, towards the ruin. I immediately felt the sombre darkness of what had occurred here. It wasn't just the icy wind which put a chill inside me. As we got nearer, I noticed the simple wooden cross, fixed to the front of the brick chimney, it's lines of grain split with age and petrified. Below the cross, which had obviously been salvaged from the remnants of the original building and bolted to the sun bleached brickwork, was a small, embossed metal plaque with an inscription:

ICI ENTERRE LES CENDRES DES MORTS
MASSACRE ET BRULE PAR LES NAZIS
L.M.P

I turned to Anna, "what does it say?"
"Here lie the ashes of the dead, massacred and tortured by the Nazis."
Gastin was looking at the centre of the building, where the floor of the shelter had been. "Its good that they have cleaned up this place and remembered what happened here. Maybe one day we will discover the truth, but we will never understand the reasons."
Gastin's words made me think of the poor, unfortunate, people who'd died here and how far they'd walked in the dark,

cold and no doubt hungry and suffering from being on the run, for weeks, or maybe even months. How could anyone be so callous and cruel to another human being? I can count myself lucky. Here I was, wrapped up in a thick fur lined coat, with boots and snow gaiters and crampons. I looked at Gastin and wondered about the weight on his shoulders. The weight of all the things he had witnessed in his life. I admired him greatly. He was looking up at the sky and for the first time today the sun had disappeared behind a thick, grey cloud.

"We'll take a quick break for food," he said, "and then we need to start heading back down the mountain."

I checked my watch. It was quarter to two in the afternoon. It had taken around six and a half hours to get here and by my reckoning we only had about four hours of daylight remaining. As we ate, in silence with our thoughts, I knew I'd done the right thing coming here. It was a fitting end and although Paul Larouchamps had not chosen this 'hard to reach' final resting place, I could now reunite Eve and Paul once again. It felt like an enormous journey, like I'd reached the end of the world. I was already planning my return visit with Eve's ashes, when Gastin announced, in his serious voice of authority, that we needed to put on our spare socks, to avoid the risk of frost bite.

Not long after we started back down, we began to run into trouble. The blast from the icy wind had become much stronger and as we walked down the glacier we were exposed to its full force. The gale was beginning to pick up the loose snow off the surface and was driving it against us. We forcibly walked along for an hour or more, with our heads down and gritted our teeth until we once again reached the ice steps above the ravines. The steps, that Gastin had cut earlier, were now completely covered over and had to be cleared before we could descend further. Anna spoke to me as Gastin worked away. "This isn't very good," she said, pointing at the descending cloud. "I'm going to suggest to Gastin that we take a detour to the Mountain Rescue emergency shelter." Once we'd descended to the ravines, Gastin agreed to Anna's suggestion, as it was obvious we had no chance of returning to the Station at Col de la Celeste that evening.

Anna and Gastin switched positions, whilst I remained the protected piggy in the middle. We were now traversing around the eastern edge of the mountain in a northerly direction. It was snowing hard. The fresh snow settled quickly over the loose shale, covering the humps and hollows. I was walking in Anna's footprints, when we were suddenly hit by a freak, ferocious gust, which took my wooden staff clean out of my hand and deposited it down a steep gulley. The power behind the gale was really startling and I instinctively dropped to my knees to protect myself.

"That was bloody scary," I shouted to Anna, who had been stopped in her tracks too. "Another six inches and I would have been over the edge."

Gastin picked me up and looked at Anna, his eyebrows had a thick layer of snowflakes on them. We huddled together for a few moments.

"How much further?" asked Gastin.

"About five kilometres, perhaps a little less," she replied confidently. "Are you okay Byrney?" The driving wind took my breath again before I could answer her.

"Yes, I'll be glad when we get off this ledge," I shouted, trying my best not to sound like a wimp, but grateful I'd packed a spare pair of underpants. We rested a few more minutes until it felt safe to continue. Whilst we waited, Gastin had taken a line of rope from his rucksack and had tied us all together, around our waists and in a line, about six feet apart.

We carried on plodding in each others footsteps for another hour, sometimes walking blindly in the white out that engulfed us. Despite the perilous conditions, Anna never wavered from her course. We were impeded further as the light diminished and for the first time I actually felt like we couldn't possibly go any further. We were staggering along at a snail pace, with just our individual torch beams to guide ourselves by. When we eventually reached the shelter, after what seemed like an achingly long time, our torches were just about finished.

Anna kicked open the door and we all stepped inside, shaking away the snow and slamming the door to, to silence the storm. I couldn't see a thing in front of me. Anna struck a match and stepped further into the room, feeling her way to the table. "There should be an oil lamp on here," she said. After a few seconds we heard the rattle of a metal handle and Anna struck another match and a welcoming glow rose up from the centre of the room, which allowed us all to let out a deep, relaxing sigh of relief. We were all suffering from fatigue, but as the light inside the room grew brighter, the feeling of doom quickly faded. We were safe at last.

Anna and Gastin examined the cupboards and placed some tins of food on the table.

"Is there anything I can do to help," I asked

"See if there is any wood in the fireplace," answered Gastin.

The shelter was well stocked with emergency ration packs, enough to keep ten men alive for two weeks, according to Anna. The cooking appliances were a little primitive and slow. Apart from the open fire, the only stove was a tiny aluminium box, which you unfolded to form the legs and the sides and in the middle you placed a firelighter, which just burnt long enough to warm a pan of Ratatouille. The hot food tasted wonderful, although if I found any meat in my dish, I'd quietly decided I wasn't going to ask what it was. The logs inside the brick fireplace were damp and the fire took a long time to get going. The heat it generated was not having much affect on the ambient temperature inside the room. Even after three hours, when we'd decided to climb into our makeshift sleeping bags, we could still see our breath, illuminated by the smoky flames from the log fire. Gastin had brought a small, silver hip flask of cognac and he insisted on sharing it with us, 'It will numb us from the cold'. Strange, I always thought it was a bad idea to give anyone suffering from exposure an alcoholic drink as it lowered the body temperature, but we'd eaten a hot meal and it seemed rude not to take a slurp as he passed around his flask.

"How long have you been crossing the mountains?" enquired Anna.

"It began forty years ago when I helped the Republicanos to flee from the tyranny of the Fascists. After the German and Italian aeroplanes had bombed Guernica, the city was in ruins. It was soon over run by the rebel army and the displaced families had somehow, to try and save themselves. They came over to France in their thousands. My father and I found a route through the mountains and brought many people to safety, to start a new life in France. At the end of 1939, when the numbers of Spanish refugees dwindled, we began taking Allied airmen and French civilians back the other way. If you sat down and thought about it, what was happening in the world…" Gastin sighed; he was lost for words. He placed his right hand up to his chest and with his fore finger and thumb together made the sign of the cross to celebrate another day on earth. He explained that he had a routine of counting each day since he'd been liberated from Mauthausen, on the 5th of May, 1945. "It took a long time for me to believe I'd survived the horrors of hell," he continued. "Even now I still have nightmares and flashbacks. Sometimes a stranger's face will remind me of a friend who had starved to death, or perhaps there is a news article and a name will leap out from the page and send a shiver down your spine. That's why I do what I do."

He distracted himself by talking about the next big fish he was on the verge of tracking down. He couldn't name names, but somehow or other he would raise the funds to go to South America and in particular Bolivia. "There are some high ranking Nazi's still enjoying positions of power there. They think they are untouchable. Every day they boast about the gruesome acts they committed against innocent victims. Well, let me tell you, they will be laughing on the other side of their cheek, if ever I come face to face with them." He shuffled about from side to side on the floor in the corner of the room, pulling his blankets up to his nose. "Bonne nuit, mes amies." he said softly.

"He takes his work very seriously," I said quietly to Anna, trying to stop my teeth from rattling. The temperature in the room was only just above freezing.

"It's not only work," whispered Anna. "It's his whole life. It sounds like it's the chase that keeps him going." There was a silence before Anna asked me if I was okay.

"Yer, I'm just struggling to get warm," I replied.

"Byrney, why don't you bring your blankets over here and get into my sleeping bag with me. It's a useful trick we've learnt in an emergency. You will soon warm up."

I grabbed my cover and pillow and squeezed inside, next to Anna. Except for our boots, we were both still fully clothed and after a few minutes our bodies were warming one another. I turned my arm over and accidentally caught Anna in her ribs, which instantly made her giggle.

"I'm really ticklish," admitted Anna. I rubbed her ribs again with my fingers and she yelped uncontrollably.

"I see what you mean," I laughed. "How do you say ticklish in French?"

"Chatouilleuse and I suppose you're not, uh Byrney?"

"Try me," I joked.

Anna dug her fingers into my side and I pretended to squeal annoyingly, but Anna stopped when we heard Gastin grunting in his sleep and we both laughed. Before we could discover anything else about our bodies, fatigue, warm bellies and the cognac took it's toll and we both drifted off into a deep sleep.

The next morning, Gastin was pinching our toes to wake us. "Come on you two bush kangaroos', it's time to get up." He had found a small axe from somewhere and was splitting some of the drier logs on the stone hearth. There were a few twigs cracking and spitting on the dying embers of last nights fire. We climbed out of Anna's sack fully clothed and put on our boots, the room and everything inside it was icy cold. Anna disappeared for a few minutes and returned with a pan of water that she'd filled from a nearby spring. She placed the pan on a fresh firelighter then went rummaging inside her rucksack. She waved a small, green bottle in front of my eyes and asked me to follow her outside.

Our wooden hut was surrounded by frost covered trees. I'd no idea they'd been there the night before. The shiny new morning was perfectly still and the sky was once again clear and as fresh as the water running in the mountain stream. Through a gap in the trees, I could see a wide track leading down from our hut, deeper into the wooded plantation.

"I've got something for you to try," she smiled.

"Yer, what is it?" She had turned away from me and was bending down to the ground. She poured a small amount of clear liquid from the bottle into the bottom of two glasses and she passed one of them to me.

"It's a traditional French drink, to set you up for the day," she said cheerily. I hesitated for an instant then I imagined I could hear Max's voice inside my head, reminding me about trying everything in life at least once. 'Here goes,' I thought. I was about to put the glass to my lips and Anna said, "No, wait. You need to add the magical ingredient first."

"Which is?" I asked, playing along to Anna's spell.

She placed her glass under a fountain of water that tumbled from a mossy flat stone beside the mountain stream and the liquid inside the glass immediately turned cloudy white. "See, now you try."

We clinked our glasses together and Anna said "Sante."

The Pastis tasted like nothing I was expecting. I liked liquorish flavours, so I was pleasantly surprised, but the flavour was really intense and had a real kick to it, which went straight to my head, in spite of it being numbed to start with, from the fresh morning air.

"Come on Byrney, down in one," said Anna, showing me how it was done. So this is what all the street merchants were drinking that day in Paris, when Fionn and I were sat enjoying our first, French 'petit-dejeuner' breakfast. However, the Parisians were missing out on Anna's secret, mountain ingredient. We slid back to the cabin, just in time to warm our stomachs again on another plate of ratatouille and a welcome cup of steaming, hot, black coffee. It was time to tidy up and pack up.

On the steady descent, down to the Col de la Celeste, our route took us through a mighty plantation of coniferous trees. It was obviously a place where local Frenchmen came hunting wildlife and was probably the source of Jacques Casson's display, back at Hotel Coraline. Every few hundred yards, I noticed there was a camouflaged tree house at the head of a clearing. Each of these hunting hides was accessed by a rear ladder. Inside there was a fire step and a shelf in front of a wide, slotted opening. It didn't seem very sporting or fair to the wildlife, but according to Gastin it was a way of life for the locals. They only hunted what they could eat and were careful not to exceed their quotas. I was walking behind Gastin and Anna who were having a deep conversation about the paths along the mountains. They were rabbiting along in French and I was only picking up the odd word here and there, but it looked to me like Gastin was very grateful for Anna's knowledge. I'm not sure how we would have survived the night had we not found the Emergency Shelter.

When we arrived back at the complex of cabins and barns at Celeste Station, there was no sign of Jacques car. Anna didn't appear too surprised.

"And I thought *we* were late," she said. "Come on, let's wait inside."

Inside, Gastin immediately became fascinated with the large wall map. He called me over and traced our route with his finger, pointing to the Col du Monde and how close we'd been to the Spanish frontier. Then he ran his finger further down the map into Spain, resting at the town of Pamplona.

"This is where I was born," he announced proudly. "And do you know what it's famous for, Byrney?"

I'd heard of it but couldn't remember why, so I shrugged my shoulders and said, "sorry, I've no idea."

"Every year in Pamplona, there is a July festival, when they let all the young bulls loose in the town and charge them through the streets. When we were kids, we used to dare ourselves, who could outrun them the longest. I always won," he smiled.

It was almost five in the afternoon before we heard Jacques car, circling the car park. We'd all fallen silent for the last hour of waiting and it had taken a little of the shine off our adventure. Anna was furious with her father when she discovered he'd actually forgotten about us. He'd been too engrossed in a game of poker with a few of his fellow veterans from his Resistance days.

Gastin had agreed to stay one more night in St. Jean, as it was now too late for us to catch the last bus back to Toulouse. Jacques remembered I needed to pay for an extra night too.

The atmosphere around the dining table at our evening meal was wonderfully energised as we relived our visit to the Col du Monde, laughing and playing down the dangers we'd escaped from, Scot-free. Jacques was interested to hear if we'd discovered anything new about what had happened there. The plaque on the chimney, he told us, had been erected on the tenth anniversary, in 1953. One of Jacques' friends in the resistance, who was actually the mayor of St. Jean at the time, had organised it through his connection with La Ministiere de Pensions. L.M.P., that was another little mystery solved, I thought.

After countless glasses of wine, I followed Anna through into the kitchen to help with the dishes. It was also an excuse for us to say a fond farewell. On listening to Anna talk about our adventure, I'd become aware that Anna had been anxiously concerned for my safety. So I wasn't sure if it was out of love, or relief, that she now placed her arms over my shoulders. Just as we were about to kiss, her father Jacques appeared in the doorway, requesting that we join him in a final toast of cognac, to remember all those who had lost their lives on the mountain. My heart sank a little at our missed opportunity and I wondered if Anna felt the same too. I was following Jacques back into the restaurant when Anna caught hold of my hand and pulled me back towards her. We embraced one another with a wonderful, passionate kiss. As we opened our eyes, Anna smiled and said, "Come on, we'd better join them, before he comes back again." We held hands unnoticed all the way to the door before letting go and Anna stepped forward to sit next to her father.

The journey back to Toulouse the next morning felt like a real anti-climax. Even the duel of death between the hairpin bends and the buses squeaky brakes failed to motivate or worry me as it had on the journey up here. Thoughts were racing through my head, like a pin ball bouncing between the buffers. I was trying to put them into some sort of order. The excitement of last night's kiss with Anna left me wanting to see her again.

This morning had not been the difficult parting I'd imagined, after lying awake half the night, pondering over what lay ahead on my next visit to the Pyrenees. Anna had offered to teach me how to Ski and prompted me about what a great time I was missing out on, during the winter months in the ski resorts around St. Jean. If only life was that simple. There were my mum and dad to consider and the stolen cash from the Post Office was hopefully still buried behind our garden shed. I'd have to recover it soon. I needed to get back to the Friary and speak to Madge and Edward about Eve's ashes. There was a very short time frame to work with if I was going to get back to the Col du Monde before winter set in and on top of that, Gastin was also planning to travel to South America in the New Year, to continue his campaign. At least I didn't have to worry about Fionn, as she seemed to be settling in to hotel life in Nice. I was looking forward to catching up with her before flying back to England, next Monday, which was now only four days away.

I was staring at the man sat next to me, the grey haired crusader, Gastin de Bourges. I thought how he'd sacrificed his life for the retribution of the victims of the Nazi's. But listening to him repeating his mantra of gratitude for survival, it seemed he didn't consider what he was doing as a sacrifice at all, but in fact a celebration. I needed to unburden a heavy weight from my shoulders and I was hoping Gastin would accept it. I was dilly-dallying about how to approach him with it. He was a man who relied upon justice and I still needed his help and guidance with Eve's ashes. I'd come to the conclusion I would just have to blurt it out, but Gastin struck first. It seems he was conjuring with his own conscience too.

"Remember I told you that my father died on the Col Du Monde," he said, "on the same journey as Paul Larouchamps?

Well, three days ago it was confirmed that my father was murdered."

Wow, I wasn't expecting that. "How do you know?" I asked.

"Remember the two bodies that Anna told us about, that had been found on the Glacier di Aureola earlier this summer? They have now been identified. One of them was my father. Just before I returned to St. Jean, two days ago, I was shown evidence at the Gendarmarie in Toulouse. They had a few possessions that had been found in his clothes, a gold cross and his watch."

"But how do you know he was murdered. Maybe he just fell from a ledge or something?"

"It's incontestable." There was a gravely, serious look to Gastin's expression. "There was a bullet lodged in the back of his skull. It was the same with the other body too. The bullets came from a nine millimetre calibre, German Luger."

I tried to envisage how it had happened. "I'm sorry to hear that. What are you going to do now?"

"Knowing how my father died isn't necessarily going to make it any easier to find out who killed him," he said. "When the Germans retreated from the South of France, they were very thorough at destroying all their records. They burnt many villages to the ground too, as they retreated. Prisoners were removed from their jail cells and taken into the woods and shot. In the last days before the Liberation it was a time of total chaos. The Resistance acted over zealously too in their thirst for reprisals. A lot of old scores were settled, even a handful of their own supporters were shot by mistake, in the hasty confusion. During the last thirty years, I haven't discovered anything new about our betrayal that I didn't already know back in 1945."

"But do you still believe a member of your organisation had helped the Germans?"

"Without doubt, that dark day when the members of our escape line were rounded up by the Gestapo, it only took them a few hours. I believe that, whoever it was, perhaps he or she had not survived the war. Without any fresh evidence, finding who it was is impossible. And so, I continue to move along in the hope I will find something, but it's difficult to obtain funding for someone who played a very minor role in the war. We have to catch the big, fat fishes first."

Our bus was now entering the low-lying outskirts of Toulouse. In around twenty minutes time, we would be back at the Central Bus Depot. It was now or never, I thought.

"Gastin, I think I might be able to help you with a large donation, if you want to accept it?" Gastin turned to face me with a crooked, inquisitive, frown.

I took a deep breath, I knew that total honesty was the only way to converse with Gastin. So I told him the whole truth about the raid on the Post Office in Crowston, from start to finish. I also confessed about the guilt I'd felt and how I was still feeling alienated by the experience of it all. Unsurprisingly to begin with, he found my story incredible. He was clearly shocked at discovering I was a crook, all be it a manipulated one. It was only after I'd relayed to him my suspicions that Eve had probably allowed the robbery to take place by throwing a faint and that she had also possibly sowed the seeds for how to carry out the raid with my girlfriend, that Gastin showed any sign of wanting to understand what I'd done. He just offered me a wry smile and I hoped he could see how desperate I was to make amends.

"Back in the early days of the war, it wasn't uncommon for members of The Resistance to steal when they had to. So I'm no stranger to what they did," he said knowingly. "But that's not the same as what you did." He paused for what seemed like a very, long time. I held my breath - he was going to drop me like a hot potato.

"Alors que sera," he said. "What is done is done. Unfortunately, no one can turn back the clock, more is the pity, but luckily I have never been a fatalist, tu comprends?" He paused again, "I can understand what has brought you here and I can see how Eve would have wanted to give her approval."

Gastin related to me some of his own memories of Eve. He'd seen her taking enormous risks during the war, hiding and moving escapees. He'd admired her fighting spirit and her unflinching hatred of the Nazi's. She was someone he would have risked his own life to save, had the situation ever arose. It was a timely reminder that he had promised his fellow inmates at Mauthausen Concentration Camp that he'd do all he could to see that those responsible for the unspeakable acts of cruelty inflicted upon them, would be brought to justice. If that meant using stolen money as a means to an end then he felt it was justified. Taking his campaign across to South America was going to be very costly if he was to be successful. As I was now the only living person who'd taken part in the Post Office raid, I assured him the money was completely untraceable and that I doubted anyone was still looking for it.

"Where is your money now?" enquired Gastin in his usual serious, business like manner.

"Back home in Lancashire, but I've no idea how to bring it to France, so that I can hand it over to your organisation."

Gastin was silent for a few minutes as he mentally trawled through his contacts, connections and acquaintances. Then he raised his finger, "I think I know how we can do this," he said, displaying one of his rare smiles. "Byrney, have you ever heard of a town called Barnoldswick?"

Chapter Seven

Tumbling Dice

Stepping back inside the Hotel Les Moulins, in the old port of Nice, felt like a moment of triumph, after my twelve-hour journey from St. Jean-Les-Bains. I was feeling really pleased with myself; it was like I was in sole possession of the answer to a really important secret and I couldn't wait to tell Fionn about my adventures in The Pyrenees. I spotted her elf-like face through the glass window, before I reached the front door. She was sat in between Jean-Paul and Patrice, at a table inside the coffee bar. As I walked in through the open entrance, Patrice was the only one who'd noticed me arrive.

"Bonsoir Byrney. Ca va?" he said in his deep, friendly voice.

"Oui, un purr fatty gay," I replied, in my best Lancastrian French. Then Fionn let out a shriek of delight as she heard my voice.

"Well if it isn't Edmund Hilary," she joked. "Did you forget your razor?"

I rubbed my chin and felt the soft stubble of hair. "More like Sherpa Tensing," I said laughing. Actually, it was the first time I'd thought about shaving, as I'd not seen my reflection since the morning I'd left Nice, almost a week ago. When I did eventually see myself, later that night in Patrice's bathroom, I had to chuckle at my reflection - it's Shaggy from Scooby-Doo, I thought.

After the usual round of French kissy-kissy hello's, I realised I had a raging hunger.

"Let's all go to Club Americain, they make the best burgers on the Riviera," suggested Jean-Paul, excitedly.

I walked alongside Fionn as we followed behind Patrice and Jean-Paul, on our way to the centre of town. Fionn was skipping along. She looked very pleased with herself too.

"So what's been occurring whilst I've been away?" I enquired. Fionn was really enjoying her time in Nice. Everyone was so friendly. Then, she blushed, as she admitted to being on kissing terms with Jean-Paul. Nothing new there, I thought, even I'm on kissing terms with Jean-Paul.

"We've been out on a few dates. He's a really nice, caring boy," she said.

"I'm pleased to hear it, nice one Fi," and I put my arm around her shoulder, for an instant and gave her a loving squeeze.

As we ate our hot, juicy burgers, inside the busy bar, I told everyone all about my prowess in the mountains, trying not to mention Anna's name too often in case I was placed under some sort of embarrassing scrutiny. For the time being, I wanted to keep my enjoyment of Anna to myself, before it all came out. In any case, we weren't strictly having any sort of a relationship, although I was already looking forward to seeing her again at the end of this month.

When I told them about the storm and losing my wooden staff, Fionn looked genuinely worried. "Weren't you scared?" she asked.

"It was a bit hairy at times," I said, playing down the dangers, "but once we were all tied together, I felt surprisingly safe." They all looked at me disbelievingly.

After a couple of drinks more, I noticed Fionn and Jean-Paul were engrossed in one another's company and I wasn't looking forward to staying at Les Moulins and playing gooseberry for the next four days. Patrice was stood next to me and I think he guessed what I was thinking.

"They have become inseparable," he said. "If you want, you can stay at my studio? I have a sofa bed that you can use. It's free of charge to my friends."

"That's very kind of you, why not."

I enjoyed listening to Patrice's stories and I had noticed from previous visits that he had great taste in music, which was something I'd badly missed listening to, ever since I'd left England.

I collected my rucksack from the locked coffee bar at Les Moulins on our way back from Club Americain and said goodnight to the two 'Love birds', who were too caught up in a fit of giggles with one another to argue with my decision.

When Patrice had finished furnishing his sofa bed with a pillow and a spare duvet, I was just about 'done in'.

"There are bottles of water in the fridge. If you want one, just help yourself." Patrice disappeared up the iron, spiral staircase to his mezzanine and I slumped down on the sofa. Earlier in the day, I'd arranged with Gastin that he would give me a call, once he'd organised for a person he could trust to collect my stash of cash. I'd given him my home number and said I'd be available everyday from next Monday, between six and eight p.m. I took his business card out of my wallet to check I'd not misplaced it. The card had a blue, white and red background, symbolising the French flag and each of the three colours supported the letters: A.T.C. Below this and across the centre of the card, in a simple black type face, were the name of Gastin's organisation and his contact details.

AGENCE TROUVER LES COLLABORATEURS
M. GASTIN DE BOURGES
14, Avenue Frizac, 31017 Toulouse
Tel.61.70.11.07 - Telex 531635

Gastin knew there were regular, weekly shipments taking place between Toulouse and Barnoldswick. These were on behalf of two aerospace companies, who had a string of joint projects between them: most notably Concorde and the new A300 airbus. Engine parts were picked up from the Rolls Royce factory in East Lancashire and we'd decided between us, it wouldn't be much of a detour for a transporter to swing by Cayburn, on the return journey from Barnoldswick to the port of Southampton. I was so relieved Gastin had gone along with my proposal. It was as if someone had removed the hangman's hood from my face and I could begin to breath again at last. All that was left for me to do was dig up my stash when the coast was clear and hand it over to the French lorry driver, whom Gastin was organising - what could possibly go wrong? According to Gastin, the French lorries, transporting shipments from Rolls Royce, normally had one of Her Majesties Government Customs seals across the rear doors. So, when the lorries arrived at Southampton Docks, the Port Authorities only ever needed to check that paperwork was in order. 'So we can hide anything inside the cab'. He joked, touching his long Gallic nose.

****

Atkinson was sat behind his desk and not for the first time in the last twelve months, was regretting his decision to transfer from the cut and thrust of the busy city station headquarters at Preston, to the boring back waters of his present environs. It had been a fairly typical week in West Lancashire; he could hardly contain himself, he thought. 'Two RTA's, road traffic accidents, one shop lifter at Booths' Supermarket and a case of arson at a public telephone box, out on Cockerham Road. And to round the week off, no doubt there'd be the usual bout of fisty-cuffs and handbags, outside one or other of the town centre pubs later this evening'. Then to cap it all, he'd had to explain to young WPC Alexander who Interpol were, when she'd handed him a note, which had just come through from their headquarters in Lyon, on the station Telex machine.

He was digesting the information, which they had submitted in response to his request last week about any details they held on record, regarding a certain Henri Larouchamps from Nice. There was nothing out of the ordinary and nothing that warranted further investigation. He appeared to be an honest citizen, with no criminal record. He ran a family business - Hotel Les Moulins. He'd taken it over in 1945, after the Liberation. Previously, the hotel had been run by his older brother, Paul, who had died in 1943. It was believed that he had been a victim of the Col du Monde massacre. A dead end. He chuckled at his own pun.

The buff covered file, regarding the robbery at Crowston Post Office, lay open on his desk. He picked up the top sheet of paper from the forensic lab in High Wycombe. Although there had been several partial prints found on the band of Cellotape used to tie up Mrs Herbert, none were a match for the fingerprint he'd sent in from the record sleeve he'd covertly lifted from under Byrne's bed. Nor was it a match for the only fingerprint they'd found previously. According to this latest report they could now say conclusively, due to the ridge density of the original fingerprint found on the Cellotape, it was definitely from a person of female sex. He dropped the single sheet of paper back on top of the file and retrieved his note-book from his breast pocket, flicking through the relevant pages to see if he'd missed anything. 'So', he thought to himself, 'Byrne's gone off to France with his new girlfriend. He wasn't carrying any of the cash. As for the cash itself, it hasn't seen the light of day since the robbery and there's no trace of it at Byrne's caravan. It would appear he's in the clear.

There was just one more piece of the jigsaw left unattended to and that was a note, stuck to his telephone, asking him to meet at The Prince of Wales that afternoon, at two p.m, with Bryn Davies, a.k.a Lofty. 'Well, it's no skin off my nose to drop in for a quick pint on my way home as usual', he thought. 'But what the hell does he want to see me about? There's nothing left outstanding with Byrne's case, as far as I'm concerned now'.

**

"I didn't expect to hear from you again," said Atkinson as he placed his pint at Lofty's table, in the corner of the Lounge Bar of The Prince. The atmosphere was unusually rowdy, glancing around, this being a Friday afternoon, it had attracted a few, early weekend revellers. There was a small crowd of factory workers, stood at the bar, still clad in their blue overalls. Friday's clocking off time at the local paper mill was always one o'clock and their camaraderie was in full swing, fuelled by their slim, weekly wage packets. Small reward for the tinnitus they would all suffer from, in later life.

Lofty peered up from his paper with a look of disappointment at the sight of the single fresh pint of beer being hugged by Atkinson.

"So what's happening in your world, Lofty?" Atkinson pulled out one of his favourite, slim panatelas and rolled the tip of the cigar between his lips, before lighting up. He was doing his best not to let Lofty see how annoyed he was to be sat facing this lackey of a man whom he'd thought he'd seen the last of, especially as he'd paid him off for good, after Byrne had left the country, on the night train to Paris. Lofty had a smug look on his face. He was having trouble concealing all he knew about what Atkinson had been up to recently.

"I know about the money," blurted Lofty, confidently.

"What money? Don't waste my bloody time Lofty, I'm a busy man," replied Atkinson, clenching his hate fist.

"Come off it, you know darn well. The money from the Post Office raid at Crowston, a couple of months back. That's what Byrne's been hiding all along and that's why you've had me follow him. Am I wrong?" announced Lofty, letting Atkinson know how clever he was by waving his eyebrows.

"You're a mile off the mark, Lofty, forget it. The case has gone cold. That means closed, to the likes of you." Atkinson regretted his last words as soon as they'd left his mouth, hoping Lofty wouldn't take them the wrong way.

"Is that right?" sniggered Lofty, reaching inside his pocket and sliding a photograph across the table, making sure it was facing the right way for Atkinson to see. It wasn't the portrait of Byrne which Atkinson had given him three weeks ago. Atkinson's eyes narrowed and cut a deep furrow down the middle of his forehead as he stared at Lofty's photograph, showing Byrne's moped disappearing into the back of a Black Mariah. The face of the person pushing it was looking away from the camera, but by the state of the crumpled dark suit, it was obviously Atkinson. He was still wearing the same suit at this very moment. Atkinson's anger was rising inside him. He drew hard on the cigar and blew the smoke straight into Lofty's smug face, hoping to see him squirm.

"S.M.Y" spluttered Lofty, "smarter than you."

"Don't make me laugh. I've shit tougher cookies than you," Atkinson said, playing for time. "The only thing that photo shows is official police business. How I conduct my case is entirely up to me and me alone," he said coolly.

Lofty began to smile. "It's no good stalling, I've got you by the short and curlies this time. I've had a look inside your garage, in Churchtown Close," he said, pausing to let the final sting bite Atkinson in the arse. "I didn't know you liked renovating mopeds, some of those scratches are going to be awfully hard to polish out, especially as the frame has been sawn in half."

Atkinsons eyes were reeling. "I'll bloody saw you in half. What do you want?" he growled, sticking his chin closer to the joker opposite and automatically pocketing the photograph.

"Two hundred and fifty quid. And if you're quick, you should just catch the bank before it closes."

"What guarantee do I have you won't be back for more?"

"I'm not a greedy man, but I'm also letting you know to back off. Byrne's mine now."

"We've got nothing on Byrne that ties him to that robbery, you're wasting your time. But don't take my word for it, you can have him."

"That just leaves the Two Hundred and Fifty Pounds, then."

Atkinson stood up and accidentally knocked over his stool as he turned to leave, which attracted a few momentary, inquisitive looks from the other drinkers inside the Lounge Bar. Lofty was feeling very pleased with the way the meeting was progressing. The boot was firmly on the other foot now, S.M.Y.

When Atkinson returned, he handed Lofty a chunky envelope full of crisp, new Five Pound Notes. Before letting go of it, he announced he wanted the negative and any other copies of the incriminating photograph.

"You'll get them in a month, when I'm out of reach. I don't want any little, unexplained, accidents happening to me. If I think you're out for revenge, I'll send all the evidence I have on you, to the Chief Constable of Lancashire Police. Do you understand?"

Atkinson was taking deep breaths. He'd had just about all he could stomach from this ginger haired prick. "Whatever you say Lofty." His words were barely audible as he spoke through clenched teeth. Lofty tucked the envelope inside his blazer pocket and gave it a gentle couple of pats for luck.

"Pleasure doing business with you, Inspector." Lofty left in a hurry, leaving his newspaper behind, with Atkinson confined to his kennel. It was time to put the next stage of his plan into action. P.O.P - 'piece of piss'.

****

It suddenly became very cold. My fingers and toes were numb. Had I forgotten to change into a clean, dry pair of socks? I couldn't remember. A blast of freezing air hurtled towards me and swept me up off my feet. I could feel myself sliding down a slippery slope, face down and feet first. I had no idea how far and how fast I was falling. I was frantically clawing at the soft snow to find a hold, which would brake my descent down the mountain, simultaneously kicking and digging in with the steel crampons which were fixed to my boots. I came to rest, dizzily hanging over the edge of a precipice. I still had a rope tied around my waist and the other end was attached to my rucksack, hanging below my feet. The weight of it was slowly pulling me over. I looked up and saw Gastin, who was abseiling down to rescue me. He was shouting at me to untie the rope and I could also hear Fionn's frightened voice asking, "Aren't you scared?" I grabbed the knot around my waist with my free hand, but when I looked down again at the other end of the rope, I could see Max. She was desperately hanging on too, saying, " save me, save me." But her words became lost in a storm of hailstones and her pale face slowly disappeared behind a shower of icicles that ricocheted against the exposed rock, making a sizzling sound. I could smell food and the sound of sizzling and it was coming from a frying pan.

102

Where was I? - Patrice's studio. What day is it? This took me longer to work out, but it was definitely Friday, or was it Saturday? I flipped the duvet across my body to cover my cool, bare legs. If my nightmare was anything to go by, I was still beguiled by a deep sense of guilt. Guilty for stealing the Post Office money and guilty for not doing more to save Max from killing herself - 'Just the here and now' I said to myself, trying to break the spell.

I could see two glasses of orange juice on top of the nearest workbench, which also had two bar stools set out in front of it. Patrice's studio style living was really cool, I thought. Just needed a pool table in here to finish it off. I could understand why he enjoyed living and working under the same roof.

"Bonjour Byrney, ready for some petit dejuener - breakfast?" shouted Patrice from behind the galley partition.

"Smells good. What is it?" I asked as I began slipping into my jeans and grabbing a clean t-shirt from my rucksack.

"Croque Monsieur. It's a hot sandwich made with ham and cheese. Help yourself to some orange juice and I'll get the coffee machine started." - Mmm, nice.

"Got any plans for today?" he asked, as he walked in, carrying the frying pan and placing the hot toasted meal on my plate."

"Nothing urgent, how about you?"

"Fridays I like to finish early, so I only have two deliveries to Villefranche and Beaulieu. You are welcome to come along, if you want."

"Cheers, I will." - It's definitely Friday, then, I thought. I waited for Patrice to sit down before tucking into my hot sandwich, which tasted fabulous and I made a mental note to myself to add it to my short list of 'okay' French foods. The hot toasted sandwich reminded me of the Friary. Not long before I left there, they had just taken delivery of the latest in fast food cuisine - a brand new Breville Toastie machine. It revolutionised making hot sandwiches and proved to be a popular choice with all the upstairs cyclists. I'll say this for Madge and Edward; they were quick off the mark when it came to introducing new fangled dishes to their menu.

Patrice's deliveries were fairly straightforward affairs: half a dozen boxes of posters and leaflets to two galleries. The funny part was travelling in his cronky little Citroen van, which was parked up, out front. Firstly, the doors opened front to back. You opened them up and kind of, backed into your seat. As I sat in the passenger seat, I was convinced Patrice had removed the original seats and replaced them with canvas garden chairs, but he assured me, they were the correct ones. Then he pulled an 'L' shaped lever, which came straight out of the front dash and began changing gear with it. I was beginning to think I'd actually felt safer on the bus journey up to St. Jean, as Patrice revved the balls off the engine to make it go. Jokingly, I told Patrice that I'd made better box carts during my junior school holidays than this concoction of a vehicle. We rolled, swerved, rocked and bounced along the twisty coast road, as I gripped the metal frame of my garden chair. There were no seat belts to cling to, of course. Citroen had probably calculated the extra weight of having them would have been an unnecessary drain on the engine power.

After the two deliveries had been made, to two of the poshest looking Art Galleries I'd ever seen, we headed out of Villefranche-sur-Mer towards a small headland. At the top of the hill we turned into a circular residential crescent, of half a dozen large houses with basement garages and swimming pools in their gardens. Exactly half way round it, Patrice stopped in front of a pair of spectacularly tall, ornate, iron gates. He pointed to the adjacent wall and said, "Do you see that sign, what it says?"

I read the simple French name out loud "Nell .. cote". What's that?"

"This, Byrney, is a very famous place," he announced proudly. "Five years ago, this is where The Rolling Stones were living - Villa Nellcote. They even had a mobile recording studio, parked up on the chemin and this is where they recorded their album 'Exile On Main Street'. I'll play it for you when we get back to the studio. If you like The Stones, I've got all their albums."

When we returned to Rue Lazarette, Patrice turned across the pavement next to his studio and stepped out to open a large, painted, wooden door, which concealed an arched entrance. I studied the paintwork. It was a typical example of most painted, wooden structures in Nice, bleached by the sun and curling and peeling away in lumps. Building maintenance is, understandably, low down on the list of priorities when there are so many other exciting things to do, living on the French Riviera. I could spend all day just watching all the beautiful people, walking up and down the promenades.

Patrice fastened the open, arched door against the wall and rushed back to his van, just as the handbrake was beginning to lose its grip on the brakes. I understood, at last, why he'd chosen this ungainly contraption, as it was able to fit perfectly through the narrow gap between his studio and the adjoining building. The narrow passageway lead into an enclosed cobbled courtyard, which looked far too inviting and interesting to be permanently shut off from the outside world.

Back inside his studio, Patrice grabbed a couple of bottles of Heineken and handed one over, then he climbed up the spiral staircase. After a few minutes, he returned carrying two cases of LP records and placed them down on the workbench and unlocked them. Inside the cases, the LP records were immaculately kept. As I stared at the glossy vinyl, I felt ashamed of the way I'd looked after my own records, piled under my bed, half of them inside the wrong covers and some loosely stacked without any dust covers around them at all.

We listened to 'Exile On Main Street' as Patrice talked about how The Stones had left England under the threat of bankruptcy and had holed up in the villa which Keith Richards had rented with his girlfriend. "It was a very notorious situation and all the locals were talking about it," continued Patrice. "Every day, the Gendarmes would be watching people come and go and write down all the car number plates. Lots of rumours went around about orgies and sex parties. Probably most of them were made up by the nosey neighbours." We were looking at the collage of photos of the guys on the record sleeve. There certainly looked to be a lot of musicians involved. The Album had a real loose, relaxed feel to it. One track really stood out for me – 'Tumbling Dice'. Hearing the opening few bars of music, Keith's guitar and Mick's voice, setting the tone, just picked me up and dropped me down right back to the middle of the summer with Max. It gave me a different take on how things had been shaped. Like a game of chance, we'd played in our own time, to our own rules. It struck me that life was sometimes a gamble, like a tumbling dice. Max, Gastin, Eve and Paul Larouchamps, they'd all rolled different numbers. And towards the end of the song the way the last line rolled back and forth between Mick and his girl, backing singers was like an addiction, like a game you couldn't escape from. Is that what had happened to us? You have to deal with what life throws at you and ever since I'd arrived in France it felt like it had been all double sixes so far.

"Hey Byrney, you know we have some really great Casinos here on the Riviera. Would you like to find out what it's like to go tumbling dice for real? We French are very proud of having opened the first and most famous Casino in the world - Monte Carlo. The thought of winning wads of money didn't hold any appeal for me at all, but I could tell Patrice was sold on the idea. "I'll give Jay-Pay a call, maybe Fionn would like to join us too, if they don't mind riding in the back of my Citroen camionette. Oh no, not twice in one day. I was regretting it already.

By seven p.m, we were all bouncing back along the twisty coast road around the headlands and inlets of Villefranche and Beaulieu as we headed out towards Monaco. Fionn and myself were sat astride some cardboard boxes, collecting fresh bruises, in the back of Patrice's van. We parked up outside an old fashioned bar on the side of road, which led up into the centre of Monte Carlo. The bar was named after its proprietor, Rosie. The interior was lavishly adorned with historic posters and photographs of the Monaco Grand Prix. I had a huge grin on my face as I studied them all in detail.

"These are great," I said to Patrice.

"I knew you would find all this interesting," he replied. "This bar has been here since 1929 when the Grand Prix first came to Monaco."

I looked at the grey haired lady behind the counter, who was serving us our stubby glasses of beer from a single pump at the bar and scraping off the top of the froth with a broad blade. Gosh, if she's been here since 1929, she must be nearly eighty years old. It didn't matter how old she was as she was obviously delighted with our company. I think I would have preferred to stay here all evening but, after just one drink, we were all striding out, up the hill towards the glistening, floodlit fountain which marked the centre of Casino Square.

Outside the famous Casino, the parking spaces were full of gleaming red Ferraris and Porsches. I was beginning to feel nervous about stepping inside as we climbed the stone steps towards the smartly dressed stewards, guarding the front door; but, as we approached them, to my surprise, they bowed and wished us a good evening and politely opened the door, in time for us to enter without pausing. The entrance hall was like stepping inside a royal palace. The size and detail was breathtakingly rich. It looked to me like everything was made of twenty-four carat, solid gold. At the entrance to the games room, Patrice was talking to the steward guarding the door, who was pointing towards me.

"I'm sorry Byrney, but you need to wear a jacket to go inside." I tried to hide my disappointment and embarrassment. I'd come this far; it seemed a shame not to experience what was going on behind the plush, padded, doors. "Don't worry," continued Patrice, "You can hire a jacket for the evening from the cloakroom."

Once I was correctly dressed, we were allowed to proceed into the gambling hall. It was incredibly busy inside. I noticed that the games were all laid out on separate tables. I recognised the roulette wheel from the many James Bond films I'd seen. Beyond the animated croupiers, I could see a crowd of excited gamblers, whooping and cheering in front of a fenced table.

"That is the Craps table," said a smiling Patrice, "tumbling dice?"

I saw that Fionn and Jean-Paul had walked over to the far wall and were busy filling up the one-armed bandits with Francs. Patrice's voice cut in above the hustle and bustle, "First we have to buy some chips."

"I'm not all that hungry."

"Not those sort of chips," he laughed, moving towards the cashier's desk. "How much money do you have?"

"Five hundred Francs." I passed him five, One Hundred Franc Notes.

"Perfect." He passed me a handful of glassy painted rectangular tokens. They looked so smart that I wanted to keep them. 'Much nicer to look at than paper money', I thought.

We watched the gamblers and the casino crew around the Craps table. It was all happening so fast, I couldn't make head nor tail of what was going on.

"I'll show you what to do, watch me." It was Patrice's turn to roll the dice. He pointed to the puck, which read, OFF. "Place your chip on the pass line and if we roll a seven, we win double our bet. Patrice threw the dice across the table and bounced them of the fence - Seven, everyone cheered. Patrice's next roll produced an eight. He placed a chip on the COME square and passed me the dice. "You have to throw an eight before you throw a seven." I did my best to imitate Patrice's roll. The dice bounced back off the fence - double one. There was a groan from everyone around the table. "That's snake eyes, the bank wins." I could feel everyone's eyes on me.

"I'll let you roll," I sighed. "I'm not a lucky gambler."

"Now you tell me," he said, still smiling.

When we walked back past Rosie's place, at the end of the evening, the bar was in total darkness and the wooden window shutters had been folded to. 'An early night must be the secret to a long life', I thought. Every one of us had spent their last centimes. Apparently, the Casino used to be the only source of income for the tiny principality, and the citizens of Monaco are still not allowed to gamble there; which goes to show what a outrageous fix it all was.

The journey back home seemed uneventfully short. Back inside Patrice's studio, we were all invited in, for one last beer to drown our sorrows. Although all our pockets were empty, I'd saved my last chip as a souvenir. It was safely tucked away inside my wallet. Patrice placed an old, cardboard chocolate box on top of the workbench, after passing around four bottles of Heineken. "Take a look inside," he said to us all.

"I know what this is," said Jean-Paul promptly and reached over to remove the lid. To my surprise it was a collection of old photographs.

"These belonged to my father. Have a look Fionn and Byrney. There should be some of Eve and her husband Paul."

"Oh, how exciting," said Fionn as she eagerly tipped over the contents of the box, spilling and fanning the photos across the bench top.

We passed each one around as if we were a panel of judges at an art competition and occasionally Patrice, or Jean-Paul, would make a comment about one of the figures they recognised. I recognised a few of the photographs from copies I'd seen at Eve's cottage, in Crowston, like the one of Paul Larouchamps's parents. "Grandmere et Grandpere," recalled Jean-Paul, nostalgically.

There was a wonderful photo of Eve and Paul, sat side by side, next to a grand piano. It had probably been taken at Les Moulins before the war. Although I'd never clapped eyes on this photograph before now, there was something strangely familiar about Eve, but I couldn't work out why. I stared at Eve's elegant, smiling expression with her arm around her husband's shoulders, looking quietly glamorous as usual. Then I saw, in the centre of the image, what had been staring at me in the face all along. Hanging from Eve's neck was an identical necklace to the one that Anna kept in her bedroom, inside her mums music box. It seemed an odd coincidence, the same aubergine shaped pendant, which I'd held in my hand only a few days ago. I hung on to the photo.

"Could I borrow this for a while please, Patrice?"

Chapter Eight

No Going Back

Patrice wanted to see me safely delivered to Nice Airport. My return flight home was due to leave at seven-thirty a.m. so we had a quiet drive along the Promenade d'Anglais. I tried to talk him out of taking me. It would have been easier and less of a worry to have simply gone by taxi, but he had a surprise gift for me, a copy of his Rolling Stones poster that I'd so admired on his studio wall. I had a list of things to do, once I was back in England and the list was getting longer by the day. Fionn had asked me to call and see her mum, to let her know that her only daughter hadn't been kidnapped and dragged off to a hareem in the North African desert. It's true; all mums have some strange ideas.

On the drive up to the airport along the Bay of Angels, Patrice and I were chatting. I asked him had there ever been a Mrs. Patrice? He told me he'd never desired a woman in that way. "As you English say, I bat for the other side." He'd spoken in a candid way that seemed quite blunt to me, but he was just talking naturally and relaxed, so I asked him why he was attracted to men and he replied, "Why are you attracted to girls, Byrney?" I was quiet for a moment. I remembered all the times I'd worked with Max over the summer, all the times we'd been together in the same room and I'd not been able to take my eyes off her. I pictured Max, the way she looked, the way she moved and her incredible smile.

"Well, in my limited experience, I'd say it's because girls have such power over me; that's what I feel."

"Well that's exactly how it is for me with men," replied Patrice. I felt like he'd wanted to explain all along, not because he fancied me, or anything. It was because I thought he felt comfortable around me and he could trust me and trusted that it wouldn't spoil our friendship. Instead of the kissy goodbye thing that Jean-Paul was so fond of, Patrice gave me a wry smile and we shook hands and gave each other a hug.

"Let me know when you are returning and I'll come and meet you here," he offered.

"Yer, that'd be great. Cheers Hardhat," I said, cheekily. I watched his rusty, old, bouncing jalopy rock from side to side as he exited the roundabout. When it had slipped back onto the highway, I slung my rucksack over my shoulder and caught the first rays of the rising sun reflecting through the long glass panels at the front of the slick looking, modern entrance hall, of Nice airport. I was booked on an Air France flight to Ringwood, Manchester.

The temperature in Manchester was shockingly damp and cold. The free bus ride from the airport dropped me off at Chorley Street coach station and I walked down to the regional railway station, on Oxford Road. The first thing I saw when I stepped off the pavement was a large brown rat crossing the road in front of me. 'Welcome to Lancashire.' I thought.

By the time I walked into mum's fashion shop, it was almost four-thirty in the afternoon. I'd forgotten how drab and dirty the old stone buildings were in Lancaster and the busy, endless, looping lanes of traffic, all chugging out their exhaust fumes and filling the high street with poison. It was quite a come down from the brightly lit, azure sky and chalk coloured stonework in Nice. Initially, mum almost didn't recognise me when I strode into her shop. "You look taller and leaner, she said, and you need a shave."

"It's nice to see you too mum," I replied, humorously, as I gave her a hug.

"Your father will be pleased you're back too and our Anthony."

I was immediately shocked when I stepped back inside our tiny mobile home. It seemed so much smaller and my bedroom had actually less space in it than one of the built-in wardrobes at Les Moulins. Coming home and seeing my family again felt a bit like going back to your old school after you'd left. You recognised everything, but you realised you didn't belong there anymore. I'd missed everyone, of course, but somehow, in just a few weeks away, everything had changed and to begin with I couldn't settle. Something inside me was changing too. It wasn't only the fact I'd just returned from living in the same environs as frequented by rock gods and the very beautiful, but I found the differences between us unbridgeable. My parents' life and the one I wanted to be a part of now were worlds apart. A rebellious instinct had crept inside me. I kept thinking I must have my own space to function in correctly. Maybe I was being too harsh on them. Their love had always been unconditional and perhaps I was guilty of taking it for granted.

Dad had filled our fridge with my favourite beer and I thought I almost detected a tear in his eye when he greeted me. I was feeling guilty again, about wanting to be as far away from here as I could get.

"So the wanderer returns," he announced. "Great to have you back again, son." I was spoilt rotten that first evening. I was told to sit down on our leather corner sofa and everything was brought to me, even our Anthony seemed amazed to see me and his voice sounded deeper than I remembered. I'd only been away two and a half weeks and yet it felt longer than a school term. I broke the news to them that I would be returning to France as soon as possible to deliver Eve's, Mrs. Herbert's ashes. They were under the impression that her husband's grave was somewhere within easy access, like a cemetery beside a main road, so I let them carry on believing that's how it was. Had they known about my prowess in the mountains, I think they would have tore up my passport, there and then.

When I woke inside my shoebox the next morning, I was completely alone. Even on a weekday, our mobile home park was incredibly quiet. Most of the residents at our end of the site, like our neighbours, The Taylors, were retirees. There were a couple of written notes for me on our kitchen table: one from mum, reminding me not to forget to visit the Police Station to report my stolen moped and one from dad, asking me to do a bit of shopping at Booth's supermarket. 'So much for being treated like a king last night - still it was nice while it lasted, I was lucky to be loved by them', I thought.

After breakfast, I'd more urgent things to attend to. Whilst everyone was out of the way, I was going to dig up the stash from behind the shed. I noticed the unkept part of the garden behind the shed was still being used as a dumping ground and someone had been recently dropping fag ends. Don't tell me our Anthony had started smoking now; he's going to be in debt to our newsagent for the rest of his life. There were also a couple of spare lorry tyres and a drum of diesel. When I'd cleared the area around the two concrete slabs and lifted them, I was relieved to see the metal ammo box underneath the sheet of tarpaulin. The bundles of cash inside the carrier bags were still more or less dry as a bone. I'd nothing to back fill the hole with, so I just put a few loose bricks inside the ammo box to fill the void left by the cash. Sitting in the bottom of the ammo box, still, was the stolen number plate, which I'd nicked with Max that day at Cockerham Sands. I could still picture her silhouette on top of the sand dunes, staring out to sea. I left the number plate in situ, underneath the bricks. When everything was returned to it's normal, dumping ground look, I scattered a few more fallen leaves around for good measure. Once the stash was stored inside my rucksack and hidden in the back of my wardrobe, I picked up dad's shopping list and cycled into town. I was thinking about how I was going to get around without my moped.

When I rang the Friary, later in the afternoon, it was Kevin who answered the phone and he volunteered to pick me up the next morning and drive me into Crowston, to meet Madge and Edward who had news for me about Eve's ashes. The news was they were mine to dispose of, as no one had come forward to claim them.

Kev was his usual chatty self, mainly talking a lot of nonsense and the majority of his conversation floated over my head. Although I did switch on when he told me he and Vicky were going to announce they were getting engaged.

"You don't hang about. Frightened she'll run off with someone else. You're not all that good looking are yer?" I joked.

Kev responded by swerving his mini from side to side, trying to scare me as we sped down the deserted part of Gunford Lane on our way to Crowston, which seemed pretty lame after being stuck in the back of a Citroen van, on the coast road from Nice to Monaco.

"When are you planning on getting married, then?"

"Probably next summer," said Kev, enthusiastically.

"Well good luck to yer mate, you've got a great girl in Vicky."

We walked into the shop together and Kevin disappeared into the corridor between the shop and the house, presumably to hang up his coat and grab one of the blue, nylon, smocks to start work for the day. I stood next to the counter, waiting for Joanie to finish serving one of the village elders. Then she turned to me, with her arms resting on her waist, "Wow, look at you, you handsome young man. Have you come for your old job back?" She stepped from behind the counter as I moved forward to receive her welcoming hug. "Come on we'd better let Madge see you."

Madge was standing next to the fryer with her back to me as she was topping up the vats, with fresh cooking oil from a five gallon drum. "Look who's come back to see us," said Joanie. Madge turned to look over her shoulder and gave me one of her cheesy smiles. I instantly noticed that she had some blonde highlights in the front of her hair, which had been cut short and gave her a younger look, but her eyes appeared slightly weary and in need of a day off. The café only ever closed for one day a year, Christmas day. All three of them worked long hours and although they were raking in the money from the business, they very rarely treated themselves, other than the traditional family holiday, once a year and maybe a smart hair-do less freequent than that.

I was really surprised to see how pleased she was to see me.

"That's splendid timing Byrney, Glenda has just rung in sick, so there's a day's work going, jump to it." Talk about being put on the spot, whenever Madge asked for help she always made it sound like you'd no other option. Funny thing was, I'd really missed the rush of adrenalin that I'd experienced when I'd been rushed off my feet, or my brain pushed to it's limits, dealing with a room full of nit-picking cyclists and trying to make sense of it all.

"Okay Madge, you got me."

Edward walked into the kitchen as everyone was laughing. "Hello stranger," he said offering his hand. "You haven't just made the mistake of agreeing to come back for the day, have you? You'll never get away from here now," he joked.

I couldn't believe I was chipping potatoes again in the back yard. I thought, now that I was an internationalist, I should be treated with a bit more respect, some hopes. Kev was folding and tearing up cardboard boxes and loading the bailing machine.

"Don't suppose you've heard about Max's mum? She's put her house up for sale and she's emigrating to Canada."

"Good bloody riddance to her," I said. "Hope her tits freeze and drop off. She won't be missed."

I'd been thinking about going to visit Max's grave. I knew I had to do it today. She was never far from my thoughts and she'd felt really close to me when I'd walked through the café earlier. It was the first time I'd been amongst the dining tables since the day before Eve's funeral.

The day passed really quickly. There'd been lots of funny comments aimed in my direction like, 'who's the new guy?' and 'does Fionn know you're here?' Maybe some of the comments had been deliberately aimed to help me along and at the end of the shift, Madge led me into their front room lounge. Straight away, I noticed Eve's urn waiting for me on the mantlepiece.

"Look after this Byrney and whatever you do, don't drop it," she said, as if she was barking out one of her orders. Then she stared straight into my eyes and in a mellow voice said, "But, more importantly, look after yourself."

"Don't worry about me Madge, I'll be back at Christmas. Wouldn't miss the 'Friary Do'. Fionn's excited already about coming back for it too."

"Well, you're both welcome, you don't need me to tell you that."

Kevin was already sat inside his Mini, twiddling with the radio/cassette player as I opened the passenger door and placed Eve's urn in the foot well.

"Is that what I think it is? Bloody hell, don't spill any," he moaned.

"Don't worry, it won't bite you."

"Well it's just, erm a bit creepy."

"Okay. Kev do yer mind driving up to the cemetery at St. Mary's for five minutes, there's something I have to do?"

"Sure mate," he said seriously, knowing exactly what I was referring to.

The old churchyard was deserted. It was almost dusk and the grey light was beginning to darken, turning the larger headstones as black as a headmaster's cape. The church steeple looked as menacing as ever; this wasn't one of my favourite places, but at least the air was dry, for a change. The bare boughs were creaking in the breeze, like a heavy foot on an old wooden staircase. There was no point in creeping about here, I thought. Max's grave was exactly where I'd guessed it would be, at the far end where all the new plots were laid out. After searching through half a dozen new monuments, I found Max's shiny, black, marble headstone. There were no clues to how, or why she'd died, so young, just a few gold letters stating her name, died 24th September 1976, age 19 years. There didn't appear to have been much love spared, so few words to sum up a life. I knelt down beside her name and took out Max's doll from my coat pocket. It was the one that she'd asked me to look after for her. I knew she'd really wanted me to find the diary that was hidden inside, so I thought I'd bring her closest companion along to keep her company. I clawed at the soil with my bare hands to make a small hole. The earth was still loose. I covered over the the doll and as I made sure the little yellow cloth dress was well hidden, I told Max about how she would have loved the freedom of the Pyrenees. I ran my finger across her name and whispered "I won't ever forget you."

****

Since the meeting with Atkinson last Friday afternoon, Lofty had been busy gathering his notes to try and piece together as much information about Byrne as he could. Besides Byrne's workplace in Crowston, he knew he'd a colleague in Firton and a girlfriend, Fionn, with whom he'd sauntered off to Paris with. Then there were Byrne's parents, at the caravan site. Somehow, he had to find out when Byrne was returning from France as it was obvious only he knew where the cash from the Post Office raid was hidden.

Lofty was reading from the notebook that he'd used to record Byrne's movements, whilst he'd been tailing him, prior to his departure. There'd been several visits to the bank, which he'd no details about, but the fact that Atkinson had been snooping around Byrne's caravan led him to believe the money was still somewhere local. He was pacing up and down inside his flat, hoping to conjure up an intuitive plan, when - eureka! An old, empty, leather suitcase on top of the wardrobe gave him an idea.

The next day, after a visit to a couple of charity shops in town, he parked up on the brick littered car park at the entrance to Bowland Mobile Home Park, at ten-thirty a.m. precisely. Just over an hour earlier, he would have spotted Kevin's Mini driving off, with Byrne sat in the passenger seat. Lofty checked his appearance in the rear view mirror and straightened his tie. There was no excuse for sloppiness. He wore a clean shirt everyday and always pressed his trousers until the creases were razor sharp. He picked up his old, leather suitcase and stood outside his car, resting it on the roof whilst he locked the two front doors. Then, he briskly marched through the entrance and veered off to the right towards Byrnes caravan. He was hoping to catch someone in. He rattled the flap of the brass letterbox and waited. Whilst he was stood on the top step, he peered

117

through the kitchen window. Apart from the echo from his knock, nothing stirred in the empty room. He looked behind him and all around; there was no one about. 'Plan B' he thought. He moved down to the next caravan and gave the door a proficient knock, which immediately startled a white poodle, scampering in the porch, snarling and barking, which, in turn, brought forth a skinny, grey-haired lady, shuffling to the door.

"Good morning Madam," said Lofty, turning on the charm and flashing his off-white gnashers. "I've come to bring you a little ray of sunshine." The fragile, old lady shooed her pet pooch inside the kitchen and shut it in. She didn't get many visitors at this time of the morning or at any time come to think of it. Her husband was sat at the kitchen table, reading the morning paper, which meant that, as usual, she'd be spending most of the morning being ignored.

"He's a lively little chap," said Lofty, referring to the desperate scratching at the door. "My name is Fred Smith, H.T.S - Home Trade Specialist. The owner of Bowland has given me permission to show my wares to all you lovely residents and lucky for you, you're my first customer of the day."

Mrs. Taylor was not taken in by the salesman's flannel, but she was enjoying having someone to talk to as she leant against the door frame to get settled in. Lofty opened his case and said "I'll bet you have a few grandchildren you'd like to spoil. These are the very latest craze going around, the shops have sold out, but I still have a few available, only One Pound Ninety-nine a pair." He pulled out a couple of plastic balls, held together with a length of cord, which ran through a plastic tablet. "These are called Clackers. You just swing them and clack them together, hours of harmless fun and they come complete with a factory, safety certificate." Lofty did a quick demo and hit his own thumb by mistake.

"Sorry, I don't have any children or grandchildren," announced Mrs. Taylor.

"Oh dear, I don't suppose there are many kids living on this site, just my luck," complained Lofty, scratching the back of his head and looking around all disappointed. Then he managed to glean some useful information about the occupants in the caravan next door, as Mrs. Taylor explained she was on chin wagging terms with Andrea Byrne next door. Over the past year or so, they had shared many an intimate detail about each other's marriages, whist hanging out the washing. Mrs. Taylor was well aware how much Andrea doted on her children, always proudly telling her about their exploits. "There are two boys next door, although one has left school now. He gets about a bit. Been to France he has and just returned two days ago." Lofty could not get away quick enough. He gave the old lady a spongy rubber dog toy for her pet and waved good-bye. 'So Byrne has returned.' He said to himself as he pounded back to his car. 'If he's only just got back, I don't suppose I'll have missed much yet.' He made a mental note to start his C.O.M routine immediately - Classic Observation Mode.

****

Mum and dad were pleasantly surprised when I told them I'd spent the day working at the Friary.

"At least you won't be having to cadge any brass of us," said dad.

"Actually, I might need to borrow a bit, to buy my return ticket to Nice."

They both stopped eating and looked at one another. Mum broke the silence. "So, you're still planning on going back then? We were hoping you'd changed your mind." The atmosphere around the table was like a blow dried bonfire, just waiting for one of us to light the touch paper.

"What about your job with the RAF?" Dad asked, angrily.

I wasn't sure how I was going to get my own way with them this time around. It'd been much easier last time, when they could both see I needed to get away after Max's suicide. I told them about Fionn and how she was enjoying working at the hotel in Nice. There was a job there too for me, if I wanted. It was a half truth, but I also mentioned Patrice and his studio and how much I admired his work/living style of life. He hadn't offered me a job, but I knew that if he ever needed an assistant,

119

it was an opportunity I would leap at. But, the main reason for going back was to take Mrs. Herbert's ashes back to her husband's family. I told them about Eve and Paul's exceptional lives and how I'd been to see the ruins of the shelter, in the French hills where Paul's life had come to an end.

"Can't you just post them the damn things," screamed mum. "This story of yours is beyond belief." It was dad who calmed her down.

"If our Mark is determined to do this, then it's up to us to support him."

Later that night, when it was just the two of us talking about life, I told him how I didn't feel I belonged at home anymore; it was time to flee the nest. My adventures had given me the drive to find my own way.

"You were always like that," he sighed. "Even as a little boy, you were always alone, twenty paces in front of the rest of us."

The next day I spent at home, sorting through my things. I'd pinned Patrice's Rolling Stones poster to my bedroom wall. What a brill concert that must have been. On my bedside shelf, I placed the casino chip from Monte Carlo. It had not been that great an experience, especially as I'd lost all the bets. I quickly put those thoughts to the back of my mind and retrieved all my LP records and Singles from under my bed and decided to give them a clean and place them all back inside their dust covers and the correct sleeves. From now on, I was going to take better care of my possessions.

At seven p.m. there was an urgent phone call for me from Gastin. Mum answered the phone and handed it over, "it's some French bloke for you!" I wasn't expecting to hear from him so soon. He had been trying to reach his driver, who was already on the road in England.

"His name is Didier. It's okay. I've known his father for a very long time. He is staying in Barnoldswick tonight, so he will be passing your home, around nine o'clock, tomorrow morning. He is driving a white wagon, with the name of an aerospace company on the side, but you shouldn't have any trouble recognising him because the steering wheel is on the other side, n'est ce pas?"

"Will he be able to take Eve's ashes too?"

"Yes, that should be fine, just make sure they are inside a square box, nothing too big, okay? When are you returning to France, Byrney?"

"Next Monday."

"Bon. Call me when you are ready to go to St. Jean, but don't wait too long."

"Okay, merci. Au voir." I said. After I'd put down the receiver, mum began quizzing me about who I'd been talking too. "Sorry, that was Gastin," I said curtly. For some reason I had a sudden urge to play my Ramones LP, very loudly, but I was also wondering what to use for Eve's ashes to travel in. I rummaged through the kitchen cupboards and found a large, lidded, Tupperware container. 'Perfect,' I thought. I spread a newspaper down on my narrow bedroom floor, to catch any stray ashes as I tipped the contents of Eve's urn into the clear, plastic container. The ashes were bleached, white particles of grit that threw up tiny plumes of dust as the urn slowly emptied. The plastic container was slightly overfull and I had to squeeze down on the lid to get it to click into place, but it was in danger of popping off again. I found a roll of Cellotape, inside dad's bureau and began to wrap the tape around the Tupperware box. The irony of wrapping up Eve's ashes with Cellotape was not lost on me. What would she have said? I thought. "Don't worry it's only temporary," I murmured.

I imagined her reply - 'That's what you said last time'.

The next morning, I waited in my bedroom, with the door locked from the inside, until everyone had left. I was cutting it fine if I was to meet up with my French lorry driver. Dad eventually left, at ten minutes to nine. I already had my military rucksack strapped over my shoulders and I clutched the Tupperware box on top of my knees as I sat on the edge of my bed, waiting for the all clear. "At last," I sighed as I heard the main door slam to. I waited for the sound of his engine to start up and disappear over the speed humps. I ran down the steps, not even bothering to lock the door. I raced across the main road and waited by the bus stop, next to the old lorry park and scanned the on-coming vehicles in both directions. At only five past the hour, I heard the hissing sound of air brakes pulling up behind me. I turned around in time to see a French lorry turning into the lorry park. It was the white lorry I was expecting, with a left hand driver. The driver wound down his window and shouted "Monter!" and beckoned me to climb into the cab, through the passenger door. Once I was sat down, he introduced himself with a firm handshake. He had the largest moustache I'd ever seen, so lip reading was not going to be an option. I pointed to the rucksack and said, "Pour Gastin."

He opened the top of the centre seat in between us and revealed an empty square compartment. As I began to unbuckle the straps on my rucksack he moved the tall gear lever forward, revved up the noisy engine and drove out of the car park, down the main road. He pointed to his watch, "Rapido!" he said. I stacked the bundles of cash neatly inside the secret compartment, making sure I'd enough room left for the Tupperware box to rest on top and as I went to fix the seat back down, Didier pointed to the box and said "Quoi!"

"It's Madame Larouchamps," I said, feeling slightly embarrassed and hoping it wasn't going to be a problem for him.

Didier began to laugh, "Oh la la!"

By the time I'd finished unloading my stash, we had travelled around five miles and had reached the opposite end of the town by-pass. I asked Didier to drop me next to the road, so that I could cut back through into town on foot, which would take me past my old school. He slowed to almost a standstill and I jumped out, slamming the door behind me and shouted "Au voir" to my wonderful, French postman.

'At last!' I thought. 'That's an end to it, no more worries about being arrested or discovered, no more feeling ashamed.' The weight of my rucksack was barely noticeable, as I climbed up the old, narrow lane back into town. Very few cars came this way nowadays, since the by-pass that had been laid out around the town, about seven years ago. There were a few old fashioned, semi detached houses on one side of the road, which were now reaping the benefits of good planning. Their old established front gardens behind tall privet hedges looked very inviting and peaceful now that they had been spared from the streams of passing vehicles. On the opposite side of the lane, I could see the entrance to my old school. There were a few cars parked up next to the pavement, an overspill from the main car park. As I walked past the last car in the line, I heard a car door close and when I turned around to see who it was, I didn't see the punch coming.

**

I could hear a faint, soft, female voice saying 'He's waking up.' My head throbbed. A deeper voice said, "Are you alright lad?" I tried to focus and noticed I was sat on a park bench, staring down at my shoes. There were fresh splashes of blood around them and on my t-shirt too. I glanced around to find the school secretary, Miss Pringle sat next to me and standing behind her was the unmistakeable figure of Sergeant Swindlehurst.

"It's young Byrne, isn't it, how are you feeling now lad?" I tried to stand up, but my legs felt to light. "Steady on, just sit here a few minutes, you'll soon be alright." Then he turned to Miss Pringle and said, "he's coming to now. I'll take it from here, thanks for making the call."

After a few more minutes I was back amongst the living and talking to the police sergeant about what had just occurred and as there wasn't much I could say, I thought I'd mention my stolen moped instead. He sat me down in his panda car and together we wrote out my statement, regarding the theft. There wasn't much I could tell him about that either as I'd been in France when it'd been taken. I just needed to report its loss, so that I could make an insurance claim. He very kindly gave me a lift home, after I'd satisfied him that there was nothing at all I could remember about my attack and that there was nothing of value in my rucksack. How had he known about that? Then I realised, Miss Pringle must have seen it happen. Swindlehurst

123

was keeping a few details back from me, I thought. Thank god my rucksack had been empty I thought, when I came to realise it was still missing. Swindlehurst didn't press me for more information and he let me go. I had the impression he already knew who my assailant was.

Besides a throbbing head, I also had a few alarm bells ringing too. The guy who'd attacked me was the same guy who'd followed me to London, three weeks ago - I was sure of it.

The next few days I spent quietly at home, periodically inspecting the shiner across my left eye, in the bathroom mirror. By Sunday, it was at last turning yellow and the swelling had subsided and my face no longer ached. Sunday the twenty-fourth of October 1976 turned out to be an historic day. I'd woken early to switch on the TV, to watch the live transmission of the Formula One Grand Prix from Japan. As a TV spectacle, it was one of the most indistinguishable pieces of sporting footage that had ever been screened. Not only was the picture quality fuzzy, to begin with, but the race was a complete wash out too. After long delays, the race, unexpectedly, went ahead. All I could see were waves and waves of spray thrown up by the racing cars. It was the finale to an extraordinary season. Englishman, James Hunt, had to win, if he was to be crowned world champion. In the end, he finished third, but his main rival had retired from the race and it was just enough for Hunt to lift the title by a single championship point. It seemed a fitting end to my week too. My bags were packed and I was looking forward to getting on the move again. I'd spoken to Fionn in Nice and told her I'd be back tomorrow evening. I apologised for not calling round at her mum's, but said I'd explain everything, when I was back at Les Moulins.

My good-byes with mum and dad had been softened by spending so much time with them during the last few days and I think I'd bored them with my endless enthusiasm and talk about how great life was in the south of France, so much so, I felt it was almost a relief for them to see me go. Although I could never outstay my welcome in their eyes, in their hearts they knew they couldn't hold me back.

Chapter Nine

To Catch A Rat

Earlier in the week, Lofty had been meticulously making preparations for his much anticipated confrontation with Byrney. He wasn't going to be caught T.D. on this one - Trousers Down. He'd already invested far too much time on this project and up to now, had little reward to show for it. The two hundred and fifty pounds he'd outwitted from Atkinson had been a cleverly orchestrated little bonus, turning the tables on Atkinson and beating him at his own crooked game. The sun had gloriously shone down on Lofty since; he had also won a further, tidy little earner on the gee-gees, at Haydock Park, a day later. He felt, at last, his luck was changing for the better.

He stared at the list in front of him and was ticking off the items already in his possession, packed and ready to go. He'd also packed his International Driver's Licence and passport just in case, and for added insurance he'd pocketed his old service revolver, the one he'd smuggled home many moons ago. This unregistered firearm had been taken from a disreputable Army Officer he'd beaten at poker during his time in Aden, whilst serving as a member of the 28th Infantry Brigade. He'd also fought and taken part in a few minor skirmishes against the NFL, the National Liberation Front, in South Yemen. He'd learnt to look over his shoulder during that campaign, as the Yemeni rebels had proved to be very resourceful at murdering off duty soldiers.

Byrne was proving to be equally unpredictable. For a kid fresh out of school, so far, he'd managed to give his pursuers the run-around. He was obviously no mug. Lofty had seen how cautious and careful Byrney had been in the past and on top of all that, he'd been able to keep the large stash of cash well hidden, even making the Inspector of C.I.D. look foolish. No, Lofty was leaving nothing to chance. He was well and truly 'tooled up', for every eventuality.

He threw his car into the brick littered car park for the umpteenth time and waited. Over the past weeks he'd become very familiar with the routines of the more outwardly mobile residents of Bowland Mobile Home Park: the pot-bellied dog walker, with his pot-bellied dog; the chubby kid on his newspaper round, puffing away on cigarettes; the odd cars, commuting at regular intervals; it was all R.S - routine stuff.

"There goes Byrne's old man, in that rough looking van. How does that old thing keep running?" he asked himself. He waited for the blue haze to clear. Emerging from the plumes of exhaust smoke, like a magician, was the king of the water rats himself - bingo! Byrne was running out of the main entrance like a storm trooper. He ran across the road and waited by the bus stop. Lofty tuned his field glasses on Byrne's position. "What that he's carrying?" said Lofty, with his mouth gaping wide open with incredible excitement. The suspense was becoming unbearable. "He's even got his butties with him, must be planning a long journey." He adjusted his gaze on to the rucksack, the big, bulky, rucksack. "Bingo!" he yelled inside the car. Lofty had to wipe the drool from his chin, T.F.A. - time for action. He exited his car, just as a large, white truck pulled up into the lorry park across the road. He stood clenching his fists as he watched Byrne climb inside the cab. He waited a few seconds, frozen with indecision. Then as the truck pulled away he leapt back into his car. He stalled the engine as he hurriedly attempted to set off. Moments later the engine was screaming through the gears as he gave chase. Luckily the red traffic lights at the junction to Cockerham Road had allowed him to pull up directly behind the foreign truck. He scribbled down the number plate - 779 AG 31

The company livery on the rear doors gave Lofty some additional, useful information - Aerospatiale, Rue Rene Leduc 31505 Toulouse. He was feeling very confident. Although at this stage he'd not foreseen going as far as Toulouse, he was still pretty pleased with himself about having had the foresight to fill up his petrol tank the night before. As he followed behind the Froggy truck, at a regulation distance of ten car lengths, he started to relax into his driving seat. Then, without warning, the truck slowed down and pulled into the side of the kerb, "What's he up to now?" said Lofty, slightly rattled as he craned his neck over his left shoulder, just in time to see Byrne jump out of the cab, only a few feet in front of him. "He's getting out already, what the fuck!" Lofty quickly spotted a lay-by about fifty yards ahead and pulled in, just in time to check his rear view mirror as the French Lorry drove up past him, continuing further down the road towards Preston. Byrne was now walking back into town, but, crucially, he was still carrying the rucksack. "Right, this is the bloody last time!" said Lofty. He swung his car around and forked off to the right, passing Byrne and proceeded up the quiet lane. He pulled in at the front of a line of parked cars and made a quick assessment for making a snatch: no one around, quiet country lane; the school opposite was quiet; all the kids were in class; this would have to do. He glanced up at his rear view mirror again. Byrne was only twenty yards away. Lofty had his right hand paused over the door handle. He closed the door behind him quickly and quietly and stepped in behind Byrne's heels. He gave him a gentle tap on the shoulder and when he turned around he let Byrne have one of his pile drivers.

Byrne fell back onto the pavement, unconscious. He pulled the straps over Byrne's arms and tugged the rucksack free from under his body. It looked unusually flat. It was light as a feather. It was as if Byrne had left him a note saying, 'too late, sucker!' Lofty felt an eruption of rage rise up inside him. He jumped back into his car and checked the bag again - nothing. 'He's done a bloody switch', thought Lofty. 'The cash must be still inside that truck, which was now, probably, on it's way back to France. It would only be about ten miles further down the road.' Lofty knew that as soon as he reached the motorway he could put his foot hard to the floor and catch up. A lorry would be no match for his seven year old Austin 1100.

He was just shy of Keele Services, on the M6 Motorway, when the back end of the Froggy truck came into view.

****

When Sergeant Swindlehurst stepped back behind his desk, he'd just finished adding Byrne's statement sheet to the file marked 'Motorcycle Thefts' when Atkinson stepped out of his office, holding an empty mug. He placed it down on WPC Alexander's desk and said, "be a good girl and do the honours, milk and two sugars."

Swindlehurst turned to Atkinson. "You won't believe this, boss. Remember Mark Byrne, the young lad we thought might be involved in the raid at Crowston Post Office? He's been attacked, about an hour ago."

Atkinson pulled his lips together and frowned deeply in annoyance, then reached into his breast pocket for a cigar and said, "you'd better step inside my office, Sarge."

When Swindlehurst had finished relaying the details of Byrne's attack. Atkinson's reaction was such that he appeared to be even more unduly annoyed than usual, like he'd taken it personally. "And you're quite sure about who was responsible?" He asked.

"No doubts whatsoever. The witness statement from the school secretary, Miss Pringle, who saw the whole thing, gave us an accurate description and the colour and make of car - it had to be Lofty Davis."

"That bloody idiot," said Atkinson under his breath. "Leave that file with me. I'll go and have a strong word in his shell-like." When Swindlehurst vacated the office, he was passed by WPC Alexander entering at the same time, with Atkinson's third cup of tea of the day. When his office was empty again, Atkinson closed his door and wandered over to the window. There were dark clouds gathering over the park opposite the police station. Lofty was becoming a liability. He'd tried to warn him to stay away, only last week. Atkinson now knew he couldn't be trusted. Whatever evidence Lofty had raked up, it was now time to rub him out. If he wasn't going to listen to reason, then it was time to teach him a lesson he wouldn't forget.

****

The street lights and illuminations drifted along the Bay of Angels like star dust, falling from the night sky. From my fuselage window, it was like staring into a fairy tale world as the plane banked steeply to one side to make its final approach to Nice airport. The landing gear in the undercarriage thudded as it locked into position and the engines howled as they drew in a sharp intake of breath to settle the plane down on the tarmac. It was a perfect landing on a perfect, tranquil evening. A cool Mistral swirled across the asphalt apron. I was back in the south of France. I had a feeling of satisfied jubilation as I carried my old, school sports bag into the terminal building. The Customs Officer asked me the reason for my trip, business or pleasure? - pleasure. And how long did I intend to stay in France? - two weeks.

"Have a pleasant holiday, Monsieur Byrne."

"Merci."

Patrice was a very welcome sight, waiting for me in the Arrivals Hall with a broad grin on his face.

"Bonsoir Byrney." He asked if I'd remembered to bring Eve's ashes with me.

"Actually, that's a long story," I said.

Later when we were sat having a beer in his studio I told him the whole story. I was quietly confident his understanding nature would allow him to forgive my errant judgement in taking part in the post office raid.

"What were you thinking, Byrney?"

"I know; it was a huge mistake." I asked him how well he knew Eve. He was only a boy during the 'Occupation', but he'd liked her very much.

"She was always so very self assured, always understood the risks she was taking. Actually, looking back, she took far greater risks than my father ever did. She often helped to deliver copies of the underground bulletins, which my father produced for The Resistance. They helped to keep people's spirits up, with news about how The Allies were slowly winning against the Germans and how the Vichy French government was nothing more than a puppet that the Nazi's had full control of. When the Vichy began carrying out orders to round up the Jews, it became very dangerous for anyone found hiding them, but Eve did so, over and over. I saw her leave here with Gastin, when she made her final escape to the port of Marseille. The Nazi's were looking for her everywhere. Soon afterwards, it was her husband Paul's turn to escape. He had delayed leaving with her, to give her a better chance of getting away, fooling the Nazi's into thinking she was still in Nice. I remember he came to the studio to say goodbye to my father. He and Paul had been life long friends. It was in the middle of the curfew when he left, along with two guides. I saw my father hand all their forged documents over to them and that was the last time I saw Paul."

The next morning, after a breakfast of brioche and cheese, we both spoke to Gastin over the phone. He told us that the money and Eve's ashes had already arrived safely in Toulouse, with Didier. And if we came over today, we could collect them on our way up to St. Jean. Great! I'd already packed some woollen thermals in my sports bag, together with several pairs of thick, seaman's socks I'd bought from the army and navy surplus shop, back home. Patrice and I shared the cost of hiring a car for three days. It was quite cheap, but I had to leave two thousand francs worth of traveller's cheques as a deposit to cover for any damage. Luckily, I'd still a bit of cash left, stored in Fionn's room, inside my belongings. We stopped off at the coffee bar at Les Moulins, to say a quick hello before the eight hour journey to the Haute-Garonne.

"What happened to you last week?" Asked Fionn after we'd all done the kissy kissy greetings thing again. I pointed to the pale, grey patch, beneath my left eye.

"I got mugged, back home and some nasty sod, stole my rucksack."

Fionn looked shocked and really concerned. "What's the world coming to?" she sighed, sounding just like her mum. "Please be careful, where you're going, both of you."

"Don't worry about me, I'll be fine, Fi. After all I've got Gastin and Patrice to watch out for me." Fionn shook her head slowly, from side to side. She wasn't totally convinced.

The journey by road to Toulouse was even more boring than the one I'd done by train, but at least the Opel Ascona car we'd hired had reclining seats, which had to be tried out, although I wasn't really tired enough to snooze.

I told Patrice about Anna. It was good to have someone to talk about her with. "Are you becoming amicable?" he enquired, smiling at me.

"I'd like to," I confessed.

When we reached the grey, modern office block in Avenue Frizac, Gastin already had bags of equipment piled up on the ground floor. It looked impressive - 'expedition numbre deux', I thought.

"Well done guys, you made it." Gastin glanced at his wristwatch and announced, "Didier finishes his shift at six p.m. so we need to load up and go to his house in the suburbs right now." Gastin looked very fresh and enthused and together, the three of us looked like a professional unit, which spanned three generations. My confidence was on a high and I was feeling more relaxed and excited by the minute. Besides our imminent adventure, I was getting closer to meeting up with the lovely Anna again.

Didier's home was at the junction of the main road and a cul de sac, side street. His three-storied, gothic looking house was bordered by a six foot high, brick wall and the only way in was through a solid looking, tall, steel gate. Gastin pressed the illuminated buzzer which was fixed to the outer gate post and within a minute the gates opened, one by one. Although the light was starting to fade, I recognised the man stood holding back the second gate. Didier looked like he'd been at home all day, dressed in baggy trousers and a white vest. Besides owning the largest moustache I'd ever seen, his trucker belly was mightily impressive too, as were his tattooed arms. Beyond the steel gates, in the corner of a cobbled yard, was a pair of wooden garage doors, inviting us inside. The dimly lit interior of the garage appeared to be empty, apart from an old Citroen car. Gastin and Didier greeted one another and walked over to the parked car. The boot lid was raised and Gastin called me over. The cash had already been transferred into a long, canvas holdall. Gastin pulled back the zip. "So this is your big mistake, Byrney? You don't do things in small amounts. I've never seen so much English money. You are one, crazy kid."

I said nothing and just stood there, quietly ashamed. He pulled out two of the bundles of cash and handed them to Didier. Then he reached deeper into the boot and I recognised the Tupperware box he was holding.

"Quoi! What is this, Byrney?" he said, holding back a smile. Didier was beginning to laugh too. "Have you no shame?" joked Gastin.

"Sorry, it was all I had."

He slammed down the boot lid and did a military, solidarity hand shake thing with Didier and said, "On y va - let's go!"

I was relegated to the back seat for the journey up to St. Jean, whilst Patrice and Gastin rabbited on, endlessly, in French. Occasionally, one or the other would look around at me and smile.

"Sorry Byrney. I was just telling Gastin how you are hoping for a liaison with Anna. ('Oh great!', I thought.) But Gastin tells me you have already slept together."

"It's not what you're thinking - we were just keeping each other warm."

"Oh really?" said Patrice. "Pull the other one," which was followed by howls of laughter from the front half of the car.

Despite the total blackness of the night sky and the view beyond the beam of our headlights being an unknown entity, I started to sense that the ominous, overbearing presence of the tall mountains was creeping up on us. From time to time, I caught short glimpses of the rugged, mountain top ridges, silhouetted against the faint moonlight that peeped through the cracks in the dirty, grey, rolling clouds. We slowed down as the road narrowed into the centre of St. Jean. Gastin gave Patrice a few directions and we soon found ourselves on the familiar ground of cobblestones and gravel and further ahead was the amber glow that signalled the canopy, outside the entrance to Hotel Coraline.

I saw Anna, sat inside the little office behind the reception desk, as we barged and bumped our way in through the main door. The stuffed grisly bear looked as offensive as ever. Anna jumped out of her chair, when she heard Gastin's familiar voice.

"Bonsoir tout le monde. Oh hi Byrney," she said, when she'd spotted me. She handed out our room keys and when it was my turn she smiled and asked if everything was okay. She led the way to our rooms, saving me for last. She stood in the doorway looking exhausted. The same exhaustion I recognised in myself after a long slog at the Friary.

"Sorry I can't come with you tomorrow," she said. "We are so busy here, the hotel is almost full." That was a great shame, but I could see she was disappointed too.

"Can I see you before we leave? I have something to show you."

"Have you brought me a gift? How kind of you." I was wishing I'd been more thoughtful. "Come and see me in the kitchen, early in the morning, before the other guests come down."

"Okay, around six?" Gastin had arranged for us to take breakfast at six-thirty a.m. Dawn light wasn't going to break through until seven-thirty, so there was no point in us leaving for Col de la Celeste until seven a.m. at the earliest.

I was still lying awake at midnight, listening to the comings and goings of other hotel guests, on the landing corridor, the other side of my bedroom door and from the rooms above. I heard the sound of a car door slam to just outside, which was shortly followed by a loud knocking at the front door. I swung out of bed and looked out of the bedroom window. My view to the pavement directly in front of the hotel entrance was slightly obscured by the small canopy that hung from the wall, just below my window. I could hear Anna's muffled voice, speaking with a man in English – it sounded like another guest arriving.

****

A few days earlier, through steely determination, Lofty had eventually caught up with his quarry. The Froggy truck was slowing down into the ascending slip road at Keele Services, on the M6. 'Must be lunchtime in France', thought Lofty, as he turned the steering wheel to follow suit. He parked up, two bays behind the large white truck and watched the muscular looking driver climb out and lock the cab door and walk away up the steps, towards the bridge restaurant building, which spanned the width of the motorway to the service area on the opposite side. Through the elevated, glass panels, Lofty could see the diners, sat enjoying their Road Chef meals. The car park was half full with cars and fellow travellers were milling back and forth, with ice creams, newspapers and white polystyrene trays of potato chips. It was too busy for him to make a move on the cash and besides, there was an officious looking car park attendant, selling overnight tickets to the lingering lorries, their cab curtains already drawn shut. Most of them ignored his tapping at their windows. Lofty turned on his radio and caught the end of the BBC weather forecast. Rain was heading his way. After fifteen minutes, the Froggy driver returned, carrying a baguette sandwich. Lofty weighed up his French opponent and gave him the benefit of the doubt letting him climb back into his cab, unchallenged. He judged he might have come off second best, had he ended up tangling with the French, tattooed bruiser. 'Just bide your time Bryn, you'll get your chance soon enough'.

He was about to doze off, when he heard the diesel engine fire up into life, revving at a constant pitch, until the air pressure relief valve sounded off with a sharp hiss and the lorry instantly pulled forward again, out towards the exit. From here it was non-stop, all the way to Southampton docks. Lofty had already come to the conclusion it was odds on he would have to cross the English Channel, in his pursuit of the money. He watched the Froggy truck move into the back of the 'Freight' lane of vehicles, waiting to board the ferry.

Once he was sure of its destination, he walked across to the Port Arrivals office ,to buy a ticket for Le Havre. It didn't take him long to fall into an argument with the uniformed, Port official. The immediate crossing was fully booked. He would have to wait four hours for the overnight crossing, which took a further four hours longer than a daytime crossing. The man behind the desk was becoming impatient.

"Well, what's it to be? I haven't got all day." After Lofty reluctantly agreed to fall into line, the tired Port official placed Lofty's tickets into a red and white paper wallet, marked Townsend Thoresen. As he handed it over, he issued his final order, "Lane Four!"

Lofty vacated the office, resigned to his fate. He held open the door for an incoming customer, giving him a friendly warning, "watch yourself mate, this place is full of P.T's." The new customer looked blankly at Lofty and as he closed the door behind him, Lofty shouted back through the gap in the door, "pompous twats."

He wiped the steam from the inside of his car window and looked on enviously, as the cars and lorries in the first three lanes began moving forwards, onto the raised decking that lead to the steel ramp for boarding. "Argh well, I know exactly where you're heading, Froggy." Lofty disappeared too, but only as far as inside the terminal building, on the hunt for a strong cup of tea and a news stand - might be an idea to get hold of a map of France. He noticed the flags opposite, on the harbour wall, fluttering horizontally on their flagpoles. The wind was starting to freshen up.

The overnight crossing was one of the most uncomfortable nights he'd spent in a long time. He'd made the mistake of skimping on the extra fourteen pounds for a berth in a cabin. The leather chairs inside the lounge salon were designed to make sleep impossible. He'd tried to inebriate himself into a drunken slumber, but that had only left him with a blinding headache behind his eyeballs. He was definitely not a happy man when he and his fellow passengers were advised to return to their vehicles. He sat morosely behind the wheel of his car as the clatter and thumping sounds from the car deck stabbed at his brain like a dentist drill hitting the raw nerve of a rotten tooth.

With the French coastline and the stinking docks behind him and distracted from his pain, his mind was now concentrating on the way ahead as he ascended the steady climb out of Le Havre. Tip-toeing over the summit, the road straightened and stretched southwards, but it was in desperate need of repair. Although it was just a single carriageway in both directions, he found he was having to drive down the centre, as the tarmacadam surface along the verge had enormous humps and hollows, which had been worn away by the endless, heavy, tide of traffic. Whenever an oncoming vehicle forced him into his designated half of the road, his car bounced with such exaggeration that his head hit the roof and his stomach did back flips.

It wasn't easy driving alone either, navigating from a map and following road signs, which always seemed to disappear, the moment he needed them the most. At a pretty village called La Crouzille, having been sat in the driving seat for eight hours, his arse and stomach were starting to complain. He pulled in by the side of a lake in front of an Auberge, with a welcoming sign, Chambre d'Hotes. The sign also had the picture of a bed - 'helpful' he thought and grabbed his overnight bag. By his reckoning he was just over half way to Toulouse, from his starting point on the Normandy coast.

Lofty was raring to go the next day, having been refreshed by a pleasant kip and revived by the strong dark coffee. Yesterday, it had all been new to him. Arriving in France, for the first time in his life, he'd become bogged down and handicapped by the foreign lingo. He'd been totally flummoxed and reduced to pointing whenever he'd needed to buy anything. At the filling station, he'd almost put diesel in his fuel tank by mistake, not understanding the difference between essence (sounded girlie) and gasoil (more manly).

He'd studied his road map the night before and had written down the names of the towns along his route, the RN20: Limoges, Brive-le-Gaillard, Cahors, Montauban and finally the old Roman city on the banks of the Garonne, his destination, Toulouse.

Finding the Froggy truck was going to be a much trickier task than he'd first presumed. Toulouse was ginormous, but at least the pretty, young, female assistant at the tourist office proved to be very sympathetic and helpful and she spoke perfect English. On his second visit there, Lofty was on first name terms with young Brigitte. Now that he'd acquired a room, at very reasonable rates in one of the lesser known districts, a supply of English food from the supermarket and more importantly, a street plan of Toulouse, he was satisfied he'd shortened the odds of getting his hands on the loot. He'd also found a telephone he could use, at a corner newsagent stand, where he'd been able to call his landlady back home to explain his sudden absence.

Lofty concentrated his efforts on watching the works gates at Aerospatiale, around clocking on and clocking off times. His first attempt to follow the Froggy truck driver home had ended abruptly as he'd not anticipated so many of the factory workers used bicycles as their main mode of transport. He had followed the big moustached guy to the entrance of an alley, which was blocked off to vehicles. On the following evening, he waited at the opposite end for Moustache to emerge, then followed him the rest of the way to his home, on the outskirts of town. No sooner had he parked up close by to make his observations, than he spotted a car approaching, with three men inside. He sat quietly and patiently, to see what developed. A grey-haired, athletic looking man approached the steel gate at Moustache's house and stood waiting. The gate opened and Moustache and the grey-haired guy greeted one another and walked over to an open garage inside the courtyard. He turned his gaze to check on the two other men who were still inside the car. He was intrigued. Then, he got the shock of his life, when one of the two men got out of the rear door. "F.M.O.B it's Byrne, where's he come from and what the hell's he mixed up in." Lofty's thoughts were racing and coming up with all sorts of conclusions. Perhaps this is some sort of international drug smuggling operation. "The crafty sod!" He picked up his field glasses again and watched the grey-haired guy hand over two bundles of cash to Moustache, 'payment for smuggling in the loot', thought Lofty. Then the holdall with the rest of the cash was placed inside the waiting car and with all three guys inside, the car turned around and headed back past him. Lofty ducked down at the last second, to avoid being seen by Byrne.

Tailing the car in darkness was no mean feat. After two hours, his eyes were feeling the strain. Lofty had no other option but to follow them, as it turned out, all the way to St. Jean-Les-Bains.

****

I had the photo of Eve and Paul inside my wallet and went down to the kitchen to find Anna. She was just taking out some freshly baked bread from the oven and its aroma gave me an instant appetite. The kitchen was very well organised. There were two workstations for preparing food and there was a long, central rack, running the full length, which divided and defined the two halves of the kitchen. There were a few old orders still hanging from them. It looked like an exciting place to work. When Anna saw me standing there, she smiled and wished me good morning. I waited for her to stop what she was doing and said, "I've missed you. It seems longer than two weeks since I was last here. It's a shame you're not coming up the Col du Monde again."

"I wish I was going too," she said. "You should be okay, the snow is very late this year."

I took out the photo and handed it to Anna. "I've been dying to show you this, it's Eve and Paul Larouchamps before the war, at their hotel in Nice. Do you notice anything familiar?"

"Oh yes! It looks like maman's necklace, but it can't possibly be the same one."

"So you're not Eve's secret love child? I know she came back to France around the time you were born." I was joking, but I could see that Anna needed to think about it.

"Definitely no, I have a photo of my mum wearing the necklace, when she became engaged to my father." Anna put down the photo dismissively, but I could sense there was still something troubling her. I still hadn't been able to work out a connection, myself, between Eve and Jacques Casson. Maybe there wasn't one.

"So it's just a coincidence then," I agreed. "But it is kinda spooky though." Anna turned around and was about to start cracking eggs into a bowl. "Wait a sec," I said and I took her hand and put my arm over her shoulders and gave her a kiss.

"I thought you had forgotten how to do that," she joked.

"I wasn't sure you still fancied me," I replied, smiling.

"Yes I *fancy* you, Byrney." Her words were ladled with sarcasm. "Hey if you are not doing anything, please can you take the clean plates and cups out to the tables for me."

"Sure, I'd love to give you a hand."

Twenty minutes later, Gastin and Patrice arrived and took up position at the table nearest the kitchen. They were togged up for our little expedition, in their thick, woolly jumpers and padded trousers.

"Bonjour Byrney," said Patrice, when I emerged from the kitchen. "Trois café, tout de suite."

"Very funny."

"Is Jacques not here?" enquired Gastin.

Anna had followed me out from the kitchen, carrying a large cafetière of hot, black coffee and poured each of us a full cup of the steaming, full strength drink. The taste of it was the equivalent of receiving a jumpstart from a series of heavy-duty batteries.

"That will put hairs on your chest, Byrney," said Gastin.

"I think it's stripped them off as well," I replied, squinting at the bitterness.

Gastin was eager to talk about the next twenty-four hours. "We should be able to make speedy progress. The weather forecast is very tranquil for the next two days."

We were startled by a sudden banging sound coming from the reception area. As the front entrance door was slammed shut, we all turned to see Jacques Casson, stood in the doorway with a rifle slung over his shoulder. He held up a pair of rabbits in his hand and with a jubilant smile said, "Bonjour mes amies, back again so soon Byrney." He walked over to our table and greeted us all with a kiss on the cheek. I could see Patrice was staring at Jacques inquisitively and their greeting seemed a little more awkward after Gastin had introduced him to Jacques.

"You remember Andre Arnatte, n'est ce pas?"

"Of course, I still have one of his forged identity cards, somewhere."

"This is his son, Patrice."

"I don't believe I have had the pleasure," said Jacques as they greeted one another.

"I'm sure I've seen him before," said Patrice to me, out of ear shot of the others.

The plan was for Jacques to take us up there, as before in his car and then the three of us could unload our gear and store it there whilst we walked up to the Col du Monde and back. Anna had organised some flasks of coffee and packs of biscuits to keep us refreshed and Gastin borrowed her key to the mountain rescue station hut, up at Col de la Celeste. There was, of course, lots of tinned food available at the station hut, which we'd be able to eat later this evening. It was all part of the adventure. As we exchanged our temporary farewells, Anna handed me back the photo of Eve and Paul and Gastin caught a glimpse of the picture. He asked me what I was doing with it.

"I brought it with me for Anna to see. It's only a coincidence, but the necklace, which Eve is wearing in the photo, is similar to the one which Anna has. It belonged to her mother, Coraline."

"Let me see," said Gastin, his curiosity beginning to stir. "Mmm well, all I can say is Eve wasn't wearing it the last time I saw her, that's for sure. Most of the 'parcels' we escorted were encouraged to hide anything of value, in case we were stopped, or even robbed. Most of them used to sew their jewellery into the seams of their clothing."

Jacques appeared at the main entrance, looking slightly angry. Regretfully, he informed us his car battery was flat, having been over used to power his search lamps from last night's hunt. We would have to use our hire car and he'd take us up to Col de la Celeste in that instead. I looked at Gastin and he shook his head. "Don't worry," he whispered, "we can hide the bag of money at Celeste Station with the rest of our gear." But I sensed he regretted not having picked up the money sooner from Didier.

We double checked all our baggage and loaded everything into the boot of the Opel Ascona. We were finally on our way just as the half-light over the mountains was beginning to waken and their strange silhouettes sharpened into view. Patrice was sat on the back seat next to me, when he suddenly realised where he had seen Jacques Casson before. "I'm usually quite good at recognising people. I'm sure Jacques was one of the two guides who came to our studio that day to collect Paul Larouchamps and the two Jewish families. I remember him clearly talking to my father. He was there the day that Paul began his journey to freedom, I'm sure of it." Gastin had picked up on what Patrice had said.

"Is that true Jacques? I thought you told us you had never been to Nice."

"You must be mistaken," said Jacques as he continued to drive, peering through the rear view mirror, his eyes studying Patrice's reaction. Gastin was sat in the front passenger seat, next to Jacques. He turned around to face us, resting his arm on the back of his seat.

"How can you be so certain, Patrice? You were only a small enfant at the time."

"Actually I was eleven years old and I remember that day perfectly well. I had been helping father prepare the documents. We had been working flat out to get them ready in time."

"Okay, stop the car Jacques," said Gastin, his voice sounding urgent and business like.

"We are almost there," complained Jacques. "Let's just calm down a minute until we reach the car park and we can settle this ridiculous argument, once and for all." Gastin asked me to hand over the photo that he'd seen earlier of Eve and Paul.

"When we stop, there is something else for you to explain too," said Gastin to Jacques, who was now silent and staring at the twisty road ahead. He was deep in thought and trying not to show he'd been rattled, by driving casually, with one hand on the steering wheel. I was starting to wonder where all these accusations that were flying around were going to land. I was very relieved to arrive at the Celeste car park, still in one piece.

Jacques switched off the engine and said, "Shall we get your bags out of the back?"

"Take a look at this first," said Gastin, handing Jacques the photo.

"What am I supposed to be looking at? he said, attempting to put up a smokescreen.

"The necklace that Eve is wearing, do you recognise it?"

"Why should I. I've never met Eve Larouchamps."

"No, but you have met Paul. It's my guess he was carrying that necklace when you escorted him to Spain.

"That's nonsense and you know it."

"Then tell me Jacques, how do you explain the fact that Patrice saw you at his fathers studio the same day when Paul Larouchamps was leaving?"

Jacques had had his right hand in his pocket for some time and pulled out the gun he was holding. Before he had time to point it at anyone, Gastin made a grab for it, but Jacques was too quick and he twisted his wrist so that the butt of the pistol struck Gastin firmly on his chin, before either of us could stop him. Jacques had quickly recovered his air of command and sharply shouted, "Nobody moves!" The pistol was pointed at each of us in turn. 'Fuckin' hell!' I thought. 'How did it get to this so quickly?' Patrice had his hand on the door handle but the clicking sound of the lock alerted Jacques and he fired a warning shot through the roof of the car. The loud sound of the gun being fired sent an electric shock of fear through the whole of my body whipping the breath from my lungs.

"Stay exactly where you are!" yelled Jacques, his face turning uglier each time he spoke.

"You've just lost Byrney his deposit with the hire company," berated Patrice. "We have to take this car back tomorrow."

"Don't be stupid, Jacques. What's all this about?" said Gastin calmly. "Tell me, where did you get the German Luger from?"

You had to hand it to Gastin. He was playing it super cool. I was hoping he had a back up plan worked out so we could all get out of this mess, alive.

"It was already in my coat pocket from last night. I like to fire a few shots with it when I go out hunting. It helps to break up the boredom."

"Actually, I meant where did you get it from originally? From the Germans?"

"Very clever Gastin, trying to trick me into giving you a confession. I'm not as dumb as you think."

"Put the gun away Jacques, before someone gets hurt."

"I don't think so. Only one of us will be going back home today. Pardon mes amies. You have all reached the end of the road." He had a crazy smile on his face. The mad fucker was planning to kill us all. Somehow we had to distract Jacques so that we could over power him; it was three against one. My mouth was dry. I'd never been this scared in my whole life. I was just waiting for one of us to make a move.

"If you kill us," I said, "you won't get your hands on the money." The surprise of hearing my young voice had put Jacques off his stride.

"What's the child talking about Gastin?" he answered, annoyed at the interruption. "What money?"

"Byrney has brought a lot of English money with him," said Gastin, catching on to my train of thought. "The money is inside a holdall, the equivalent of a quarter of a million Francs."

"I don't believe you. Where is this money?"

"It's in the boot of this car," I said. "I'll get it for you if you like." I was about to open my door when Jacques fired another shot through the roof of the car.

"Merde!" said Patrice, again. This time we all ducked down at the sound of the gun being fired.

Jacques removed the car keys and pointed the gun at us all again. "I'll get out first, followed by Byrney. No one else moves." He opened the car door slowly, his eyes watching for the slightest movement, then he warily stepped back to my door and opened it from the outside.

Gastin said, "if you lay a finger on Byrney, I'll kill you myself Jacques."

Jacques replied with a few tuts as we both moved to the back of the car. "Open it!"

I pushed the lock cylinder inwards and the boot lid popped up. "It's in that holdall at the bottom," I said, pointing to it.

"Take it out!" As I bent forward into the boot, Patrice appeared from the blind side of the car and made a grab for Jacques. The gun went off again almost immediately and I heard Patrice's deadly groan as he slumped forward to the ground. He was bent double, holding his thigh. I could see blood soaking through his trousers. Gastin got out of the front seat and Jacques took a step back to cover us both with his gun. The injury to Patrice had clearly unnerved him.

Just at that moment, we heard the sound of a car approaching and a pair of headlights shone across at us. The car stopped at the opposite end of the car park with its engine ticking over. It was like a Mexican stand off.

"Are you alright, Patrice?" asked Gastin.

"Oui," he said, painfully.

All eyes were on the headlights. They remained pointing directly at us. Jacques had positioned himself so that the gun was shielded behind the raised boot lid. We heard a car door open and close, and a tall figure began to walk towards us. He was getting closer, 'whoever it was' I thought, 'he's either brave or stupid, if he came any closer he was about to have his head blown off'. Then I had to catch my breath. I recognised who it was. It was too unbelievable to be true - Gingernut. The same guy who had followed me on the train to London, the same guy who had attacked me last week and now here he was at the Col de la Celeste. It was obvious to me now what he'd come for. He stopped short about five paces away from where Patrice lay on his side. Gingernut stood perfectly still with his hands inside his raincoat pockets. He was the last person I expected to come to our rescue.

"Is everything alright?" he asked, looking down at Patrice. Then, Jacques stepped from behind the boot and as soon as Gingernut saw the gun, I heard two shots. They had both come from Gingernut's right hand from inside his pocket. He had been holding a gun all along, but his aim hadn't been perfect and Jacques was able to fire twice at the intruder and both men fell to the ground, simultaneously. Neither was mortally wounded.

Gastin picked up both pistols and handed them to me. "If either one of them moves shoot them." I had no intention of shooting anyone, so I held a gun in each hand and tried to look menacing. Gastin retrieved some rope from his bag and expertly tied the hands and feet of both men. 'He's done that before', I thought. Then I helped him put a tourniquet around Patrice's leg and we sat him across the back seat of our car. We left him Gingernut's pistol and Gastin and I went to the Station hut to use the radio. It took us a few minutes to work out how to switch it on. I'd remembered seeing Anna connecting the batteries up in the back room, so once we found the isolator switch, we were in business. Gastin spoke to the duty Policeman in St. Jean and asked for two ambulances. He described what had happened and that there were three injured men with bullet wounds.

I didn't dare go anywhere near Gingernut, in case he grabbed hold of me somehow. Whilst we waited with Patrice for the emergency crews to get here, I let Gastin know exactly who the intruder was.

"Don't worry Byrney, he won't be bothering you again from now on." I wondered what Gastin had meant by that, but I trusted him to his word. Part of me was thankful to Gingernut for showing up when he did. He'd actually saved all our lives and been seriously injured for his trouble. Gastin spoke about the significance of Jacques' German, Luger pistol. I already knew that the body of Gastin's father had recently been found. He had been shot in the back of the head, over thirty years ago, with a similar weapon and by the way Gastin was hanging on to

Jacques' gun, he was obviously thinking the same as me. As I kept a vigil over Patrice, in case he fell into unconsciousness, I was also wondering how all this was going to affect Anna.

It was a relief for everyone when we heard the sirens approaching. Gastin had taken the precaution of moving the holdall into one of the lockers at the Station hut. Neither Jacques, nor Gingernut, had actually seen it, or what it contained, so I was still in the clear, although my nerves were feeling like they'd been shot at too. Gastin assured me that everyone would recover from their injuries, as the cold air had helped to clot the blood. "Is it cold?" I said, "I was sweating like hell."

Chapter Ten

Fallout

The wooden front door at Hotel Coraline had been propped open and held back against the inner porch by a decorative, metal toggle, in the shape of a girl's head wearing a flat-topped bonnet. It's amazing what pings into view when your minds working twenty to the dozen. I closed my door and helped Gastin to remove our baggage from the boot of the police car. They'd insisted on bringing us back down to St. Jean as we would still have been stuck up at Celeste station for several hours more, waiting for a recovery truck to pick up our hire car. In any case, our little Opel Ascona was being delivered back to the police garage in Toulouse, for forensic analysis. There were two gaping bullet holes in the car roof - it wouldn't take anyone long to spot them, I thought. The two policemen from St. Jean were just as shocked as we'd been by how Jacques had behaved. They had known him a long time and often used to call in on him for a late Pastis, at the back door most likely. Gastin handed me the Tupperware box, which contained Eve's ashes and shrugged, "Don't worry Byrney, we'll take them up again soon."

The reception desk was deserted, no sign of Anna. Gastin raised his arm to stop me from walking further into the empty dining room. "I think it will be easier if I explain to Anna what has happened to her father."

"You're probably right," I agreed. I couldn't think of any easy way of telling her that her father had actually just tried to kill us. A few moments after Gastin had disappeared into the kitchen, I heard Anna cry out. She was shouting in French, the word 'menteur', which I later found out meant liar. Gastin's voice was barely audible. When the conversation on both sides had subsided, I listened quietly to Anna's mournful sobbing. I really wanted to put my arms around her. I slowly pulled back the kitchen door and Anna looked up angrily.

"Why did you have to come here Byrney? This is all your fault, digging up the past." Her eyes were reddening with grief. Her comments stopped me in my tracks. I guess she needed to blame someone. I remembered what Henri had said, that first morning in Nice, about how it was dangerous to start overturning stones from the past; it felt like he'd been right all along. Anna's slender frame stood motionless. Behind her, long beams of sunshine were bursting through the window above the stone sink. It should have been a beautiful day. Gastin spoke softly to Anna about how bravely I'd acted in trying to get Jacques to come to his senses, by leading him to the back of the car so that he and Patrice could escape. That wasn't quite how I'd remembered it, but I was hoping Gastin's comments would soften Anna's hatred towards me. Gastin sat Anna down on a stool and said, "Let me make some coffee. We have a lot of things to discuss."

Later that afternoon, the police returned to take our statements. Anna's mood became serious once more, at the sight of the uniformed Gendarmes, but at least she didn't feel threatened by their familiar faces. She interpreted my statement for them. At last, she was beginning to believe and understand what had taken place earlier that morning at Col de la Celeste. The Gendarmes examined my photo of Eve and the necklace from Anna's bedroom drawer. Then they were bagged and sealed and taken away as evidence. They informed us that Patrice was being kept in hospital overnight in St. Jean and that we would be allowed to visit him later that evening. As the Gendarmes were preparing to leave, Gastin took me aside and explained that the Englishman was being held alone, in a guarded room, at the same hospital and that I was to stay away from him.

"Don't worry, I'll be staying well out of his reach."

"From the injuries he received, he's going to be there a week or two. As of yet, the police haven't brought any charges against him. Obviously they have confiscated his gun. It's my guess he will be deported, as soon as he is well enough to leave."

I was almost beginning to feel sorry for him. He'd come all this way and ended up being shot. "Do you think we could maybe give him some of our cash, as a way of saying thank you?"

Gastin gave me one of his furrowed frowns. "I'm not sure that is a good idea Byrney." He lowered his voice, "After all, this cash of ours doesn't officially exist. I'll have to think about it." He patted me on my back and asked, "So, what are you going to do now Byrney? Back home to Lan-ca-shire?"

"Well, actually I'm going to hang around here in St. Jean and wait for Patrice. What about you?"

"I'm going to be very busy. Now that we know Jacques was around Col du Monde when the Nazi's killed Paul Larouchamps and the others, I have to gather as much evidence as possible. We know Jacques reappeared around the time of the Liberation and became a hero in the resistance. We just need to find a few more pieces in the jigsaw to fill in the gaps, then prepare for the trial."

God! Yes, of course. I'd not thought this would all have to be decided in court. I wasn't thinking that far ahead. I looked at Gastin, "There's going to be more sorrow and stress for Anna."

"She's a strong girl, just like her mother used to be."

Anna came back from the reception area. "I have to start preparing the evening meals. That's if we still have any guests. Some of them have checked out already. Having a gunman for a father isn't exactly good for business," she said bitterly, as she walked past, on her way back to the kitchen.

I walked with Gastin down to the Bus Station in the centre of town. He was telling me a story from the war about Jacques and his partner, Eduard Siguer, who had also worked for the Renard escape line. "Are you going to track him down too?" I asked.

"Sadly, he was shot and killed, in strange circumstances, at the end of the war. However, there are still a few of the old Resistance boys around. Maybe someone will come forward with information about Jacques, but I'm not sure they will speak against him."

I was really pleased to find Patrice sat up in bed, at the old hospital in St. Jean. It had once been a German Military Barracks that the French had found a better use for after the war.

"Did you bring me some grapes Byrney?"

"No, sorry, I didn't think."

"Only joking. It's good to see you." Patrice was looking in much better health than when I'd last seen him, being carried into the ambulance with blood stained trousers. His left thigh was heavily bandaged and there was a wooden crutch next to his bedside locker. "The doctor says I can leave tomorrow." He said cheerily.

"That's good news. We'll have to take the bus back to Nice. The Gendarmes have taken our hire car back to Toulouse." Patrice shook his head. "Sorry about you losing your deposit too. One day we'll have a laugh about all this."

"With a few beers," I added.

At the other end of the corridor from Patrice's ward, I noticed an armed Gendarme, talking to one of the pretty nurses. So that's where they're keeping Gingernut. I turned to go in the opposite direction and waved a salute at Patrice.

****

It was a chilly, inky, black night, in a soaking wet Lancashire. Atkinson quietly pulled his car to the side of the road, listening to his nearside tyres crunch the gravel, which lay next to the kerb. He stared at the tired, decrepit building, which had once been the old union workhouse. It was a mystery how it had survived until now and Atkinson wondered who in their right mind would choose to live in it's poorly converted flats. In the passenger foot-well of his car sat a box. Inside the box were two old, brown, beer bottles and out of their necks hung torn strips of a used tea towel. He turned off his window wipers and soaked up the silence. About fifty yards ahead of him, a lone lamplight flickered above a bus stop sign, masked by the faint, moonless drizzle. No one was likely to be standing there; why would there be, on a night like this.

It had only taken Atkinson two phone calls to learn the details of Lofty's home address. The first call to Chorley Nick - where Lofty's car had been dumped in the yard, that day Byrne was followed to London - had yielded Lofty's car registration number. Armed with this piece of information, he called the local vehicle taxation office in Preston and 'hey presto'. Here he was in Stribling Lane, Claughton, in the back of beyond. Atkinson picked up both bottles at once, gripping the Molotov Cocktails between the knuckles of his hate hand and strode over the worn stone slabs, which led up to the single, arched entrance door. On the right hand door pillar, he scanned over the illuminated doorbells: Mr. B. Davis, Flat One - ground floor, first on the right. Of the ten doorbells, only four had named occupants. Of the four occupied flats, Atkinson noted, as he stepped back outside, only one of them was currently showing a light, at the far end on the upper floor.

'What a god-forsaken hole', he thought, 'I'll be doing this place a favour'. He removed his silver lighter from his jacket pocket and had a final glance behind him to make sure the coast was still clear. He watched each of the petrol soaked wicks flame up strongly, before taking aim. Then he lobbed them, in quick succession, smashing through the thin glass panes of Lofty's ground floor window. Whatever incriminating evidence was stored there, it was now rapidly being turned to ash. Even Atkinson was surprised by how ferociously and immediate the room had caught a blaze. Dense smoke poured out of the broken panes, quickly staining the lintel above, and smothering the dark wet leaves of ivy. Departing hastily, he pulled up outside the first public telephone box and made an anonymous phone call to the fire brigade. Then, afterwards, he automatically wiped the receiver with the handkerchief, which he'd used to muffle his voice. He left rubbing his hands - rubbing out any further threat from Lofty. "That's what happens when you mess with the big boys."

However, the night did not go entirely as Atkinson had planned. After his regular jar of ale at the Prince, he received an unexpected shock, on his own front door step. Next to the empty bottles of milk, were two suitcases. 'What the hell's this?' he thought. He felt the prickly anger begin to rise, burning into his ears. He pushed his Yale key into the door lock and no matter how hard he tried, it just wouldn't fit. By now he was snorting like a trapped bull. He began banging loudly on the door with both fists. One by one, bedroom lights flashed up in the neighbouring houses and someone's dog began barking gruffly. Then the window above the door opened and in no uncertain terms Sandra Atkinson told her husband to sling his hook.

"I'm not going to waste the rest of my life stuck to you!" she screamed, caring 'not a jot' just how many of her nosey neighbours she disturbed. "If you don't bugger off, I'll call the police."

"I am the bloody police," complained Atkinson, spitting feathers.

"You're a bloody poor excuse for anything!" she screamed and slammed the window shut.

Atkinson picked up his cases and threw them into the boot of his car. "You stupid old hag, I'm bloody sick of you an' all."

****

I was secretly studying the faces of the other guests who were currently staying at Hotel Coraline, whilst dunking a freshly baked croissant into my cup of black coffee. This was the traditional French way of eating croissants in a morning. Loose flakes were floating on the surface. It looked fairly disgusting, but it tasted delicious. A young American couple were sat directly opposite me and I must have been letting my gaze linger on them. The man nodded and smiled and said, "You're English aren't you."

"Is it that obvious?" I said apologetically.

"I noticed your t-shirt, the Rolling Stones, great band man!"

"Thanks."

"Why don't you join us? We're having coffee and pancakes."

"Okay, thanks."

The curly-haired guy was called Rod and his freckle-faced girlfriend was Pamela, or Pammy, as he kept calling her. They were over here in Europe, mainly for the skiing and they'd decided to head off to the Alps, due to the lack of snow on this side of the Pyrenees. They were leaving later today, in their rented car, so I explained about my friend who was in hospital and how we'd had a mishap with our own car. "Why don't you guys hook up with us?" suggested Pamela. "We can take you part of the way, it'd be fun to have some company, wouldn't it Rod?"

"Sure, we can drop you in Montpelier. We'll be passing that way."

"Gee thanks," I said, accidentally slipping into a fake American accent. I noticed Anna pass through the restaurant and tried to catch her attention, but she hadn't realised I'd changed tables. I wasn't sure how she was going to react to my sudden departure. Maybe she needed a bit more time alone to come to terms with the shock of recent events.

I heard raised French voices coming from the reception area. Everyone in the restaurant looked up for a second and then carried on with their meals, like it was an everyday occurrence. I made my excuses to Rod and Pamela and went to see if Anna was okay. She was having an animated conversation with this prim looking, school head mistress type, who was stood with her back to me, wearing a head scarf and carrying an old brown suitcase in her left hand, which was being swung back and forth as she spoke. Either the suitcase was as light as a feather, or the old battle-axe swinging it had powerful arms. Anna noticed me standing there and looked relieved to break off her argument with the intruder, although I had the impression they had met before. The intruder turned to face me. I was ready to say something in Anna defence, but her scowl and the way she looked down her nose at me, changed my mind. Then she shook her head, unbuttoned her coat and took her case through into the tiny office behind the reception desk.

"Who the hell is that?" I asked.

"Unfortunately, that is my Aunt Simone. She claims to have spoken to my father and he's asked her to look after me. She's a real pain in the derriere." I was beginning to feel worse than ever about leaving Anna in such an unholy mess, then Anna continued. "Byrney, don't take this the wrong way, but please can you stay here for a while and help me get rid of her. As soon as she realises I can cope, she'll go back to Toulouse."

I quickly thought it through for a moment, "if Patrice is okay, then sure, I want to help you." Deep down I was really made up that Anna had decided to call a truce, even if it turned out that she was just using me, at least we could still be friends. It was a big step forward from yesterday.

For once, everything seemed to click into place. The American couple drove me down to the hospital to collect Patrice, who was fine about travelling back to Nice alone. He even managed to joke about how I was dumping him so that I could be with Anna, pointing to my blushes. I could feel my face warming as I tried to conceal the truth. He was right of course. I tried 'changing the subject'. "I'll be back myself in a few days."

Patrice placed his crutches down in the back of the American's rented car and hobbled across the back seat, "don't worry about me, Byrney."

"Okay, I won't." I said smiling and waved them all off. As their car descended the main street, I looked up at the grey windows along the facing wall of the hospital, half expecting to see Gingernut staring down at me. Happily, they were all empty.

Back at the hotel, I could hear activity coming from the kitchen, but the sound of rattling and chopping was devoid of female voices. As I opened the door, apprehensively, there was a distinct lack of smiling faces and an oppressive atmosphere hung in the air, like an empty prison cell. I looked at Simone and noticed how she had the same character trait as her brother Jacques. There was something fake about her and I couldn't quite put my finger on it. The tension between her and Anna was all too obvious. 'Argh well, things can only get better,' I thought.

Anna had worked out a simple menu for the evening meals. After the Americans had checked out, there were currently ten guests, occupying five of the nine bedrooms. Anna and Simone would be working in the kitchen and I was to tend to the tables, taking orders and serving up food and drinks. I was feeling really nervous about not understanding the customers.

"You'll be fine, Byrney," said Anna, touching my arm. "We'll run through the menu, so that you understand what it all means."

"Cheers, that should help." I was not at all convinced. My French was still very basic. Anna took me into the cellar and explained the layout. The wines were numbered and these numbers corresponded to the positions on the metal racks, so far, so good; the cold drinks, beers, fruits and waters were stored at the end, in the tall cooler.

"Okay, got it. Think I'll pop up to my room and put on a clean shirt. Is it okay to use the phone in reception?"

"Yes help yourself. And try not to worry Byrney."

Before I'd chance to pick up the phone, a trendy, middle-aged couple burst through the door and smiled. "Le clé, si vous plait."

"Right, erm, quelle chambre?"

"Vier. Pardon quatre."

I stepped behind the desk and handed them their key. The lady spoke, "Guten abend," then carried on up the stairs, on the heels of her fella, patting the head of the brown bear as she skipped past.

'German as well now,' I thought. I was beginning to wish I'd studied harder at school, instead of staring out of the window. At least I understood 'Good evening'.

I made two calls, the first to England and spoke to dad. I was hoping he would answer as our conversations normally involved less explanation and interrogation. He was pleased to hear I'd found some gainful employment. As I went on to describe what it was like here, it sounded like I was reading out a postcard. "You'd like it here, dad. There's a real, life-size, stuffed grisly bear at the foot of the stairs. Good food and a peaceful town. Reminds me of Scotland." I ended the call by promising to write to them with my address.

"Is there anything you'd like us to send you?" he asked.

"A copy of the New Musical Express would be good."

My second call, to Fionn, immediately afterwards, felt strangely closer and more warm hearted. Perhaps we were turning into brother and sister after all. I took a deep breath and explained about what had happened to Patrice. All I heard at the other end of the phone were several 'Oh my god's' followed by serious tones of 'you're joking and several are you okay's'? I told her I was staying at Hotel Coraline in St. Jean, until things calmed down. I mentioned that Anna needed my help, expecting Fionn to say 'and who's Anna?' Instead I asked her to keep an eye out for Patrice as he should be arriving back there this evening and might need some help too.

After I'd put the phone down, I realised I'd not asked Fionn about her relationship with Jean-Luc, but as she had not mentioned it either, I took it to be 'no news is good news'.

Our first evening in the restaurant started out badly and went downhill from there. Simone (and my god, could she moan) began by complaining she couldn't read my writing. So we devised a number scheme for the menu, making sure it didn't duplicate the numbers we were using for the wine list. Then she made a big scene in the restaurant, blaming Anna for one of her own mistakes. Every time she looked at me, she tutted, buffed, blustered and shook her head. 'Bollocks to her', I thought. Although she was much younger than her brother, I'd just worked out what the family resemblance was. Like Jacques, she had perfected a two-faced persona, creeping and crawling and endearing herself upon the clients, then storming back to the kitchen, scathing and bawling and leering at us both.

When the last of the guests had retired to their rooms, or had left to take a final stroll down the cobbles, 'Simoaner' as I now called her, made a huge play of tackling all the dirty dishes by herself. What a hero. Then, finally, she spouted off in French to Anna. The gist of it was how the plates and pans had never looked so clean, and how she had an early start in the morning, as the whole kitchen needed re-organising.

"I think we need a beer," I said, relieved to see the back of Simoaner as she left the kitchen, leaving the door wide open. I took two beers from the cooler and flipped off their crowns with the bottle opener, which was now part of my uniform.

"Sorry Byrney, I've been a little distracted this evening." I'd noticed it too, although I kept it to myself. Normally, she carried an air of confidence and let nothing shake her. To say she'd lived in a small village, half way up a mountain, most of her life, she was much more worldly wise than I was. "I think I need to put what's happened to Papa to the back of my mind for a while." I let her talk some more as I took a big swig of beer, straight from the neck of the bottle. "I'm not sure I like the idea of Aunt Simone re-organising our hotel. If you ask me, I think she's trying to take over."

"Well, she's got the two of us to get past first. Anyway maybe some of her ideas might actually work." I put my arm over Anna's shoulder and said, "I'm on your side, you know."

Over the next few days, the more Simoaner kicked and screamed, the closer it brought Anna and me together. Not all of her re-organisations were for the worse. She had dramatically improved our weekly supplies from the espicerie, when the quality had dropped to mere scraps in the aftermath of Jacques arrest. For all of Simoaner's unpleasantness, when it came to her brother's reputation and social standing in the town, she was one hell of a fighter. Every Saturday, without fail, Simoaner disappeared back to Toulouse to visit her brother, who was still being held in a cell at the Police Nationale headquarters. Anna had not been able to go there. She'd spoken to her father just once on the phone. She said there had been no apology, or any sign of remorse from him and that he'd acted the way he had because he'd no other choice. He wasn't going to win Anna over with that attitude.

In the weeks that followed, somehow, the three of us managed to find our own space. My French was coming on in leaps and bounds. Having Anna to teach me and with the patience and allowances of our clients, I was able to relax, to the point where I no longer felt awkward or nervous at the prospect of communicating with the next stranger to walk through the door at Hotel Coraline.

Christmas had been looming like a distant light on the shore, getting closer and brighter each day, forcing me into thinking I had to decide on which side of the English Channel I was going to drop my anchor. I foresaw the disappointment I was about to make everyone feel back home, if I decided to stay in St. Jean. I'd spoken to Anna about it and she'd left the decision entirely in my hands. There were only four guests booked to stay then and Anna was confident she could cope on her own. As for Simoaner, she had several invitations from cousins and nieces to chose from. Apparently, she was the life and soul of the Casson family Christmas. Fionn was keeping everyone happy - home for Christmas to see her mum and the crew in Crowston for the Friary Do. Then she was returning to Nice, to see in the New Year with Jean-Luc.

The week before Christmas, we'd an unexpected visit from Gastin. He'd brought some papers over for me to sign about the events at the Col de la Celeste. He later told me what had happened to Gingernut, whose real name was Bryn Davis. I'd never heard of him. After spending three weeks in hospital, recovering from his bullet wounds, he was taken to the Police headquarters in Toulouse. The Commissioner in Toulouse had decided the best course of action was to have him deported back to England. His gun and vehicle were seized and his passport confiscated. The charges against him: possessing an unregistered weapon, firing an illegal weapon with intent to cause injury and causing actual bodily harm, would be dropped if he signed a statement saying he was acting in self defence which, of course, he agreed to do. However he would now be banned from re-entering France for the next five years. "So you see Byrney, you are safe. No more sudden attacks from this guy, n'est ce pas." At last, Gingernut was out of my life. No more feeling scared of looking over my shoulder. Then Gastin informed Anna that a date had been set for Jacques trial. It would commence in less than a months time, on the thirteenth of January 1977, at the Palais de Justice in Toulouse. "It has attracted a lot of interest from the APF and the National Press Service."

I looked at Anna, who had gone deathly white. Gastin reached across the table and reassured her. At least she would get to know the truth. Then she could move on afterwards. In his usual, serious way, he said, "whatever the reasons Jacques had for his actions, you have to keep an open mind about them."

So it was settled, I was staying with Anna until after the trial. The following day, before Gastin left us, I had a chance to have a private chat with him during breakfast. He'd not had any luck in helping to build a case for the prosecution against Jacques. The Eduard Siguer lead had come to nothing. Eduard's widow had died three years ago and whatever information she might have had she took with her, to the grave. Whether Jacques had played a part in her husband being falsely identified, as a collaborator, would remain a mystery. "The best course of action," admitted Gastin, "would be to get Jacques to make a confession about the missing months of his war time activities. His solicitors are keen to do a trade, in order to have him acquitted, or his sentence suspended. If the judge drops the charges against him for the Col de la Celeste incident, by agreeing he shot Patrice by accident and that he only fired at Davis after he had fired first, then maybe we will get to know the truth about Paul Larouchamps and the others and of course, my own father. If that's the way it goes, then our statements will not be needed either and we won't have to appear as witnesses. 'Bloody hell, I hope he's right', I thought. " We're still waiting on the judge. As soon as we hear about how he's going to proceed to chambers, I'll let you know. One thing in Jacque's favour is the time gap from the end of the war and the lack of credible witnesses. It's hardly likely any Nazis are going to come forward and take responsibility for these deaths." We were so close to knowing, and yet the circumstances were still shrouded in mists of time. It seemed to me there was only one man left alive who had all the answers - Jacques Casson.

****

Lofty had been well cared for at the village hospital in the Pyrenees. His dressings were tended and changed almost daily and he'd grown attached to his carers. They giggled at his amateurish attempts to speak French and when the time came for him to leave, he'd come to the conclusion that what he really missed in life was a companion.

When the armed Gendarmes led him away to a waiting police car, he had expected to be arrested and thrown inside a cell, as soon as he reached the station. The Commissioner, who was waiting to interview him, had once been an army regular too, but he'd suffered the ignominy of having to surrender to the Germans in the Verdun, during the Blitzkrieg of 1940. As a result, he'd spent several, lean years as a P.O.W. Before making his final decision, he wanted to find out what sort of person this Bryn Davis was. It worked in Lofty's favour that he'd spent time in the army in Africa. The two ex-military men had the same vague connection. After an hour of swerving and playing dumb to the routine questioning, Lofty was surprised to find himself being driven to the nearest airport - 'home in time for tea, P.O.P'

One of the armed guards remained at his side, at Toulouse-Blagnac airport, all the way to the departure lounge. He even followed him out onto the tarmac apron. At the last moment, the guard tapped him on the shoulder and handed Lofty a brown envelope and said "Don't open until you reach England." Lofty looked baffled, but followed the policeman's order and stuffed it inside his jacket pocket, next to the letter of deportation, stamped and personally signed by the Commissioner. Without this he'd be arrested again, as soon as he touched down in Manchester.

161

As the Boeing 737 took off and the no smoking light was switched off, Lofty couldn't resist having a peek inside the bulky envelope. It was stuffed full of twenty pound notes. There had to be over five hundred pounds worth - 'F.M.O.B.' he thought.

When he landed at Ringwood, two and a half hours later, he was greeted by the usual, Lancashire, grey, wet sky. It continued to rain, all the way to Preston. The short, two-carriage, commuter train took an aeon to reach familiar territory. "Nearly home," he said, re-discovering the old familiar routine of talking to himself again. Once inside his flat, he was looking forward to having a long soak in his bath. When he jumped into the first available taxi to take him to his home in Stribling Lane, the driver queried whether he lived at the flats in the old workhouse.

"Where have you been for the last fortnight?" he said, pausing behind the wheel. "The old place was gone, burnt to the ground, demolished." It didn't take Lofty long to work out what had probably happened. He'd anticipated just such a scenario and began to laugh out loud.

"Take me to the Crown Hotel, my good chap," and carried on laughing. The puzzled taxi driver kept a close eye on him, thinking he'd picked up a right nutter.

Exactly a week after filing his insurance claim, Lofty received a big, fat cheque for eight thousand pounds. It was practically all profit. He'd only paid two hundred pounds for his flat, five years earlier, but the current price of a new-build replacement was what his insurance had been measured against. He bought an open-topped sports car and decided for the time being he'd stay put at the Crown. There was no rush to buy another place and besides he was getting on, like a house on fire, with the new bar maid down in the public bar. They shared a passion for horse racing. Lofty recognised who she was the first time he'd spotted her, but decided to P.I.B.E - play it by ear.

Sandra loved being driven around in the little white sports car and it wasn't long before they were having days out together, at the races. Lofty's decision not to rush into buying a flat finally paid off when Sandra invited him back to her house in Churchtown Close and suggested he could stay, 'it being Christmas an' all'. It was a move that provided mutual comfort for them both, with an added bonus. There was a knock at the door on Christmas day morning. Lofty opened it to find Atkinson standing in front of him, holding a bunch of flowers. Atkinson looked in a state of shock and was unable to lift his gaze from a familiar pair of old, worn slippers, which were now covering Lofty's feet. By the time Sandra reached the door, her ex-husband had stormed off up the drive, dumping the flowers in the bin.

"Well, I don't know what's got into him. He always was a funny bugger. Cup of tea, love?" she said, reaching up and kissing Lofty on his Cheshire Cat cheek.

****

The ominous cloud, which Simone cast over the hotel, was beginning to lift at last. Either we'd worn her down, or she had done the same to us. I'd bought a radio/cassette player to entertain us, whilst we worked in the kitchen and between us, Anna and I had chosen some music, which an old fuddy-duddy like Simone would find annoying. It had worked for a while. We took childish pleasure in seeing her cringe and her demands fell on deaf ears as we sung along to the lyrics, 'come on baby light my fire'.

But Simone, to her credit, eventually began to join in too. Her shrill singing voice made us laugh and even Simone saw the funny side. So by the time she left for Christmas, the kitchen felt ridiculously empty without her.

Christmas Eve in St. Jean was billed as the main Yuletide event. Anna had cooked a tradition French meal of Capon and chestnut stuffing, with Foie Gras and L'escargots for starters. After our four guests had finished, it was our turn. I liked the chicken, but no matter how close I put a slimy snail to my lips, my mouth just refused to open. That was one delicacy too far for my taste. I volunteered to find us a bottle of wine from the cellar and chose another dirty, dusty relic, with a torn label. We

163

were still drinking when we heard the church bells ringing at midnight.

"Let's go outside and listen to them," I said, carrying my wine glass through the front entrance. Anna followed and we both stood on the gravel pavement, staring up at the stars. The night sky was beautiful and positively humbling. I had my right hand in my pocket and took out the trinket box, which I'd bought earlier in the week and handed it to Anna. Her eyes widened and the dark shades beneath them instantly disappeared. She opened the lid and lifted out the simple, silver necklace. I hoped she didn't think it was too plain.

"It's the nicest thing anyone has ever bought me," she said.

"Merry Christmas," I replied, stepping up close to her smiling face and our white breath mingled as we kissed.

Above us, the stars glistened like jewels. We both spotted a shooting star, darting across the sky and away over the rooftops.

"You should make a wish," she said teasingly. I closed my eyes. "What did you wish for?" she asked excitedly. I looked straight into her star-lit eyes and said, smiling confidently.

"Take a wild guess."

Anna was the first girl I'd slept with. Our nights together were like a true voyage, a voyage of discovery around our young, naked bodies. I christened our bed 'The Crystal Ship' after the love song by The Doors. Lying together, night after night, was electric. Each gentle touch lit up a thousand flames, a thousand thrills, a million ways to kiss goodnight.

Chapter Eleven

The Trial

In between Christmas and New Year, the harmony at Coraline was interrupted by a phone call from Fionn. She was back in France, but her relationship with Jean-Luc had turned sour since she'd returned from spending a week away in Lancashire. 'He's turned into a green-eyed monster', were Fionn's exact words. Jean-Luc had become struck with jealousy and whatever else his slightly warped mind had concocted during Fionn's absence. He had changed for the worse and Fionn had had to take up temporary residence in Patrice's studio, although she was still working at Les Moulins during the day. Jean-Luc's mother, Juliette, confessed to her that her son's girlfriends normally dumped him for this sort of thing, sooner or later.

"Now she tells me," complained Fionn. "I think I'm cursed to only ever date boys who turn out to be right loonies." I put my hand over my mouth to muffle my laughter as she went on to ask if she and Patrice could drive over to St. Jean and see in the New Year with me and Anna. "I'd really like to meet her."

Anna thought it was a great idea. There was plenty of room available at Coraline. "So they won't be sleeping together?" she enquired. I must have blushed at the thought and Anna began to laugh, "What? Have I said something funny?" After I'd explained Patrice's preference, Anna went on to say, "Well it could still happen, it only takes a tiny spark of desire - have you never read Dangerous Liaisons? It's a French classic."

We made up two separate bedrooms next to one another. "That's probably the best thing to do."

It was around four in the afternoon, on New Year's Eve, when I saw Patrice's little Citroen van, with it's two small, round, yellow, aging eyes for headlamps, chugging up the high street towards us. Evidently it was still miracle time of the year. Fionn jumped out of the passenger door and did one of her flying leaps, landing on me with her arms around my neck and her legs gripping my waist. Not surprisingly, I fell back into the doorway and Anna and Patrice looked on in amazement.

"That's not usually how we do things in England," I said, putting Fionn's feet back down on the ground. "Who is this woman? I've never met her before." Patrice hauled me to my feet. "Cheers, great to see you, Patrice, you're looking fit and well." Then turning to Anna I said, "let's show Fionn and Patrice to their rooms."

"But Byrney, you haven't introduced me to your friend." Anna was smiling and looking eager to greet Fionn.

"Sorry. Fionn, this is the lovely Anna." I smiled proudly. They greeted one another with an air kiss on each cheek. I could tell by Anna's relaxed smile that they were going to get along great.

Patrice was first to walk back down into the restaurant. He looked like a rock guitarist in his denim shirt, jeans and chisel-toe boots. He greeted the other guests and began chatting to a French couple at the nearest table. After a few minutes, I served him with a fresh glass of beer and explained the dish of the day.

"Look at you Byrney, speaking French," he teased. "You actually sound as though you know what you're doing."

"Yer well, I'm okay with food and drinks. It's just everything else I struggle with." Fionn who had just sat down opposite Patrice said the same thing applied to her too.

"I can't believe Jean-Luc hasn't taught you any rude words, Fi."

"He has, but I always forget them five minutes later." We all laughed.

During our meal together, I had an opportunity to talk to Fionn about her week back home. "What was the Friary Christmas Do like?"

"Oh, you would have loved it. We went to the Seven Oaks at Stalmine. The coach was packed solid. Everyone had so much to drink. The older ones were worse than us young ones. There was also lots of canoodling going on, on the way back.

"Oh aye," I said. "What did you get up to?"

"Nothing, I was sat next to Rhonda. But Kevin's younger brother Ian, kept pestering me on the dance floor half the time." I didn't know Kevin had a younger brother working at the Friary. But, there she goes again, still attracting the loonies, I thought.

"Ian started working at the Friary just after we'd left. He was too young for me really and besides I was behaving myself for Jean-Luc. Wish I hadn't bothered now."

"Jean-Luc'll get over it," I said smiling.

"He can bloody well swing. As far as I'm concerned, it's over between us. I always knew there was something slightly creepy about Jean-Luc. Oh, I almost forgot," she said. "I bumped into Lewis whilst I was back in town. He asked how you were doing and to remind you to keep in touch."

"Blimey, Lewis. What's he up to these days?" I'd not spoken to him since I'd left. Sometimes I think I don't deserve any friends. I always get so wrapped up in my own surroundings.

"He sounded a bit fed up actually. He's still working in his dad's business and he said he'd been learning to drive one of their vans." I was impressed.

Anna suggested we should all walk down to the main square to watch the annual firework display. We all knocked back our glasses of wine and took our dirty plates into the kitchen and left them piled up in the two, large, stainless steel sinks. "Leave them. We'll catch up tomorrow," she said and herded us out like stray sheep. "Come on let's go - on y va."

There was lots of activity in the busy town square in St Jean. There were gangs of children running around, which seemed a little odd, to say how late it was. The cinema had just closed it's doors for the last time this year too, but there were several tented stalls still open, selling Frites and Saucissons and Vin Chaud - hot spicy wine. Fionn was really going for it, I thought, as she returned to the back of the queue for another round of drinks.

The cold temperature was starting to make the ground glisten. In the night sky the stars were out in their thousands. They never ceased to amaze me with their incredible patterns. The more I stared at them, the more I saw. As Fionn walked slowly back, with four more paper cups of wine balanced in her gloved hands, Anna suggested we needed to climb on top of the old Roman wall to get the best view. I could see lots of family groups already gathered up there and huddled together and chatting excitedly.

"Don't throw your cups away," said Patrice. "I have a surprise for us later."

As the crowd counted down the last seconds and the town clock struck the hour it was the signal for the first rocket to be launched and the crowd roared with approval. There were voices from the spectators on top of the wall and from every hidden place all around. The fiery display built into a crescendo of orchestrated explosions, all timed to perfection. The sky was slowly being filled with cascading globes and fountains of tiny coloured flares. A constant stream of pale smoke drifted across the rooftops; the noise was perforating. The finale lit up the whole town in the most brilliant, white light as cascade after cascade rained down in a wave of ashes as thick as a glacier, whilst the last explosive thunder faded to an appreciative applause.

Minutes later, the air was still filled with falling grey specks of ash, as steady and condensed as a snowfall.

"Happy New Year - bonne année," said Patrice, waving a bottle of champagne, which he'd produced from beneath his coat. "Pass me your cups." I gave Anna a passionate kiss whilst we each took it in turn to hug one another as the champagne bubbles tickled our noses. Looking around at our fellow revellers, we weren't the only ones celebrating with a bottle of fizz. It looked like some sort of ritual.

We chatted about the New Year – 1977; I couldn't imagine living in a more exciting time. I studied Fionn as she shared a joke with Patrice. It was great having them both here tonight, but seeing Fionn again reminded me just how far we'd both come in such a short space of time since leaving school. Back in April, during our final months, I'd envied my mate Lewis, leaving at Easter to join his family business. He had his future all sorted. But, standing here with my friends, amongst the giant mountains in a far-flung corner of France, felt like I'd reached the ends of the earth. I was overwhelmed with elation. I put my arms around Anna and whispered "Je t'aime."

The first dawn of 1977 commenced with the thickest headache I'd been savaged by, so far in my life. I had to claw my way through the morning. Thankfully, I wasn't the only one. Patrice slumped into his chair at the breakfast table, just in time for the last cup of coffee. We were still sat there when Fionn arrived an hour later, with all her shirt buttons fastened in the wrong holes. She had her hair tied up, but had completely missed one half of it.

"You look like I feel."

Fionn closed her eyes as she fell into one of the two empty chairs, almost finding the gap in between them. "I need some black coffee." What she really needed was for the next twenty-four hours to be cancelled.

"I'll make us a fresh pot," I said, levering myself into an upright position.

In the kitchen, Anna was half heartedly attempting to wipe the work surfaces clean and doing her best to ignore all the dried up dirty plates from last night and a few additional ones from this mornings breakfast. "Leave it for now, come and have a coffee with us Anna." I'd no idea how she'd managed to drag herself out of bed earlier that morning, to see to the four, paying hotel guests. I was dead to the world.

We sat quietly, with the restaurant to ourselves and drank cup after cup of strong black coffee. Having revived ourselves enough to have a coherent conversion, I noticed Anna and Fionn were discussing make-up, whilst Patrice and I were going through the pages of my New Musical Express. "This year is going to be really exciting for music," he said. "There's a new sound heading to Europe from New York. There's a band called The Ramones."

"Yer, I've heard some of their stuff already."

"There's going to be a punk revolution, lots of kid's doing their own thing. Even Johnny Halliday has got a new haircut."

"Johnny who?"

Our peaceful afternoon came to an abrupt end with a sudden, icy, gust of air being blown into the restaurant from the front entrance, announcing the return, of Aunt Simone.

"Oh shit," I whispered as our nemesis stood in the doorway, clutching her suitcase, with her smug expression bursting at the seams and gushing to reveal what a wonderful holiday she'd had.

By the end of the evening, we all had lockjaw from forced smiles, listening to her endless reminiscences. None of us had a clue as to whom she'd been talking about. Fionn's face had frozen, with a glazed expression. Mind you, to be fair, it'd been like that most of the day already. As the three of us climbed the stairs, leaving Anna to lock up, I could hear Simone's piercing comments. She'd obviously noticed the state of the kitchen - 'la grande bouche Simoaner' was back. 'Here we go again', I thought.

Since helping out at Hotel Coraline, I'd become used to the habit of saying farewell to our guests, a smile, a wave and they were on their way and the cash register was all the more healthier for it. When it came to saying goodbye to close friends however, it always made me feel sad and hollow inside. I'd loved spending time with Patrice and Fionn. Anna joined me on the step outside the entrance and we linked arms like an old married couple to wish our friends a bon voyage.

"I hope Fionn will be okay, working again with Jean-Luc."

"Fi can handle herself pretty well," I said reassuringly and picturing the day she'd thrown classroom swat and bossy britches, Belinda Hunt, into the school pond. It made me smile.

We could hear Simoaner, calling to us from inside the kitchen. "She's two streets away and we can still hear her," I joked.

As the week wore on, I sensed there was a different kind of tension building. Aunt Simone's blustering and bullying was no longer rubbing me up the wrong way. I'd grown used to her need to re-organise and order us about, whereas Anna had just grown tired of Simone. It was easier to allow her to have her own way. Objecting to her determined ideas was pointless. With the trial of Anna's father, Jacques, almost upon us, I could see Anna withdrawing deeper into her thoughts. She no longer cared about what became of her home. Simone had finally taken over. What worried me more was the way Anna appeared to be pulling away from me. Our intimacy was cooling; perhaps I was imagining it; perhaps she was even growing tired of me too.

Gastin telephoned, two days before the trial was due to commence. He had very generously organised a room for us in Toulouse, which was only a short walk from the Palais de Justice. With Gastin close at hand at least I would have someone to confide in, on how Anna and I were getting along. The other upside to Gastin's arrangement was that at least we didn't have to share with Aunt Simone any longer. She had her own place to stay, at her daughter's home.

On the first day of the trial, I was feeling nervous, but Gastin had assured us that we wouldn't be required to stand in front of the court to give evidence. So we were able to sit with other members of the public.

The Palais de Justice building lay behind a large, ornate, wrought iron fence and a pair of tall iron gates. They looked very imposing and impossible to climb. Along the enclosed courtyard, several thick, black cables lay across the stone cobbles, like snakes in the bottom of a pit. A camera crew was going through their set up checks in front of a red and white van, next to a single tower of floodlights. The two camera men were adjusting their position and were being closely followed by a guy holding a large, woolly sock at the end of a metal frame. The van had three steel aerials sticking out of the top of its roof, which didn't add up as the logo on the side of the van read - TV Antenna 2. "Arn tarn deux," said Anna as we hurried past, stepping over the cables. Above the arched, entrance door, I noticed an old stone clock face with Roman numerals; it was five minutes to nine. I held Anna's hand as we stepped inside the grand hall, past the two, armed policemen who stood guard at the main door, glancing up and down, at everyone who approached. The cavernous hall was heavily decorated in almost the same luxurious style as the casino in Monte Carlo, only the ceiling was much higher and the walls were painted dark red. It wasn't a room that I felt comforted by.

At school, we'd been taught about the French Revolution, how the citizens of Paris had turned on authority and run riot on the fourteenth of July 1789. Perhaps the same thing had occurred in Toulouse. Perhaps this hall had been painted with the blood from their grovelling victims.

I could see Gastin, stepping briskly towards us. It was a relief to see a welcoming, friendly face. He led us up the grand staircase, then along a wide, carpeted, corridor to the main courtroom, on the first floor. There was a queue of people waiting to be let in, some with notepads, some carrying attaché cases.

"This is where we'll be everyday this week," said Gastin, shaking my hand and looking at Anna with a deep frown. "Are you okay?" he asked calmly. Then, sensing he wasn't going to receive a reply from her, he continued with his instructions. "If I'm not here one day, just join the back of the queue, in the morning, before nine o'clock. For one day only, I have to give evidence about my father." We both nodded and moved forward into line. I could see more armed police at the entrance to the courtroom itself, checking inside bags and briefcases.

They were being very cautious. We gave our names as we passed them and Gastin lead us to our seats. I was expecting to be sat in a gallery overlooking the courtroom, but to my disappointment, we were all sat in rows of wooden benches, which were lined up, facing the judge's platform. To the side of the platform, at ninety degrees, were two rows of seats in a separate enclosure. "Those are for the Jurors," explained Gastin. Behind the two rows, a door opened in the wood panelling and out walked twelve men and one woman. They filed quietly into the courtroom and took to their seats as the buzz of chatter from the members of the public around us began to hush. From the side of the platform appeared two more armed policemen. Between them, I spotted Anna's father. I felt her hand tighten its grip on mine as everyone turned their heads in unison to face him. He sat, about twenty feet away, on the front row, next to his lawyer.

The entrance door behind us, at the back of the courtroom, closed shut and a few seconds later opened again to let in one other person. I looked around to see Simone walking towards us. I'd never seen her looking so smart, in a purple, two-piece suit and matching beret. She'd obviously had her hair done too. I turned away hoping she'd not seen us and comforted myself that at least our bench was fully occupied, or so I thought. Needless to say, she stopped at the end of our bench and insisted everyone 'hutched up' to make room for her.

"Bonjour Byrney, bonjour Anna," she purred and turned to face the platform. The only answer she received was from the clerk, asking us all to rise as the judge and his secretaries stepped into the room and sat behind the platform. The big, comfy chair was for the judge, of course.

The procedure seemed a very long-winded affair. There were discussions between the judge and his two secretaries, then, the two lawyers, one for the defence and one for the prosecution, stepped up to the platform. The judge had a sharp nosed, shrewd looking face, which reminded me of the front of a Concord jet and he appeared to be a stickler for procedure. He kept raising and lowering his glasses, to check the paperwork. Blimey, he's coming in to land, I thought, but he just repeatedly passed reams of paperwork back and forth to each secretary until he seemed satisfied. At this rate it was going to be a trial just to stay awake. The judge drew in a deep breath through his droop snoop and appeared to wince as he nodded to the prosecution lawyer to commence. The young 'no nonsense' looking lawyer leapt forward and eagerly addressed the Jury, pausing over each of the charges against Jacques to allow the seriousness of each alleged crime to hit home. As he emphasised each charge, I could see Simone getting restless in her seat and true to form started huffing and puffing. When she heard the lawyer read out the word 'traitor', she couldn't prevent herself from rattling out a rapid rant at him, halting his delivery. The judge banged his gavel to bring the court to order and spoke very calmly to Simone and she immediately flopped back down in her seat.

"What was all that about?" I whispered to Anna as the prosecution lawyer recommenced his address, with one eye on the jurors and the other on Simone.

"My aunt said my father was completely innocent and that this was no way to treat a hero of the resistance. The judge asked her to calm down as there is a long way to go." I looked at Simone again. She didn't look to me like she was going to take any notice of that.

Anna had taken it upon herself to summarize for me, at each break in the proceedings, when the two lawyers took it in turn to speak. After the defence lawyer had spoken to the jurors at the end of his opening address, there was a loud gasp from the people in the seats around us.

"Jacques is pleading not guilty to all the charges," whispered Gastin. "That is no surprise. It only means it will take a little longer for us to get Jacques to change his mind."

As we filed out, at the end of the afternoon, my backside was as numb as a nail. I was looking forward to getting back to our room and having a bite to eat. As we left the main entrance, several reporters stampeded towards us and tried to speak to Anna. Gastin stepped in to push them away. It was obvious they'd learnt who Anna was. How I wondered? Then, I noticed Simone being interviewed in front of a television camera. She was enjoying standing in the spotlights. I wanted to kick her derriere.

We were sat having a meal later that evening and Anna protested, she couldn't go back inside the courthouse again. I tried to persuade her that she had to hear the truth, so that she could put her life back together. It was Gastin who managed to sway her to go back again the next day.

"It's so important for you to go back. It will put pressure on your father if he knows you are there."

I asked Gastin how Jacques could possibly plead not guilty, when all the evidence was so heavily stacked against him. Gastin briefly explained about a similar case in France, about five years ago. "There was a notorious political fugitive called Pierre Voyou, who had worked for the Vichy government. During the occupation, he had been responsible for rounding up hundreds of Jews in the French free zone and packing them off to the concentration camps. Somehow he escaped justice after the liberation and even took up a post in the new De Gaulle administration. When he was eventually exposed, in 1966, his lawyers argued that too much time had past since he committed his crimes and claimed a twenty-year statute of limitations. He escaped the death penalty and was eventually pardoned in 1971, by President Pompidou." Gastin shrugged his shoulders. "The national press called it 'un badigeon'. But, as we speak, he is still a free man. However, there are now more powerful organisations in France today, which have the backing of the European courts. Collaborators, like Pierre Voyou, will soon be made to answer for their crimes, no matter how long ago they were. The problem in France is that there are very few people who can claim they didn't share some of the guilt for how our country behaved during the occupation."

It still didn't seem right to me. I'd not encountered politics interfering with justice.

"It's how nations are born and die," said Gastin sombrely.

On the second day of the trial, Gastin got his chance to deliver some of the evidence he had collected against Jacques and confirmed his father had been one of the Spanish guides who had been discovered a few months ago on the Glacier di Aureola having lain undiscovered for over thirty years. The ballistics report had also confirmed that the gun, which Gastin had taken from Jacques after the shoot out at Celeste Station, was the same weapon that killed his father. They had been able to recover enough of the bullet, which was still embedded inside the bones of the skull. This latest evidence was beginning to tip the scales in our favour.

Not surprisingly, on the penultimate day in Court, the judge finally lost his temper at Aunt Simone's interruptions and she was quite literally, thrown out of court. It took two armed policemen to lift her off her feet and carry her out with her legs swinging, kicking and screaming. We could all still hear her protestations long after the door was closed. When order was restored, I felt the whole courtroom breathe a sigh of relief. It was also a turning point in the proceedings. After a long recess, Jacques Casson finally took to the stand. He had at last agreed to make a full confession. As he spoke, I could see he was looking directly at Anna. He looked broken, his shoulders were hunched and the judge had to ask him to speak up, several times, as his mind drifted between the past and the present. He spoke in French. When Gastin translated it for me later, it was eerily compelling.

" My downfall began when I was arrested during a routine check, after the German authorities had crossed the demarcation line and had taken over the whole of France. I was taken to Furgole Prison, where I was introduced to one of their spies. I recognised him as someone who had asked for my help, a few days earlier, to take his supposed family across the border. I'd no idea he was a German. So they knew I worked for the Renard escape line. The Gestapo threatened to torture me and have my entire family arrested, unless I agreed to work for the Nazis in their fight to liquidate all the escape lines. They gave me money and demanded I handed over every single member of our group, by laying a trap for them. Whenever I was meant to take over the 'parcels' from the guides, I made sure the

Gestapo were waiting to intercept them, before they reached their rendez-vous. That way the guides would not suspect I had betrayed them. That is how Gastin de Bourges was eventually caught. I was moved into the Nice sector. When the day came to collect Paul Larouchamps and the two Jewish families, I was praying that this would be my last time. When I arrived in Toulouse, to make the hand over to young Eduard Siguer, he had failed to show. He'd clearly been tipped off. The Gestapo left me no choice other than to deliver the 'parcels' to the Spanish guides myself. They wanted the Spanish guides locked up too. When the German patrol arrived at the shelter on the Col du Monde, they'd not anticipated being so far from their base at St. Jean. One of them followed me to meet up with the Spanish guides. We ambushed them and tied them up. The German soldier wore the uniform of the Wehrmacht. He handed me a Luger pistol and ordered me to shoot them.

The next day, the German patrol grew restless. They had no intention of taking their prisoners back with them. During the night Paul Larouchamps had begged me to help him. He gave me his watch and jewellery, but the only person I could save was myself. During the massacre, I was able to escape and headed towards Spain.

Months later, when I heard about the second Allied landing in the south of France, I came out of hiding and linked up with a resistance group, who were poised to drive the Germans out of St. Jean. During the fighting and repercussions, I was eager to prove myself. I had nothing to lose and everything to gain. I was not afraid to execute collaborators. In the confusion of those frenzied days of the liberation, it wasn't surprising that a few innocent people were shot by mistake. One of those was young Eduard Siguer. I wasn't there that day, so I was unable to stop the others from shooting him. I wanted to hand myself in to the new administration, but instead, I was given a high-ranking job at the mayor's office and later I was handed the empty hotel on the high street, as a reward. I found myself in such a respected position within the community that I could no longer own up to the truth. The longer it went on, the more difficult and impossible it became to be anything other than the man I am today."

The jury retired to deliberate their decision. Gastin thought the prosecution lawyer had missed an opportunity to challenge Jacques about the roll he'd played in the death of Eduard Siguer, during the violent aftermath of the Liberation. It had worked to his advantage, to silence Eduard before he could expose Jacques as the real collaborator. But Gastin had been unable to dig up any evidence, which would stand up in court, to support his theory. With the lack of any former members of the local resistance coming forward and the death of Eduard's widow, there was nothing anyone could prove.

When the Jury returned to the courtroom the next morning, Patrice and Henri Larouchamps were also present to hear the spokesman of the jury read out the verdict. Jacques was found guilty of aiding the Germans, but not guilty of murder.

The judge sentenced him to four years in prison, but as he'd co-operated by submitting a full confession, it was reduced to one year. He would be free again in six months time.

I tried to put myself in Jacques' shoes all those years ago. How would I have acted? I don't think anyone truly knows about themselves until they are put in a similar position. How could I even begin to imagine? I'd learnt my lesson about breaking the law. I'd got away with it lightly by comparison and I wasn't just thinking about the punishment side of it. I was thinking about how it had affected me: how I'd felt I couldn't breathe or even face myself. As they led Jacques away from the courtroom, I knew he'd get in touch with Anna again soon. Gastin was more philosophical about the scale of the punishment handed out to Jacques. He was disappointed he'd been found not guilt of murdering his father. Whether Gastin felt angry about it, he never let it show. Like Anna he just wanted to draw a line under it. He said, "There is comfort in knowing."

Afterwards, it was so strange, no one actually felt like celebrating. Gastin had invited us to his favourite back street café for a farewell meal. Patrice and Henri joined us too. I'd been slightly shocked to see them earlier in the day, but so pleased they'd come all this way to represent Paul Larouchamps. I was hoping a little of my happiness would rub off on Anna who, unsurprisingly, was still feeling lower than the rest of us. I'd agreed to return to Coraline with her, the next day, to talk about our plans. We were all sat in this slightly dodgy looking café; at a long, red, Formica topped table; by a window, which looked out onto the quiet, narrow, little lost street. The bar inside our café was lively enough. Customers were coming and going, fairly rapidly. Our waitress rested her hand on Gastin's shoulder as he went through his usual routine of asking about every item on the menu, before ordering his usual. We all had the same dish: bouillabaisse - fish stew. I was taking a mental picture of Gastin, smiling away in the midst of all our companionships. To a stranger, Gastin always came across as a bit of a loner. He was unmarried and very much focussed on his work, but seeing him on his home ground, he was very much a people person.

The barman brought over a tray of demi beers and Gastin spotted the news on the TV behind the bar. When the barman turned up the volume, we listened to the female reporter who had stood outside the Palais de Justice earlier in the day. Then who should appear on screen next to her, but Aunt Simone and we all cheered. Watching her, made us laugh with her expressions. For some reason, I found myself admiring her. She wasn't afraid to stand up to the highest authority in France and tell it how she saw it, even if it was her one sided view of the world. Patrice and Henri were astonished to learn she'd been ejected from the courtroom.

"I wouldn't like to get on the wrong side of her," joked Patrice.

I could definitely agree to that.

Chapter Twelve

End Of An Ending

It's funny how no matter what huge sets of circumstances I find myself in: trials, unsolved murder, betrayal etcetera, mother nature finds a way of putting all of this in the shade. When the first soft flakes of snow began to fall on our bus journey back to St. Jean, it was a gentle reminder that we were still living in the grip of winter and an unpredictable one at that. There were only a handful of passengers with us, making the same intrepid journey along this bumpy, winding road. The morning had started out bright and sunny, brilliantly illuminating the snow-capped mountains, which formed the distant, almost impassable barrier, between France and Spain. But in these altitudes I'd already seen how quickly changes to the weather could descend and threaten the lives of those unlucky enough to be caught up in them. I was hoping we'd reach our destination before the real, thick, heavy stuff covered the surface of the road. I eyeballed the snowflakes hitting the screen head on. They were so hypnotic I had to force myself to look away. The driver had no choice other than to stare at the same view through the front windscreen, with only a pair of window wipers dragging away the white, splattered spots for help. I'd no idea how he could see where he was going, but he appeared not to show any sign of nerves. He was busy working his way through the gears and his head constantly moved from side to side, measuring the distance to the edge of the road as he feathered the brakes, slowing down, in ample time, to take each switchback bend as the bus struggled on, higher and higher.

We'd not seen another vehicle for miles. The snow was falling even faster now and the tyre tracks we'd been following were becoming more and more obscured. Our journey was forced into an unscheduled stop when the bus slewed around a steep, tight, hairpin bend. The wheels span, lost their grip and we failed to make any further progress. The handbrake hissed in annoyance as the driver looked back at us and made an announcement.

"What's going on?" I asked Anna.

"The driver needs to fit some snow chains to the tyres, don't worry, it's just routine. We'll soon be on our way again."

We heard the luggage compartment door open at our side of the bus. I wiped the steamy window next to me and stared out into the abyss. We were stuck inside a cloud.

My mind took me back to a similar wintry situation with my dad, when I was about eight or nine years old. He'd bought an old Bedford van from a car auction, somewhere in deepest, darkest Yorkshire. Mum had been pressganged into taxiing him to collect his latest acquisition. Our journey back to Lancashire had taken us up a steep bank. Mum and Anthony had been in front of us and had shot on ahead. The old van dad and I were travelling in had only got part of the way up the hill when it lost its grip on the frozen surface and we could go no further. Dad let the van roll backwards and we had another run at the gradient, but only making it a few yards beyond our first attempt. After three more go's it was obvious the old van wasn't going to make it. If only we had more grip. My young mind began to worry I'd never see my home again and to make matters worse, Mum and Anthony would probably already be tucked up, nice and snug, in front of a roaring fire.

Lucky for us, Dad rooted about in the back of the van and found a pair of snow chains, which he fitted to the rear wheels. This did the trick and we were able to reach the summit. I felt an enormous sense of relief. I asked him what would have happened if he'd not found the snow chains. He said, "Oh, no problem, we could have gone another way. It would have just taken another ten minutes longer." That was typical of dad. Once he'd got an idea in his head, there was no going back.

The bus driver appeared again on the steps. His cap and shoulders were covered in a coating of snow. He looked around sympathetically and began speaking to no one in particular. Anna stood up and grabbed my arm as she made her way down the aisle, "Come on Byrney, he needs our help."

The thick, heavy chains were laid out flat next to each wheel. The driver asked us to lift them onto the top of the tyre whilst he scrambled underneath the bus and clipped the links together at the back of the wheel. Once it was fixed, we joined the links at the front of the wheel and helped him to fit the tensioners. The steel chains were freezing cold. I blew on my fingers to keep them warm whilst Anna helped with the next wheel.

We were soon on our way again and the bus was behaving as it should, all be it at a slower pace, but at least we were getting closer to St. Jean. Anna explained that whilst the snow was still fresh we would be okay, provided it didn't get too deep. The bus continued carving a path up the centre of the road. We had the road all to ourselves. There was something about being amongst these mountains that left me feeling anxious, like my life was in peril. It's true I'd had a couple of scares on my two previous visits to St. Jean, but now that Jacques was locked up behind bars and Gingernut was back in England then surely I would be out of danger once we'd reached our destination. When we drove into the outskirts of the hillside town, there were snowploughs busily at work, making huge piles of snow on every street corner. It was obvious the bus would be going no further. The wind was rapidly blowing the snow back across the square and undoing the work of the ploughs. After the handful of passengers left the bus and disappeared into the gloom, Anna offered to put up our driver at Hotel Coraline, until the road back down the valley became passable again.

"We can sometimes be cut off for days," she explained. "It all depends how quickly the wind dies away."

That night, after Pascal, the bus driver had retired to his room, Anna began to discuss her plans for the future. "I've decided that it's only fair for you to have a share of the hotel takings." I wasn't expecting that. So far I'd been happy to work for my meals and board. It's true I'd not earned a single Franc since I'd arrived in France. The cash I'd hidden in Fionn's room in Nice had kept me going until now.

"If you're sure you want to do this, thank you, that's great."

Anna took a deep breath, straightened her shoulders and tried to force a smile. "Listen Byrney, I've been thinking..." My heart suddenly felt hollow. I'd been half expecting for Anna to say how she truly felt about seeing her father being led away from the courthouse and put into jail for six months. So far she'd only spoken about being unable to forgive him for living a lie and hiding the truth from her, probably from her mother too. Anna put her hand on top of mine and said, "I'd like to go back to America when my father returns. I've realised I really want to finish my studies. I'd like you to come with me, but I'll understand if you don't."

I didn't know what to say. I'd not thought that far ahead. I looked at Anna and I could see now what had been troubling her for some time: that she needed to get away from here. We talked for the next couple of hours. Her college was in a place called Syracuse, in New York State. It sounded great, but at the back of my mind I'd been hoping Anna might have wanted to come back with me to Nice.

Pascal, our friendly bus driver, ended up staying with us for four days, all paid for by his company, which earned me a half share of his Five Hundred Franc bill. Once the road down to Toulouse was opened up again, I was dreading Aunt Simone making a reappearance, but Anna confirmed she wouldn't be joining us until her father was due to be released. So we had the place to ourselves.

The clients and ski lovers trickled back to St. Jean and to our little hotel too. I was hoping to tempt Anna away for a weekend break, back to Nice, but as soon as the hotel looked like being empty for a few days, more customers turned up out of the blue.

It carried on like this for the next couple of months. The highlight for me came on the twenty-eighth of February, my seventeenth birthday. Anna had intercepted my post, recognising it might be birthday cards and had rung Fionn, who'd confirmed the exact day. Anna took me up to the ski slopes for a days skiing, which was mainly a day of me falling over and rolling down the slope in my heavy boots, helmet and goggles being chased by a stray pair of skis. I was about to give up, when Anna encouraged me to have one last try. Incredibly, this time I managed to stay upright, with both ski's pointing in the same direction and it felt really exhilarating as we both glided down the slope, side by side. "That was brilliant!" I shouted, catching my breath, when we levelled out at the foot of the slope.

In the evening, the hotel guests sang 'Happy Birthday', in the candlelit atmosphere as Anna carried a cake to my table. She'd also bought me a present too - a pocket radio with headphones.

"Wow this is superb. Thanks so much." I caught my reflection in Anna smile - it had been a great day.

"Is there anything else you'd like," she said, looking like the best birthday present I could wish for.

"Well, apart from the obvious, there is one thing I've been aching over, which is I'd really like to go back to the ruins on the Col du Monde and scatter Eve's ashes."

"I've been thinking about that too," admitted Anna. "Perhaps we can try again in two weeks time, when the avalanche season has finished. I'll check with the mountain rescue team and make sure it's safe up there."

When the day came, we climbed aboard Anna's Mobylette scooter and headed up to the Col de la Celeste, just as dawn was breaking. The station hut was already open. Anna introduced me to Capitaine Georges, who ran the mountain rescue team. He was just in the process of routinely checking the large radio set. He asked Anna about when she was coming back to the team again and advised us about which path to follow up to the Col du Monde. He handed Anna a hand held two-way radio for emergency use, but assured us the risk of avalanches along our route was very small.

I'd got Eve's ashes with me, tucked away inside my rucksack and I was just so pleased to be finally doing what I'd set out to achieve, all those months ago when the idea first struck me, whilst standing on the summit of Ingleborough Hill, at the end of my road trip in North Yorkshire.

Anna tested her radio, set it to channel six and clipped it to the front of her parka. Once again the sun was shining down favourably upon us, and it felt like we'd all the time in the world. We'd left Aunt Simone in charge at Coraline. I knew she wouldn't be able to stay away for six months. Still, at least having her back had allowed us to take a few days off.

Our route was unrecognisable from the one we'd taken with Gastin, back in November. The snows had transformed the barren, lunar landscape into a white, silvery, sparkly covering, which stretched out for miles in front of us. Occasionally, we had to stop to attach our snowshoes when we stepped onto fresh snowdrifts. Then once again, on top of the Glacier, we changed into our crampons. The day was beautifully still and silent. The only sound came from our breathless panting as we climbed onto the high ledge where the ruins were hidden, inside the basin like cutting in the face of the Col du Monde.

I'd forgotten how spectacular the view of the Southern Pyrenees was, so clear, so boundless.

At the base of the weathered, brick chimneybreast, beneath the charred wooden cross, we scraped away the snow to reveal fresh, pale shoots of grass. Anna removed a clump of earth with her ice axe and I watched as she dug out a small hole. Then she removed her glove and unzipped a small pocket.

"I've brought this - I think it's right that Eve should have it again." She held out the palm of her hand and slowly opened her fingers to reveal the aubergine pendant that her mother had worn. It had been returned to Anna after the trial. I'd completely forgotten all about it. It was a wonderful, generous gesture.

"I think Paul would be pleased too," I said, imagining him looking down on us. Anna placed the pendant on the dark soil and then covered it with the small clump of turf. I removed the lid from the Tupperware container and tipped Eve's ashes on top of the grass shoots. Then we both covered them again with snow.

"Do you think we should say a few words?" I asked.

"Yes, if you like. She was your friend."

I felt a bit silly, as I'd not thought of it until now. I pictured Eve in her charming little cottage in Crowston, surrounded by her treasures. Then I said, "Well, if there is such a thing as Heaven, then I know Paul will be waiting for you." I looked at Anna and we both nodded in agreement, "Farewell Eve."

As Anna and I made our way back down the glacier, we were both wrapped in our own silent thoughts. For me, saying 'farewell' after scattering Eve's ashes had made me think of Max, how I'd wished we could have parted on friendlier terms. In saying 'farewell' I'd understood how final the word sounded. I was too young to think about finality, hoping that I wouldn't have to use the word again for a very long time. The temperature was cooling and I rushed to catch up with Anna and ask if we could go to the hunting bothy where we'd stayed on our first trip to the Col du Monde. "I really loved that night when we all stayed there. It was so safe and cosy."

The shelter hadn't been used by anyone since we were last there. It looked exactly as we'd left it. The hurricane lamp was still sat in the centre of the table and I went to break some sticks for making a fire. As the bare room began to thaw and the air filled with a mixture of steam and wood smoke, we settled down, zipping our sleeping bags together.

"At least we don't have to listen to Gastin snoring away," I said, feeling a little nostalgic by his absence. I looked upon him as a substitute father figure. He was always full of sound advice and seemed so indestructible. "I hope I'm as fit as he is when I'm older. Imagine Gastin being the feature in a Hollywood film. Who do you see playing him? Burt Lancaster?

"Non, Yves Montand. He's more handsome." She laughed. "It was something Gastin said to me which helped to make up my mind about my future," continued Anna. Her breath was still visible. Her happy face shone brightly in the glow of the fire. "I asked him about his plans to go to South America, whether he thought he could do it, you know."

"What did he say?"

"He said I should never be put off by how far away a place is. It's the same principle as going to the boulangerie for a baguette - all you have to do is put one foot in front of the other. He made it sound so easy."

We'd been lying together in a warm embrace, listening to the logs crackling and burning. I felt Anna turn onto her side and heard her familiar, long, sleepy breaths as I watched the glowing light from the fire flicker, making the shadows dance around the rustic room. I recalled Gastin's last piece of advice, 'stay out of trouble, mon ami.' But it actually sounded to me like he was the one more likely to find it, where he was heading, knowing how someone of Jacques Casson's lowly stature, in the murky world of war crimes, had dealt with being exposed. Imagine the sort of fight he'd be involved in with catching a really big fish. I'd hoped to see him again at some point in the future. 'You're welcome to come with me to Bolivia, he'd said, now that you have mastered the art of capturing collaborators. Our organisation could use someone like you.' I wasn't sure if he was joking or not. He'd looked serious at the time, but there again he always did.

With Aunt Simone's irremovable presence reinstalled at Hotel Coraline, the writing was on the wall for us. Not content with taking over the everyday running, it seemed to me that her latest objective was driving a wedge between Anna and me. What was it about these Casson siblings? If they couldn't win, then Jacques and Simone hated to see anyone else succeed in life. We were both desperate to leave St. Jean. We travelled together to Toulouse, for the final time. Anna followed me to the train station before heading off to the airport. She was in floods of tears as we waited on the platform for my train to arrive. We kissed and hugged as we said goodbye, promising to write to each other and that we'd meet up again back in France, later in the year. I was convinced that once Anna had settled in America, she'd soon forget about me, or meet a boy who could give her the happiness she so desperately needed. As much as I loved Anna, I'd never pictured myself being together with her for the rest of my life, in the same way that I had last year with Max.

On the train journey back to Nice, I'd come to the conclusion that a change had taken place in me. I was no longer overtaken by fantasy. Living with the stigma of being a whopping great thief, with a hoard of cash buried outside my family home, had affected me badly. The dream of owning and escaping to my own island had gone forever, but I had still so much to look forward to, with a clearer conscience. As for work, there was no immediate need to rush into anything. The last four months at Hotel Coraline had been a much more prosperous adventure than I could have wished for. The lessons in hard work I'd learnt at the Friary from Madge, Joanie and Edward had stood me in good stead at Coraline with Anna. We'd stuck it out through thick and thin. So, for the time being it was back to making myself useful, either at Patrice's studio or with whatever else came along.

Monday's were Fionn's day off from Les Moulins. We'd met up on the beach, in front of the Promenade d'Anglais and watched the vast space around us fill up with the usual cast of glamorous bathers. As Fionn lay in the sand next to me, with her back to the sun, I asked her how she'd been persuaded to return to working with Jean-Paul after their relationship had broken down. Juliette, Henri's wife, who always looked to me like a school PE teacher with her hair tied back tightly - all she was missing was a string necklace with a whistle attached to it - had sat Fionn and Jean-Paul down together and had made him apologise to her. Juliette always saw Jean-Paul as still being a bit of a baby and Fionn as the more mature one. She explained to her son that jealousy was an ugly trait, which would eat him from the inside out if he didn't put an end to it; that before he did so, he must learn how to forgive and this he could start by apologising to Fionn.

"Anyway it's all behind me now. I've been offered a new job," continued Fionn.
"Really, when did this happen?"
"Last week, just before you came back. I've been offered a place on one of those posh charter yachts. I can't wait. It has an all English crew. I met the captain last week and he told me the boat was fully booked for the summer season by the 'Young Presidents Organisation' in America. So, you never know, I might get to meet some real millionaires."
"What exactly will you be doing aboard this yacht?"
"Mostly house-keeping type stuff - a sort of a cabin girl."
I began to laugh, "I'd be very careful how you phrase that when you tell your mum."

I looked out to sea and watched the water skiers and pedalos, splash across the water and popped on my headphones and tuned into the English speaking, local radio station - Sovereign Radio. I heard this amazing song called 'Roadrunner'. It was from the east coast of America. The new sound invasion had arrived as Patrice had predicted.
As the warm sun and the endless rushing of the waves ran out onto the shoreline, I had a question for Fionn.
"You know when something really cool happens and you say, that's music to my ears. Well, what do you say when you already have music in your ears and things are going great?"
Fionn lifted her head from her pillow of folded arms and said, "life doesn't get any better than this."